LIBERATED BY SIN

THE SEVERED SIGNET

BOOK 4

ELLE MALDONADO

Editing: Mackenzie Letson of Nice Girl, Naughty Edits

Cover Design: Haya In Designs

Proofread: The Blue Couch Edits

Author's Note

Liberated by Sin is a dark romance. It contains explicit content such as on page sexual assault, sexual violence, and mentions of sex trafficking. None of which occur between our main characters.

Please guard your mental health.

A full list of triggers can also be found on my website: www.authorellemaldonado.com

It is intended for readers 18+.

CONTENT WARNINGS

Sex Trafficking
Non-Con/Rape (On page. Not between MCs)
Sex Auction
Assault
Captivity
Confinement
Drugging
Sexual Assault
Whipping
Attempted Sexual Assault
Graphic Violence
Knife Violence
Eye Trauma
Arson
Body Set On Fire
Death
PTSD
Disassociation
Attempted Murder
Kidnapping
Suicide Attempt

Suicide Ideation
Genital Mutilation
Dismemberment
Blood
Torture
Murder
Gun Violence
Explicit Sex
Explicit Language
Graphic Blood Play (Not Between MCs)

For the lost. The broken. The healing.
For the survivors.

······································

PLAYLIST

······································

WILDFLOWER by Billie Eilish
Lilith by Saint Avangeline
The Castle by Chris Grey
Taste of the Divine by Shaker, Azee, COBRA
Bring Me To Life by Evanescence
The World We Made by Ruelle
I GOT YOU by Chris Grey
Aimed to Kill by Jade LeMac

View the full playlist here: www.authorellemaldonado.com

ONE

Athena

PAST

I dragged my teeth across my bottom lip as a tingle of nerves traveled up my spine. After months of sneaking around, fleeting touches and kisses, and late nights on the phone, Ezra and I would finally be together for the first time.

My first time.

We knew the risks. If Ronan found out, he'd have his nephew's head. But I wasn't a child anymore. I hadn't been one for a very long time. And outside of my brothers, no one had shown me love, comfort, and understanding the way Ezra had. He was a few years older than Derek, but despite our age difference, we were perfect for each other. We lived and breathed this life. No secrets. No hiding. I convinced myself that, eventually, Ronan would understand. They all would. They'd have to.

"What are you doing in here by yourself, birthday girl?" Kai slid onto the stool beside me and grabbed my drink, downing the liquid in one swallow.

"I needed some quiet," I said, stealing back my glass. Neither one of us was legally old enough to drink, but that didn't matter when we'd been trained to snipe a man from 400 yards—then go home, make a sandwich, and watch the news coverage as if it was just another Tuesday.

And it truly was for Kai and Derek. Maybe for me, too, up until six months ago.

But after meeting Ezra, I realized I wanted more out of life: a family, kids someday, and *love*.

"Most of the guests are gone, and Derek and I are heading out. You want to join us?" he asked, shoulder-checking me. "A little after-party."

Peering at the time, I shook my head and smiled. "I couldn't tell my brothers about Ezra yet. They were so protective, I didn't trust they wouldn't make my boyfriend disappear."

"I feel a headache coming on. I think I'll stay in and get some sleep."

"Sleep?" We whirled around. Derek leaned against the entry-way, a drink in one hand, the other tucked into his pocket. "On your birthday? Unacceptable."

My boys.

I didn't know where I'd be without them. Eight years ago, I was nearly dragged onto a plane, ripped from the bloodied hands of my mother and father. Too young to understand what was happening, all I could do was cry and hope to die the way my family had. Until the night Kai brought me a chocolate chip muffin and a wad of rolled-up tissue from his back pocket.

I still laughed at the thought because it was such a *Kai* thing to do. Meanwhile, Derek lingered by the door, stoic and unreadable. Not much had changed with those two, except now we were as close as any real siblings. However, nothing about our relationship had ever been conventional.

Trauma bonding was a bitch.

"I doubt you'll find the solution to your headache at the bottom of that glass," Derek teased as he pried the refilled drink from my hand. "Let's get you something to eat, and then Kai and I will give you your birthday gift."

"So you didn't forget about me, after all."

"Oh, come on, blue! We bought you cake, didn't we?" Kai slid my stool away from the counter, tugging on my arm until I stood. With a sigh, I relented. Ezra wouldn't be by for another two hours anyway, so it couldn't hurt. And turning down free food and a birthday present was sure to raise alarms.

"Fine. But I want tacos from that food truck on 5th Ave."

I poked Derek in the chest and winked, knowing exactly how he felt about street vendors. Kai and I had a bet going that he'd had tainted food once and was forever traumatized by whatever unholy transgressions followed. But we knew he'd take that secret to the grave.

"Fuck, Athena. Really?"

"It's my birthday. You can't say no," I quipped, backing out of the kitchen—right into what felt like a brick wall.

I twisted around, and the sharp, familiar scent of Ronan's cologne hit me before I even saw his face. Call it vibes or intuition; his presence had always sent my heart racing in all the worst ways. Thankfully, I only had a few more weeks before I was out of here for good.

"There you are," he said in a sing-song tone that was equally unnerving as it was cringe-worthy. "I've been waiting all night to catch you alone and finally give you your gift, but you've been the center of attention." He cast a glance down my body that I hadn't missed. "And rightly so."

Stepping back into my boys' protective circle, I forced a smile. "It looks like you'll have to wait just a little longer. Derek, Kai, and I were heading out," I said, swinging around and jumping onto Kai's back.

"It will only take a moment." Despite his smile, I caught the twitch in his left eye. It was a tick of his, a reaction to frustration.

"She said later," Derek countered, stepping in front of Ronan as Kai and I maneuvered around them and into the hallway.

There was a brief back-and-forth between the two men, though not unusual. Derek and our adoptive *father* butted heads more often than not. And I had a gut feeling that one of these days, one would end up dead at the hands of the other.

My money was on Derek.

We spilled onto the front steps, the cool summer air caressing my face as I closed my eyes and tasted the petrichor lingering from a light evening rain.

"Are you riding with me or Derek?" Kai set me down and tossed me a helmet before straddling his new bike. He had discovered his love of motorcycles two years ago and hadn't looked back. It suited him.

The Cain brothers looked nothing alike, but each was handsome in his own way. Wherever they went, they drew the attention of a swath of women. And the three of us together—well, I wasn't conceited, but once I was old enough to understand the world, I realized Ronan hadn't handpicked us just for our potential.

"I'll ride with Derek. You've only got one helmet, and I'd hate to be the reason you messed up that pretty face."

"You're in luck," he chuckled, climbing off his bike—Gloria, as he'd curiously named her—and reaching through the open back window of Derek's car. He pulled out a black helmet, its side detailed with hot pink wildflowers.

"For me?"

"Well, Derek wasn't a fan, so why not?"

I swatted him with the helmet and tucked it under my arm, rising to my toes to peck his cheek

"Thank you. It's beautiful."

"Come on. Hop on."

Hanging my new gift on the handlebar, I slid behind my

brother and rested my head against his back. "How long do you think Derek will be? I can't be out all night."

"What's wrong? You got somewhere else to be?"

I glanced at my phone again, expecting a response from Ezra, but there was nothing.

He must be busy.

"No, it's just that headache, remember?"

"Sure."

"Kai?" I whispered, staring at my dark screen, willing a text to appear. "Do you ever think about leaving all this behind?"

He remained quiet for a moment and reached for my hand. "Maybe someday, blue."

"Yeah, someday," I said with a sigh, giving him a squeeze.

I used to hate that nickname until it grew on me. Some dumb boy on the playground once called me a freak for having different-colored eyes, and for pretending Derek and Kai were my brothers. I was still a kid, so naturally, I cried. But they had my back and reassured me we were family, no matter what. And that even though we didn't look alike, we all had blue eyes, even if I only had one.

The boy went home with a bloody nose that day.

"Athena." It was rare for Kai to call me by my first name unless it was important. I stilled, waiting for him to speak. "Promise me something," he said. "If you ever decide to leave... take us with you."

I laughed and ruffled his hair. "Why? You'd miss me?"

But Kai didn't laugh. He was strangely serious.

"I mean it."

Again, I lay my head against him and wrapped my arms around his shoulders.

"Okay, Kai bear. I promise."

He belted out a laugh at the old nickname I used to call him when we were kids—*Bear* had been one of the first English words I learned.

There he was. The Kai I knew.

———

I stumbled through my bedroom door and nearly tripped over my own feet, blindly patting the wall for the light switch. Between the dark and the alcohol in my system, the usually simple task felt nearly impossible. Maybe I should have cut back on the shots. But it was my *fucking* birthday, and Ezra wasn't answering a single call or text. Screw him. I drank my feelings until I could barely walk straight because I knew I'd be safe with Kai and Derek. They had their suspicions something was up, that I was keeping a secret, and that said secret was feeding my need to drink. But even this drunk, I wasn't about to out our relationship or admit Ezra ghosted me on my special day. The last thing I needed was a lecture from my overprotective and homicidal brothers.

"When you said a little later, I didn't think you meant 4 a.m."

Ronan's voice jolted me damn near out of my skin. My back crashed into the wall at the sight of him sitting at the edge of my bed, as if he'd been waiting there for a disturbing amount of time.

"What are you doing in here?"

Blood pumped a little faster as I steadied myself, feeling as if the effects of my drinking binge were wearing off, overtaken by adrenaline.

"I told you I had something for you."

"You can't just come into my room, let alone sit here in the dark. Don't you see how fucking creepy that is?"

"Did I scare you, *mo stoirín*?" he asked with a devilish grin, pushing to his feet. "I thought I taught you better than that. Always be ready."

As he approached, I squared my shoulders. "I wasn't expecting anyone, least of all you."

"Well, that was your first mistake." His breath fanned the back of my neck, but I refused to give him what he wanted and didn't turn around. Although my instincts were not as sharp, I was ready.

Ronan had never overstepped. The vibes he gave off were just that. And while I knew what he was capable of, the line in the sand had always been clear. But tonight, something about his demeanor, his words, and the sinister way they slid off his tongue had me on alert.

"Listen, I'm tired and—"

"You've been drinking," he said, now in front of me. "Heavily."

"So what? You've never cared before."

He shrugged. "And I don't now. My only concern is—why?"

"I was celebrating with the boys. I don't understand your line of questioning."

Ronan said nothing for a beat, his eyes on mine, and then he slowly brushed his thumb down my cheek.

"What were you crying about?"

My mascara.

I remembered my reflection in the bar mirror, my face streaked with makeup after I had cried over Ezra. Kai and Derek tried to get me to confess, but decided to let me sleep it off and question me when I was sober.

Pulling away, I motioned toward the door, ushering him out.

"We can talk tomorrow. I told you I'm exhausted."

Again, a stretch of uncomfortable silence settled between us, until he jerked his bearded chin toward the bay window, where a brown box sat on my desk. The once-warm room turned cold, and the hairs on my arms stood on end. I couldn't guess what was inside, but instinct warned me to keep my distance. Still, curiosity was a bitch.

My gait was unsteady as I approached the box and rested a hand on the lid.

"What is it?"

"The faster you open it, the faster you find out," he said with a slight chuckle. "Not exactly what I had planned, but I think you'll love the upgrade."

Malice laced his tone, and I hesitated, exhaling a heavy breath before tearing the box open. I instantly regretted it. The air I'd just forced from my lungs left no space to breathe. The room turned suffocating, and my throat collapsed in on itself at the horrific sight before me.

Ezra.

My boyfriend—reduced to a tiny box in the cruelest and most horrific way. His head, severed at the neck, lay on its side, eyes swollen, his skin mottled in hues of purple and ash. As I took a shaky step back, the contents of my stomach rushed up and splashed at my feet. I'd seen death. I'd doled it out without remorse for the last two years.

But this was different.

"Run away together, huh? And you let him call you...*Dollface?*" He chuckled wickedly. "Would've almost been sweet if the two people I cared for most weren't betraying me and plotting behind my back. My nephew knew the rules when it came to you."

Ronan crept closer, but I was frozen in place from shock and mortification, my eyes still fixed on Ezra's lifeless ones.

"W-why?" I managed to choke out.

His lips ghosted over my bare shoulder, and another bout of nausea rolled through me.

"Because you're mine."

He didn't need to elaborate. His claim on me wasn't that of an overprotective father. My intuition all these years had been right.

"You're sick."

"I'm glad we've cleared that up." When he leaned in for another kiss, it was the spark I needed to make a move. Dropping to the floor, I reached for the Sig under my bed, but my blood ran cold when I came up empty.

Ronan's cruel laughter echoed from above me.

"Looking for something, darling?" In a flash, his hand tangled in my hair, and he yanked me to my knees. "I can give you the world, Athena. All you have to do is let me."

"Fuck you!" I cried, thrashing against the pain of his grip. "I'll never be yours. You're going to have to kill me...or I'll kill you first."

His eyes widened when I drove a blade into his side. Before I could plunge it again, he grabbed me by the throat and hurled me over the bed with brutal force. I crashed to the floor on the other side, pain ripping through me.

My mouth fell open as I struggled to draw breath.

"F-fuck," I whimpered, slightly dazed as I pushed my chest off the hardwood and watched as blood pooled below me from a gash on my head.

"So you want to do this the hard way." Ronan rounded the bed and pulled the knife from his body with a grunt. "Let's dance."

"When Derek and Kai find out, they're going to kill you."

"Who's going to tell them? For all they know, you ran away with that headless bastard over there. Left this life behind without saying a goddamn word. Isn't that what you wrote in your little messages?"

Ronan's hand was around my throat again. Maybe if I hadn't had so much to drink, I'd have more of a fight in me. I'd taken on men his size in the past and won.

"You can lock me up...torture me, but I'll never be yours. And I'll *never* stop fighting you."

"I know you won't." He swept his tongue up the side of my face, where blood was still flowing in a steady drip. "That's why, as much as it pains me, I'll have to break you."

TWO

Athena

Was it possible for the room to spin while my eyes were closed? Not that I had a choice, because it felt like my eyelids were glued shut, or made of lead. The heaviness radiated to my limbs, reminding me of when I convinced the boys to ride the Graviton at the state fair. A terrible decision we all paid for, doubled over behind shrubs, puking up our lunch.

The boys...

Visions of their faces floated in my thoughts like a hazy memory I couldn't quite reach.

Where was I? What happened?

The rush of a highway registered first, then the sensation of movement beneath me. I was in a car, speeding fast. And I didn't need my sight to know I was shrouded in darkness.

Realization hit me with the force of a bomb.

Ronan.

Every sensation came rushing forward at once. My arms and legs were bound tight, but even without the restraints, my body felt too weak to fight back or attempt an escape. Worse, a creeping numbness was spreading through every inch of me. And the scream blazing its way up my throat escaped only as a muffled whimper. I thrashed and clawed—at least in my mind—but my body refused to listen..

There was no telling how long I'd been out, how far I was from home, or where the fuck I was heading.

No, no, no...

Tears slipped from my eyes as the truth sank in. I was truly fucked.

Drugged. Beaten. Tied up like an animal heading to slaughter.

I will have to break you. Those were the last words he'd said before my world caved in on itself.

At the thought of what was coming, a soundless sob tore through me. I knew Ronan well enough to mistake his threats for empty promises. Whatever fresh hell waited at the end of this ride, it was meant to break me. Or kill me.

I didn't have a second to dwell on my fate. The car jolted to a sudden stop, and I was thrown hard against the rugged interior of what I could only assume was the trunk.

Pain exploded behind my eyes as my head struck a sharp edge, metal or something worse, and I knew, without a doubt, it had left a gash. Between the adrenaline and whatever sedatives were still in my system, it was impossible to tell how bad the damage was. For all I knew, I could be bleeding out. And I wouldn't even feel it.

"Get the girl inside. And remember what he said: no one touches her." The command came from a gruff voice right outside the trunk. "I'll be back in the morning. Try to keep that bitch alive. She was bleeding all over my fucking car."

A second man responded in Russian.

Fuck, fuck, fuck.

Then came a loud creak, followed by a rush of cool air.

I stiffened and held my breath, waiting for him to make a move, but seconds crawled by in suffocating silence.

What the fuck was he waiting for? I could feel his eyes on me and nearly jumped out of my skin when his rough hand fell over my hip. But I forced myself to stay still and feign uncon-sciousness.

Until the sudden blaring of a horn caused me to jerk.

"There you are," he said with a heavy accent.

"Sasha, hurry up and get that bitch from my trunk before I send you the cleaning bill."

The man chuckled deeply and plucked me up like a rag doll, tossing me over his shoulder and telling him to go fuck himself in Russian.

No more words were exchanged before the car peeled away, the screech of tires and stench of burned rubber flooding my senses.

"P-p…" I swallowed hard, bracing myself to speak as I fought to find my voice. "Pl-please…" I whispered on a raspy breath. "L-Let me…go."

The man barked a laugh as he dragged me forward, grass whispering beneath his feet as we moved toward some unknown destination.

"Even if I wanted to, I can't do that. Don't be foolish."

The slam of a heavy door, followed by the sharp click of a deadbolt, tightened my chest. I knew then that my fate was sealed, and there would be no escaping.

"No…please."

"I'm just here to get paid, pretty girl."

Without warning, he tossed me on a bed and tugged my arms above my head, where he latched my restraints to metal rails.

"Can't have you trying to run."

Every second that ticked by brought me closer to a fate worse than death. Like some twisted premonition, I could feel it.

"Open your eyes," he demanded, ripping off my blindfold so callously that he tore several strands of hair from my scalp. "I want to see if what they say is true."

I wasn't sure if it was out of defiance or just the fact the world was now far too bright, but I squeezed them tighter and shook my head as more tears slid from the corners.

"Don't get bold. Do as I say."

His large hands gripped my throat, forcing my eyes wide and my mouth open, while his boisterous laughter echoed off the walls of that dank room.

"That bastard, Kirill, wasn't lying." The hazy vision of his face neared mine, and a deep crease drew his eyebrows together. "Demon eyes...*ved'ma.*"

Something in his gaze shifted and darkened, as if whatever shred of humanity that had once lived inside this man was gone now.

Ever since I was a child, I'd gotten used to the stares and double takes my heterochromia always drew—the stark contrast between one blue eye and one brown. Yet in my eighteen years of life, no one had ever looked at me the way he was, as if I were no longer a person but an object to be loathed and used.

When his eyes drifted over my chest and down the length of my abdomen, I followed his gaze, and gasped in horror when I realized I was naked.

Not even the night my parents died had ever made me feel so utterly vulnerable and helpless. The sadistic tilt of his mouth and the gleam in his narrowed eyes sent me spiraling into despair. My only consolation was that the other bastard had warned him I was untouchable. But he didn't seem the type to follow anyone's rules.

I bit back a sob, refusing to give him the satisfaction of seeing me cry.

You won't break me.

"You know, witch," he said with a morbidly amused tone, tracing a rough hand up my thigh, "boss wants you cleaned up and pretty for tomorrow."

I yanked at my restraints, desperate to crawl away from his touch. "Let me go. You don't have to do this. Please."

"I know." His shrug was callous. "But I do need to get paid."

Thick fingers gripped my chin, the metallic taste of blood spilling into my mouth.

"What do you say? Bath or shower?"

"Fuck you!"

Searing pain exploded across the side of my face when the back of his hand connected with my cheek. I clamped down on my jaw and muffled a scream as another steady drip of liquid rolled into my ear from a laceration, most likely from a cut caused by his signet ring.

"That's always an option, too. Don't tempt me."

As much as I wanted to lash out or even beg him to kill me, I couldn't afford to be stupid or lose hope. I was still breathing, which meant there was still a chance to escape this nightmare. Kai and Derek were out there. They had to know I wouldn't just leave and cut them off.

Didn't they?

I squeezed my eyes shut, fighting back tears, and listened as his footsteps faded, followed by the heavy creak of the door closing. It wasn't until the silence settled around me that I realized I'd been holding my breath.

A gasp of relief escaped my trembling lips because even if only for a moment, I was safe. Alone.

Now, I needed to plan, strategize, and use every ounce of my training to figure out how the fuck I'd get out of this mess.

Tilting my head, I tested the chains against the wrought-iron bedpost. Both were solid.

The cuffs binding my wrists were too tight to slip free. Not even the desperate thought of breaking my thumbs could set me loose.

"Fuck!" I screamed, kicking my legs, but they were too weak. "This can't be happening."

My voice cracked as pain and despair surged like a dam breaking. I cried out, each sob louder than the last...

Until I was drowning, water seeping down my nose and throat. My lungs were on fire, the pain magnified by violent spasms and coughing. I heard his barking laughter before my eyes snapped open to find the bastard standing over me, an empty bucket in his hand.

"That should shut you up." He sneered with a laugh.

My chest heaved as I tried to regain my breath, but another splash of ice-cold water left me voiceless and frozen in every sense of the word.

"Oh, fuck. You should see your face, witch." He doubled over, his vicious laughter hammering against my eardrum. "I'd heard stories about you, but now I know those were lies."

He dug his thumb into my cheek, reopening the cut inside my mouth, then squeezed, prying my jaw open. I couldn't hold back the whimpers. My suffering only fueled his cruelty.

"We aren't supposed to sample the merchandise. But tell me, little witch—who would know?"

Before I could register his words, his mouth slammed onto mine—aggressive and unforgiving.

I raged beneath him, fighting to break free, my legs desperate to shatter the prison of sedatives. When his tongue slid inside, I bit down hard, and his howls vibrated through my body.

Another sharp and heady slap rocked me into near unconsciousness.

"Bitch!" he roared, his newly acquired lisp twisting the word.

Through the haze of pain, a smile curved my lips as blood poured from his mouth, dribbling down his chin.

I spat blood and a small chunk of flesh. "Coward. Why don't you free me so we can play."

His eyes narrowed to slits, glaring at me as he pulled a key from his pocket like he was calling my bluff. I could take him on a good day, armed with a blade. But my muscles were weak, and I wasn't sure I could even stand. I was trained to never show weakness, even facing death. But regret churned inside me as he approached.

"You're fucked," he growled, tossing the key across the room and flipping me over.

"Wait...I'm sorry. Please..."

"On your knees."

The sound of his belt sliding free from the loops cracked through the air like a whip and sent me into a panic.

"Sasha...please," I begged between shuddering breaths, bracing for what I knew was coming.

"*Sasha?*" The fire of the first lash stole my breath, and the third and fourth, my soul. "On your knees. And call me sir."

Two more strikes blazed against my ass and the backs of my thighs, ripping a scream from my throat.

"On your knees, witch!"

Every slash threatened to send me into unconsciousness.

"Stop....please!"

"Call. Me. Sir."

Seven. Eight. Nine. Ten.

My shoulders. My back.

"I said, get up."

Eleven. Twelve.

My ass.

Thirteen. Fourteen. Fifteen. Sixteen. Seventeen. Eighteen. Nineteen.

"Do it!"

The sounds of leather on skin were wet now.

"F-fuck...s-stop," I sobbed, my voice stripped raw.

"Knees."

Trembling, I tried to lift myself off the mattress, but the pain forced me back down. Every inch of me felt shredded, like I'd been set on fire.

"Say it," he growled through heavy breaths. Not slowing, not stopping.

Twenty-three. Twenty-four. Twenty-five.

"S-sir...s-stop.

"But the blows kept coming. Until the edges of my vision darkened, and his ragged groans and the sounds of tearing flesh faded into a distant echo, pulling me down into nothingness.

THREE

Athena

"You goddamn bastard. He's going to slit your throat!"

The gravelly voice dragged me from the depths of darkness. But even as awareness surfaced, my eyes refused to open.

"Bitch nearly took my tongue. Had to teach her a lesson."

At his words, the part of me that had fled from the pain came crashing back, igniting every nerve to the agony of ruined flesh. I stifled a cry into the damp mattress, praying they wouldn't notice. But brutal fingers tangled in my hair, yanking my head up so hard I thought my neck might snap.

"Fuck. How will we explain this?"

"Easy. Get rid of her."

He released me, and I collapsed face-first onto the hard bed, whimpering like a wounded animal. The idea of death was almost a welcome comfort compared to the unrelenting pain tearing through me. I hated to think that giving up was my only option, but there was only one way this would end, and I would rather die than become someone's property.

"And what do you propose we tell Cain? She got away? That you killed her? None of those scenarios end well for either of us."

"Fine," Sasha huffed, sounding almost like a child denied

their turn. "Take her to Polina. She'll clean her up like she does the other girls."

"No! Kill me. Please." My voice broke, so choked with pain that the words barely made it out.

Sasha laughed and brought a heavy hand down on my ass. My mouth fell open in a soundless scream as I curled into myself, shuddering at the torturous shock wave that ripped through me.

"Put her to sleep."

I shook my head furiously. *Not again.*

"No...no. Just kill me."

The sharp sting of a needle pierced my arm. Ragged screams and whimpers tore from my throat until even the sound of my own voice felt miles away.

And then, slowly, I began to melt into the mattress.

———

Harsh Russian blared through a speaker, yanking me from the depths of another fog. This time, it was a woman. I didn't need to understand the words to know she was angry.

"I was given orders not to leave her. Have someone else do it."

Another blast of obscenities filled the room, but their argument faded into the background as I took in my surroundings. I was no longer on a wet mattress. They'd moved me somewhere new. Time and distance were meaningless now. For all I knew, I'd been unconscious for days...and carted across the country.

My wounds still pulsed like living entities, but as I mentally took stock of my body, I realized I was no longer bound.

My arms rested by my side beneath a thin blanket. But I remained still, refusing to alert her that I'd come to.

"Shit. I'll be there in five." She muttered something under her breath before a cell phone clattered onto a hard surface, ending the call.

Silence engulfed the room as I felt her draw closer. My heart pounded faster with each step, and for a moment, I wondered if she could hear it slamming against my ribs.

"Don't you move," she snapped, sliding the chair back as she stood. The moment the door clicked behind her, I exhaled, my muscles relaxing against the cot.

My eyes flew open as much as the swelling would allow.

The room was small and dimly lit, without a single window to offer an escape, not even a six-story jump to salvation.

I didn't know where the fuck I was or what awaited me on the other side of that door, but it was my only shot. I wiggled my toes and tested my feet, gauging my strength. The drug's effects still lingered, but I managed to bend my knee and brace myself against the edge, pushing into a sitting position.

"Oh...fuck!" Every wound lit up, stealing my breath and forcing me to tense. Black spots danced behind my eyes as I fought through wave after wave of unforgiving pain.

"I can do this...I have to."

Blinking away tears, I huffed and rolled over, slowly at first.

"That's it," I whispered.

But between my wounds and the drugs, I overshot, unable to stop in time. Instead of falling toward the floor, it felt like the floor exploded into me, knocking the last bit of oxygen from my lungs.

Was it karma? Was this punishment for everything I'd done? The men I'd killed? Was I already dead, trapped in hell? It had to be the only explanation, the only justification for the misery swallowing me whole.

"Get...up."

My tears mixed with the blood droplets on the floor.

"Get up...goddamn it!"

You're stronger than this.

I wasn't weak. Never weak.

On a long pull of air, I pushed to my knees and reached for the cot.

Just a little more.

My ankles wobbled as I stood, but I gripped the edge to steady myself. Pressure lifted from my back, and I became aware of the tightly wrapped bandages. A shred of gratitude flickered for the woman. I hated to imagine how much worse my raw skin would have felt, exposed and untreated.

Days.

It had to have been days by now.

Were Derek and Kai searching for me? What had Ronan told them?

The messages.

No.

They'd believe him. He'd show them our talks about leaving.

I promised you, Kai. Please remember.

But with both Ezra and I gone...

As if my brain had locked away the trauma, the memory of Ezra's severed head was all I could see. A sudden rush of adrenaline propelled me toward the door, and I stumbled into an empty hallway, desperate to escape the nightmarish images.

The walls were stark white and bare, like some clinical facility. I followed a row of recessed lights and turned a corner into a longer corridor, where a red emergency exit sign glowed at the end like a beacon. Leaning on the wall for support, I moved as fast as my legs would carry me.

Almost there.

Renewed strength and a glimmer of hope fueled me as I swung around the corner. But instead of freedom, I slammed into a broad chest, the impact sending me crashing backward onto my ass.

Every human body had a threshold of pain before it shut down—passed out or went into shock. I wondered how close I was to that limit.

"And where the fuck do you think you're going?" My attempts to scoot away were pitiful. He pulled me by the front of my gown. And another wave of searing pain tore through me, but I didn't have the strength to even cry out.

I expected Sasha to come barreling down the hall and finish me off, but an unfamiliar man with silver-capped teeth grabbed my arm.

"She must have gotten out during transport. I'll escort her back."

Through my haze, I locked eyes with the first man, and his dark gaze flickered with confusion.

"I don't remember this one."

"That's 'cause her face is fucked to all hell."

"That must mean she's trouble, doesn't it?" Again, he assessed me cautiously, and my eyes fell on the black scorpion tattoo on his neck. "Get her to the truck before they take off."

The taller of the two dragged me down the hall.

But something wasn't right.

Transport?

We reached what appeared to be an abandoned hangar, where a white delivery truck was starting to pull away. The man whistled loudly near my ear, grabbing the driver's attention. They exchanged words, but I was trapped in a haze, their voices fading into indecipherable echoes as the ringing in my ears grew louder...Until the latch on the back of the truck popped, and the metal door slid open.

"Get in!"

Inside the haul, a group of women and girls were crammed together. Some were awake and crying, while others lay sedated, their faces vacant and distant.

"No." I shook my head. "I'm not supposed to be here."

"Me neither, princess. My lunch break was nearly an hour ago. Now, get your ass inside before I throw you in."

"No! Get your fucking hands off me."

I thrashed against his grip and clocked him with a right hook to the nose. Swallowing thickly, I swung again. And when he doubled over, I snatched his gun and fired into his shoulder.

Screams erupted behind me, and I let off another round until he went still.

"I *don't* belong here."

The driver's footsteps jerked me around, but before I could react, a sharp prick to my neck burned through the fog. I stumbled, slowly cupping the spot where it stung.

"Fuck!"

My legs buckled beneath me, the world tilting at a nauseating angle as I staggered toward a wobbly door.

"No... please, no."

Blindly squeezing the trigger, I fired wild shots into the hangar—a last stand, frantic and aimless. I collapsed to my knees, vision swimming, the gun trembling in my grip.

With the final thread of consciousness slipping, I pressed the barrel to my temple and shut my eyes as tears carved down my cheeks.

Death was mercy.

Click.

Fuck. Me.

Cold concrete slammed against my face as my body gave out.

The blurry images of Kai and Derek dimmed as I tipped into the abyss.

Come find me.

FOUR

Athena

Never stop fighting.

"Sleeping beauty. Wake up!" Sharp slaps against my cheek forced my eyes open to blinding white light. I recoiled from the bright rays of a sun I hadn't seen in…in…

I didn't know how long.

Days? Weeks?

Moving, locked up. Sleep, sleep, and more *fucking* sleep. I was dead to the world more than I was conscious. But maybe it was better that way.

"Now that you look more *presentable*, it's time to start earning your keep." Her graying brown hair was pulled into a tight bun. She was tall, with an accent I couldn't place, and muscled arms suggesting she followed a strict workout regimen. When the woman effortlessly lifted me off the cot, bridal style, and carried me to a walk-in shower, she confirmed my suspicions.

"Let's clean you up. You're a young one, aren't you?"

I said nothing as she stripped off a gown I assumed had once been white.

"I heard you've been keeping the guys here on their toes." I ignored her, staring off, too mentally drained and still swimming in sedatives to care. But she had my full attention when her fingers knotted in my hair, yanking my head back. "If you don't start cooperating, they'll toss your ass into the nearest landfill. Do you understand me?" She twisted harder when I didn't answer fast enough.

"Y-yes." I barely recognized my own voice. The last thing I remembered was screaming until I tasted blood. Then they drugged me again.

"The only reason you're still alive is because you're young and pretty." Her calloused fingers tilted my chin. "You have these strange eyes, and you're a virgin."

My eyes snapped to hers, stomach twisting. "What?"

"Your hymen is intact."

I blinked furiously, unable to understand how and when... and *who?*

"Oh, come on. Don't act surprised. You thought they wouldn't check? Do you know how much you're worth? It's the only reason you haven't been sent to the Pit. And trust me, that's not somewhere you want to be."

The question hung on my tongue, but I chose silence again. I believed her. The name alone was enough of a warning.

A spray of cold water tumbled over my body.

"I don't know what you did to deserve these," she murmured, fingertips gliding over the shredded skin of my back. "But it's nothing a little makeup won't fix. Some of my homemade balm will help fade the scars."

Her tone was calm, playful, as if she hadn't just been talking about selling my virginity to the highest bidder.

Every time they drugged me, I fought when I woke up. Screamed. Clawed. Begged.

But no one listened. They wouldn't kill me. And they wouldn't let me go. This nightmare was never-ending, like a revolving door to hell on earth—and somehow, I knew I hadn't even gotten to the worst part.

"Please," I whispered, voice cracking. "You have to help me. I'm not supposed to be here."

The woman's rough fingers paused in my hair, and she tugged my head back again. "Do you think the girls here volunteered or won some fucking lottery?" Her laugh was cruel. "In a perfect world, honey, none of us would be here. Not even me."

More cold water crashed over my head, trailing down my shivering body.

"Magda!" A man's voice boomed from the other side of the door, followed by the heavy thud of his fist. "He's here."

"You dumb fuck. No names!" As if his slip had been *my* fault, she forced my face under the freezing spray until water flooded my lungs. I thrashed, choking and coughing violently.

"Now, come on. Tonight is your night. We have a client with *very* deep pockets waiting for you."

"No," I wheezed, still struggling to breathe. "Kill me."

"If you get another dose today, you may never wake up. So I suggest you calm down and get comfortable."

"Do it!" More than wanting to die, I *needed* it. I craved it, the numbness it brought. It was the only time the pain stopped and the voices faded. "Do it, please! Do it!"

Her backhand came fast, a brutal crack that set my right ear ringing.

"I have kids to feed. Your tears and your pleas mean nothing." She dragged me across the cold floor by my cuffs and tossed me into a chair. "I only have twenty minutes to get you looking like some virginal fucking offering, and your hair is a disaster. This"—she gestured wide—"*this* is your reality now. Whatever life you had before, the people you knew, friends, family, all gone."

Magda spun me toward a mirror, but I dropped my head, refusing to look. Tears dripped down my thighs.

I was afraid of the girl staring back, the one I was losing piece by piece.

Every single day.

———

Another fog began to lift, slowly dispersing as I clawed my way back to the surface. I didn't want to. I wanted nothing more than to sink and never wake up. Magda must have given in.

Had I fought her, after all? I couldn't remember.

"Nice of you to join the party."

Fuck. The client. The monster.

"I know you can hear me. Go on, now, open your eyes."

I bit back the bile rising up my throat when his hand fell on my thigh. Even if I had the strength to swat him away, my wrists were chained to the bedpost.

I was unaware of their drug of choice. The one keeping me compliant, slowing my body, and clouding my mind.

But I welcomed it.

Strong fingers gripped my face, nails cutting into skin as he forced my eyes to meet his.

"Beautiful," he said with a twisted smirk. "I'm a little pressed for time tonight, but I couldn't pass you up. So, excuse me if this goes a little faster than you can tolerate. I wasn't expecting the cuffs, but I heard you've got a spark in you. I like that."

They'd sold me like livestock to a man who would take the last strip of my dignity. Inside my mind, I was screaming, clawing for freedom. But bound and drugged, I was helpless to save myself.

I jolted when he pinched my nipple.

"Stop," I whispered as he tweaked harder. "No, stop!"

"It's okay," he reassured me, ignoring my cries and kissing my neck.

"No...no, please."

"*Relax*." His low growl brushed against my ear as his hand cupped between my legs.

"Don't touch me!"

Coarse fingers split me open and slid toward my entrance.

"I'd love to feel how tight you are, sweetheart, but I need to see how pretty you bleed on my cock."

Oh, god.

He jumped off the bed, stripping as he stroked himself, eyes dark and lecherous.

"Please...don't." I shook my head and turned away. But I should have known better. Never take your eyes off the enemy. He flipped me over and hauled me to my knees, kicking my thighs farther apart.

"Stop! You son of a bitch!"

I heard him spit, then he slapped my ass three times, each strike burning like he'd set my skin on fire.

Yelping into the mattress, I twisted, desperate to escape, but he gripped my hips and pressed his weight against me.

"I told you to relax," he rasped in my ear, his cock now at my entrance.

"No! Don't—"

The words died in my throat as he mercilessly shoved inside. I thought I knew pain, that we'd become well-acquainted over the last few weeks, but fuck, was I wrong.

Red hot flames scorched me from the inside out as he brutally pistoned inside me.

In and out, his fists tangled in my hair.

The satin sheets muffled my sobs as he continued his assault.

"Oh, fuck, sweetheart...look at you. That's the prettiest fucking shade of red I've ever seen."

Blood-streaked handprints smeared across my back, my ass, and the mattress. That sick, sorry bastard. He was so fucking proud.

But my body wasn't his to take, to violate, and desecrate. I didn't belong to him.

I was yours, Ezra. But you left me here.

The world faded to black, over and over, day after day. Each time I woke, my soul dimmed a little more—a new face, a different set of eyes staring down at me...until they all blurred into the same monster.

FIVE

Athena

A loud, drawn-out grunt vibrated in my ear as he pumped the last of himself inside me. His breath was vile and hot on my neck. I closed my eyes, silently begging he'd leave without a word, without extra favors. But when had luck ever been on my side?

My prayers had long since drowned in an endless sea of tears and despair.

"Just give me five minutes, sweetheart, and I'll come back for this," he said, pushing his thumb against the tight rim of muscles in my ass.

I shuddered at the thought of the pain waiting for me. It wouldn't be the first time. Mr. H was a fucking sadist. He thrived on tears, pain, and blood. The night he took my virginity, he'd made sure I bled far more than necessary and proudly wore what he stole like war paint.

There were others, of course, but he was consistent, always coming back for more. I begged for the day he'd take it all and end me.

"I had some meetings scheduled tonight and a three-day business trip over the weekend," he said casually, slicking back his hair in the mirror. "But it turns out, we had last-minute cancellations. *And* since the wife and kids are out of town, you got me for the next four days." He slammed the comb down on the dresser, then turned with a wicked grin, his eyes roaming the length of my naked body.

Four days.

Surviving twenty-four hours with this man was a feat in itself. But four days...

It's what you want. Let her die.

"I have some fun planned for us, sweet girl." Mr. H slowly dragged his hand along my inner thigh. "Are you excited?"

He'd never demanded I speak before, so I didn't see a reason to reply. It wasn't until he flipped me over, face inches from mine, and three fingers buried so painfully inside me that I realized his twisted game had upgraded.

"Y-yes," I breathed.

His eyes, light green flecked with gold, framed by pale lashes, reminded me of Ronan. The way he masked depravity with dark humor.

Ronan.

I hadn't thought of that name in so long.

Then again, I hadn't thought much about my life at all.

Because not thinking, not feeling, was safer.

But suddenly, my blood ran warmer, faster. A flush of anger rose, heating my cheeks hotter each time Mr. H's fingers slid back and forth. When he pinched my face and forced me to watch him suck those intrusive fingers clean, I decided it was time for him to die.

No one would come looking if he were slated to spend the next four days with me.

Play the part.

"My wrists. Just for a little?"

I met his gaze, following it down to where my hands were bound, cuffs digging deep into raw, torn skin. If Mr. H didn't kill me soon, infection would.

"You know that's not allowed. Naughty girl."

"What if I begged?"

He chuckled. "You know what I like, don't you?"

I nodded. "I do."

Sometimes, we didn't know what we were asking for. And when he flipped me back around and lifted my ass in the air, I instantly regretted the sacrifice. But as he plunged inside with just a drop of saliva for his benefit, it became clear: my suffering was a means to an end.

His end.

There was no guarantee he'd keep his word, but I had four miserable days to convince him.

———

I'd always taken something as simple as scratching my nose for granted. But that morning, or night, or whatever the fuck time it was, that small, once trivial gesture was a godsend. The metal cuffs lay on the nightstand, no longer biting into my wrists.

Mr. H slept beside me, one arm draped possessively around my waist.

With a slow, steady exhale, I eased onto my back and slid off the edge of the bed, moving as silently as I could manage.

Hitting the floor, I rolled onto my hands and knees, fighting the lingering fog of the drugs.

Two days in that bed had stolen what little strength I had left, and my legs trembled as I stretched to my feet. Once fit and curvy, the ghastly sight of my rail-thin body and sunken eyes in the mirror made me pause. Magda, that bitch, fed me just enough to keep me alive...or whatever this existence counted as.

I snatched a key card and his black comb from the dresser, snapping the teeth off one end.

My eyes locked on the door. I could just walk out. Take my chances. Trying to kill him in his sleep with a broken plastic comb was reckless, maybe suicidal. But letting him live wasn't an option either.

When I straddled his abdomen, his hands instinctively found my thighs, and a faint smile curved his lips.

"Good morning to you, too, sweet girl."

"It's a good morning to go to hell."

The moment his eyes flew open, I drove the sharpened edge of the comb into his jugular. His first instinct was to claw at me —at my skin, my arms—but my hand came down again, and again. Two more times, until the plastic snapped under the pressure. By then, I was soaked in his blood. It painted my chest, my hands, my face, warm and metallic as he gasped and gurgled through the torn mess of his throat.

But it wasn't enough.

He'd violated me. Invaded my body without permission. Desecrated my blood like it was his fucking right. It was only fair that I paid him with the same disrespect. Mr. H didn't deserve a quiet, suffocating death on the floor of this godforsaken place.

His pale brows shot up in shock, nearly to his hairline, when I reached into the gaping wound at his neck and tore. Flesh, tissue, tendon, anything I could grasp as he shuddered beneath me. A final gift for the monster who thought I'd never fight back.

He wasn't deserving of mercy. But maybe his death would bring a sliver of peace to the wife and children he pretended to love. And when the light finally faded from his eyes, the feeling was damn near orgasmic.

With Ares, my marks had always been just names on a contract, and I'd grown numb to the sound of their final breaths. But this moment fractured something deep inside me.

An unnerving sense of déjà vu crept in as I shuffled toward the door and twisted the knob. But there was no turning back. My fate was freedom or death, only I wasn't sure which of the two I desired more.

Bloodied and naked, I staggered down a dim hallway, turning left toward a pulsating red light above a metal door. Cameras blinked in every corner, and I knew it was only a matter of time before I was spotted. My legs still trembled, weak from days in that bed, but I forced them into a slow, clumsy sprint until I crashed through the door and straight into a torrential downpour.

The slanted rain was thick, slicing through the night sky and against my skin. I dropped to my knees and let the storm wash me clean—of his blood, their imprint, the filth of every violation.

But it was all in vain. Their hands still stained my soul, and their voices had found a permanent home inside my mind.

She's too far gone.

I collapsed, head bowed, wet hair hanging in limp strands around my face as the tears came.

"What the fuck are you doing out here?"

Strong arms plucked me from the mud. I knew that voice.

"You're supposed to be with Mr. Halstad."

"He's dead."

Magda's hand shot to my throat, squeezing until I saw stars. "Come again?"

"Fuck..." I gasped, then slammed my forehead into hers, "... him. And fuck you too."

The impact caught her off guard, and she stumbled back, slipping in the mud. I hit the ground hard, ankle twisting beneath me. Pain flared, but I wouldn't stop.

I *couldn't* stop.

I'd be damned if I'd gotten this far just to let her drag me back to hell. I limped toward the chain-link fence, her footsteps pounding behind me.

"You're going to fry, bitch!" She lunged, grabbed my hair, and spun me back around, her fist cracking into the side of my face. Sparks of light exploded behind my eyes, and I nearly dropped.

God, I wanted to stay down. To let it end.

But I trained for eight years in hand-to-hand combat.

Never stop fighting.

I ducked her next swing and drove my fist into her gut. She

gasped, winded, groaning from the blow, but her fingers still clung to my hair like a damn leech.

"You want to get bold, huh?"

Another blow to my jaw had me spitting blood, but I gave it right back and reveled in the sickening crunch of cartilage. Red sprayed from her nose, slicking down her chin...and she smiled through it like the sadistic cunt she was.

"That was cute." In a flash, her arms locked around me, and she slammed my back to the ground, the air fleeing my lungs in a harsh gasp.

"You'll pay dearly for what you've done," she growled, pressing her weight into me, pinning me like prey.

"Fucking kill me!" I spit in her face, and she slapped me hard, then backhanded me for good measure. "Is that...all you got?" I wheezed, grinning through the blood.

"I'll see you in the Pit."

Fuck.

The Pit was worse than death. A free for all. Where everyone took a turn and lived out their most depraved fantasies while others watched.

I'd found that out the hard way.

"Look at you, taking all of us so good."

With the last of my strength, I shifted my hips upward, throwing her off balance and over my head. Magda landed with a heavy thud. I quickly straddled her, and snatched a rock. Her front teeth shattered under the first blow, dazing her.

"You're a disgrace. What you do to these girls..."

The jagged edge crushed her face with every punch.

One.

Two.

Three.

Four.

Until her flesh was mangled beyond recognition.

"Hey!" a man roared from the door. Another flanked him. Both were armed and sprinting straight for me.

No, no, no.

I dove for the fence, heart slamming against my ribs as bullets screamed past me. My hands scrambled up the slick metal where barbed wire crowned the top, tearing into my flesh when I tried to scale the razor-sharp edge.

I swallowed the pain as skin split and peeled away.

Then crack...

A bullet clipped my side, and I slipped, falling, and hitting the ground hard.

I cried out, my lungs burning but I flipped over and bolted, legs pumping through the dark until I crashed through a thick wall of trees. Behind me, the gate groaned open.

"Oh, fuck."

I stumbled, nearly went down, but kept running.

Because this was it. My last chance.

If they caught me, they wouldn't kill me. They'd *keep* me. Break me. Torture me until I begged to die, then do it all over again.

I won't go back.

Shouts echoed behind me, voices closing in no matter how fast I ran. I cupped the wound at my side, slipping in the mud as I finally broke through the tree line and reached an embankment. Headlights approached like a godsend. I tried to climb the hill, but the slope was too steep. Too wet. Every step I took, I slid back down into the ditch.

"Fuck!" I sobbed into the darkness, the sound echoing through the trees.

I'd just given myself away.

"You have to keep moving, goddamn it!"

Using both hands, I gripped at the slick roots, my feet digging into the mud, slipping, sliding—but I *pushed*. One desperate shove at a time until I clawed my way over the edge and rolled onto the cracked shoulder of a highway. Cold asphalt met my skin, and I crawled forward a few feet, dragging my body inch by inch.

Then collapsed.

I couldn't stand. Couldn't breathe. My limbs trembled and gave out. So I lay there, blood soaking through my side, and I whispered a prayer.

Please let me die before they find me.

"Oh, my God! Lorenzo, call for help!"

A sharp hiss tore from my throat when a woman flipped me over, cold fingers brushing wet, matted hair from my face.

An angel.

Soft eyes. Warm voice. She couldn't be real.

"Honey, what on earth happened to you? Where did you come from?"

I shook my head, vision blurring.

"They're coming. Please...don't let them get me."

"Who? Who's coming?"

Rain blurred everything. I clutched her jacket with shaky fingers as I fought to stay conscious.

"We have to go...Can't...stay here."

"It'll be okay. We'll get you help."

Why was she talking funny? And why were there two of her now?

Everything was spinning, and my body gave out. Her voice faded, a gentle hum swallowed by the storm.

Then...nothing.

SIX

Athena

The Castle – Chris Grey

Faint whispers and distant beeping roused me awake to sterile air that clung to my skin, sending a shiver rippling down my spine. Then it hit me.

The blood.

The mud.

The rain.

Magda.

My breath caught and panic surged. I clawed at the sheets and pushed myself upright.

"Hey, hey, it's okay." A pair of hands gripped my shoulders. "Easy. You're safe."

I thrashed against them.

"N-no…" My voice cracked, raw and foreign to my own ears.

"Hey, look at me. You're in a hospital. No one's going to hurt you."

But that wasn't true.

I'd learned that nowhere was safe. Not beds, not locked doors, not even inside your own fucking skin.

I twisted, ready to fight again until I blinked against the brightness pouring through a nearby window, and the woman came into focus. The light behind her flared like a halo.

My angel.

Sinking into the pillow, a calm I hadn't known in so damn long washed over me as her warm brown eyes met mine with a gentle smile.

"It's okay." She paused. "How do you feel?"

Like I'd been hit by a freight train, then run over by a bus. Chewed up and spit out. Every inch was fiery and bruised.

I tried to speak, but my throat was sandpaper-dry.

"Water," I rasped, eyes on a white Styrofoam cup near the windowsill.

She moved without hesitation, lifting the straw to my lips and holding it steady while I drank.

"The nurse is supposed to make her rounds soon," she said softly. "But if you want me to go grab her, I can."

I shook my head. Instant regret. Even the smallest movement made the ache pulse harder, like my body was begging to be sedated again, desperate for the sharp kiss of a needle.

"No, not yet. I just need to...breathe."

"I understand," she murmured, reaching for my bandaged hand with careful fingers. "You've been through a lot. Three days ago, I wasn't sure you were going to make it."

"Three days?"

Her smile faltered.

"Yeah. You're pretty banged up. God, I'm so sorry for what they did to you."

"You don't even know me, and you stuck around for three days."

"Maybe...I've been in your shoes. And I remember wishing someone had been there for me when I woke up."

Tears welled in my eyes at her kindness. She could have

dropped me off and disappeared—or worse yet, kept driving. And if the roles were reversed, would I have stopped?

"Thank you."

"Of course. I'm Cambri, by the way."

"Thank you, Cambri. I'm..."

The name withered before it ever left my lips. That girl was no longer here. They'd murdered her. Every trace. Just thinking her name made my skin crawl. It didn't belong to me anymore.

That name was weak. Gone.

Athena was dead.

But if I wasn't her...then who the hell was I now?

The question echoed as I forced myself upright, muscles screaming, and skin splitting.

"Hey, you're hurt. Please, lie back down."

When her hand reached for me, I slapped it away. Hard.

"Don't touch me."

The words came low and deadly, punctuated by the memory of chains, rough hands, and cold floors, ripping away the security I'd felt just moments ago.

She froze, hands up in surrender. "I'm not going to hurt you."

I shook my head as Cambri's image blurred behind tears. Maybe she was a good person. She had to be to stop for a bloodied stranger on the side of a dark highway. But there wasn't a soul on this earth I trusted. And the only people I gave a damn about probably thought I'd abandoned them.

I can't go back.

Ronan...

His name lodged in my throat. Just thinking of him triggered a fresh surge of panic. He had some of the world's most dangerous people in his pocket. Kai and Derek wouldn't stand a chance.

"I-I need to see..." Fingers tore at the IV in my arm and every goddamn piece of medical equipment. My legs felt boneless when I touched the floor and tried to bear weight. But I had to get up.

"You really shouldn't be doing this. But if you insist, at least let me help."

I hesitated, then gave a shaky nod and held out my hand.

But she didn't take it. Instead, she moved in close and gently swung my arm over her shoulder.

"Bathroom?"

"Please."

Step by step, we made our slow, agonizing crawl across the tile.

Every motion sent sparks of pain across my ribs, my side, my legs. I bit down on a cry, my jaw clamped shut.

"Can you hold yourself up?"

"Yes," I breathed, hunched over the sink, knuckles white as I gripped porcelain and stared down the drain. "Go."

"Are you sure?"

I wanted to scream, to tell her to fuck off. To unleash the fury rotting inside my bones until the whole fucking world burned for what it did to me. But Cambri didn't deserve my wrath.

"I'll let you know."

She nodded, retreating quietly out of the small space. The second I was alone, I grabbed the strap at my back and untied the gown. It slipped to the floor and pooled at my feet. Slowly, I lifted my gaze to the mirror. The person staring back was unrecognizable. Matted hair, stiff with blood and debris, while bruises and slashes painted every inch of my skin.

There was nothing left of the girl I used to be. Even my eyes were empty.

Dead.

The name Jane Doe was scrawled on the white bracelet on my wrist.

I'm no one.

I licked at my cracked lips, watching my reflection blur behind unshed tears.

But maybe...Maybe I could be anyone.

My life had been plagued by pain, loss, and death. But there was a time when the ugliness of the world hadn't touched me. Hadn't carved into my body. And hadn't taken so fucking much.

A memory flickered. Two little girls building sandcastles on a sun-drenched beach in Rio de Janeiro. My childhood best friend.

Amara Carvalho.

AMARA IS HERE NOW...

EIGHT

Santino

Slow Down – Bobby V.

"I was starting to think you wouldn't show."

Luca stood taller, filling out his suit more than when I'd seen him last. He wore a broad smile and outstretched his hand as he greeted me from the entrance of his late father's establishment. Uncle Lorenzo was still cold in a morgue while his firstborn was all business and grins, summoning me at first light to sign over the rights to Illusion. As co-owner, I was here to forfeit my share or take on full ownership. While I wasn't usually in the business of giving up assets, I didn't particularly care for the responsibility of a gentlemen's club in Miami.

I had plans to move back to Italy and lay low for a few years.

"Flight got delayed," I said, pulling my younger cousin in for a hug and hard clap to the back.

"Glad you made it."

"I'm sure you are."

He pushed open thick metal doors and chuckled. "Oh, come on, Santino. I'm happy to see you. It's been nearly four years, and we're practically brothers. *Papá* always saw you as a son, and I know he'd be honored that you came to say your goodbyes."

"I'm not staying for the service."

I was no stranger to death. It was as natural to me as breathing. We all had an expiration date. And Uncle Lorenzo's time had run up.

Every second that ticked by was one closer to death's door. And I was simply trying to be on a beach somewhere in the Mediterranean and, hopefully, buried to the hilt in good pussy when it came time to atone for my sins.

"Where are you off to in such a hurry?"

"Home, *cuginetto*," were the last words I spoke before music engulfed us, drowning out whatever rebuttal he tried to toss back as we stepped into the darkened lounge.

Red lights gave life to the crowded space, casting a pulse over everything it touched—the well-stocked bar in the distance, the velvet booths lined in shadows, and the stage lit like a fever dream.

A topless dancer commanded the pole, her fire-red hair snapping through the air as a glittering thong caught every beat of the strobe lights. She bent low, tempting the front row with every calculated move.

Thick smoke plumed from the patrons surrounding her, eyes glued, drinks sweating in their fists. Some shared their seats with women who clearly worked the floor, dancers, maybe. Escorts, more likely.

"Cambri," Luca said into my ear, his voice sharp over the bass. "One of our best. You should stay a while, *cugino*—enjoy the show."

Not that her tits weren't pretty, pierced with diamond barbells big enough to catch my attention from across the room, but jet lag was creeping in, and right now, a hot shower and a stiff drink sounded a hell of a lot better.

"Maybe next time I'm in town."

"At least let me hook you up with a private dance. It'd be a damn shame for you to come all this way just to turn around and leave without so much as tasting the merchandise."

I shifted my gaze back to Cambri, who now had her thong stretched around each ankle, arms raised above her head, fingers gripping the cold metal pole as she undulated her bare cunt toward the crowd.

Maybe I could stay a while longer.

"I can clear her schedule for you tonight. Get you one of our rooms upstairs. On me," he offered, pulling out a stool at the bar.

"You *that* happy to see me?" I chuckled, lighting a Fuente and leaning against the counter.

Luca had always been an ambitious son of a bitch. Hell, I wouldn't be surprised if he'd had a hand in his own father's death just to inherit the empire, the millions, the power he thought he deserved. Lorenzo knew exactly what kind of man his only son had become.

Stupid.

The old man had spent the better part of the last decade bailing him out of debt, bargaining for his life, expunging records, and dragging his ass in and out of rehab.

I gave this place a month before he gambled it away or burned it to the ground.

"You didn't have to come, so I'm thankful you decided to do right by my father."

I snorted, remembering how he practically begged me on the phone. My uncle would roll in his grave if he knew I was signing over Illusion to his fuckup of a son.

Luckily for Luca, I didn't give a damn. And Lorenzo was dead.

"So, what do you say? You up for Cambri?" he asked, waving over one of his staff and whispering in his ear.

The dancer was nowhere to be seen on stage now. The lights had dimmed, and employees in skimpy leather uniforms were collecting her winnings.

"I'll pass this time," I said, drawing short puffs from my cigar.

He shook his head in disbelief. "You're still interested in pussy, right, *cugino?*"

I shook my head in exasperation, eyes drifting back to the empty stage without a word, letting the comment slide.

The red bulbs suddenly pulsed with the shift in music, a sultry tune ready to lure the next clientele.

"You called for me, sir?"

The voice pulled me in. No need to see her face or memorize the glittering jewelry to know it was Cambri. Red waves tumbled over her shoulders, and the scent of vanilla filled the tight space between us. Her dark eyes met mine, a jeweled smile breaking across her lips as she took in my suit and watch.

Typical.

"I did. My cousin's on the fence about a private with you. Think you can convince him?" Luca settled back with a smug grin plastered across his face.

Dick.

Cambri's fingers traced my lapels as she slid between my legs, tugging forward just enough to make the point. "I'm sure with a little persuasion..."

The venue's noise faded around us, the rising beat pulsing louder. Drawn to the stage, I twisted, eyes locking on a new woman. Taller this time, draped in a skin-tight black suit, a curtain of dark curls cascading down her back.

A foreign fire smoldered low inside my chest, watching her command the stage like she owned every inch of it. Like she *knew* all eyes were hers, hanging on every flick, every sway.

What about this particular woman captivated me, setting her apart from Cambri? I couldn't say. But I'd heard whispers about a caliber of woman who could dominate a man with a single glance, lure him with the swing of her hips, and devour him with venom dripping from her lips.

"Who is she?" I demanded, pushing to my feet and nearly toppling the redhead in front of me.

"Amara," Luca said, the tightness in his tone impossible to miss.

Releasing Cambri, I pushed through the crowd, threading between patrons toward the stage, never once breaking eye contact with the woman in the black mask—her partially hidden face only added to her allure.

There was a moment when she swung around the pole, and I thought we connected. Maybe she felt the fire behind my stare and hesitated. Or maybe it was just my head playing tricks. But suddenly, having her attention was all I craved.

I reluctantly tore my gaze away from her and swept across the room, rage coiling tight in my muscles. Cambri had drawn plenty of eyes, maybe even more, fully nude, but irrational as it was, for the first time, a strange surge of possessiveness flared inside me for this woman.

"She's spectacular, isn't she?" Luca's hand landed on my shoulder.

"Tell me about her," I said, eyes locked on Amara's toned legs and fluid twirls.

Amara.

Her name fell like honey from my tongue.

"*Papá* took her in a few years back. Started out as a waitress. He caught her practicing one day before her shift, and here she is." He leaned in. "She doesn't take privates, but I'm sure I can pull some strings and get her for you. *Papá* had a soft spot for her, let her call the shots. But now that I'm in charge…Well, I can break her."

I shot him a cold look, curiosity sparking at what his insides might look like if I cracked him open.

"That won't be necessary."

He laughed, exhaling a sharp, exaggerated breath. "Santino, you're one tough son of a bitch. Even when I dangle pussy as pretty as two of our top dancers, you still won't budge."

Luca clapped me on the chest again. I fought the urge to rip his hand off.

"Come on, then," he said, nudging me toward his office. "Let's sign these papers so you can be on your way."

His head snapped up when I didn't follow, eyebrows knitting in confusion as I shot him one last look before turning my full attention back to the stage.

Amara stepped out of her bodysuit and dropped to the floor, arching her back with perfectly round tits thrusting toward the ceiling. Red, glittery pasties covered her nipples, making my jaw clench with the urge to tear them off with my teeth.

"Santino?"

"I'm not selling," I said flatly, shaking off Luca's grip.

Maybe Miami wasn't so bad, after all.

"What the fuck did you just say?"

The music died instantly as those words left his mouth. Every eye in the place turned to us, but suddenly they all blurred into the background. Because this time, there was no doubt.

I had Amara's full attention.

"Where have you been?"

Cambri barged into my dressing room, heels stabbing the tiled floor like she wanted to crack the foundation. I caught her wild eyes in the mirror as I wiped away makeup and glitter.

"I've been right here. What's got you so worked up?"

"Luca was escorted off the property. By our own security."

I froze mid-wipe, turning to face my friend now leaning against the vanity, red wig in hand, waiting for my reaction to the news that our temporary boss had been kicked out of his late father's club. As much as I loved her, Cambri had a knack for dragging out suspense like it was a goddamn soap opera.

Luca being gone would be the highlight of my night. He was crude, an absolute dick, and so far up his own ass, I was surprised he could see straight. Every day, I'd come to work and wonder if it would be the one where he would end up with my blade sticking out of his face.

"Are you going to tell me what happened, or do I need to beat it out of you?"

She laughed, shoulder-checking me.

"Apparently, the mysterious co-owner of Illusion finally

showed up. He and Luca got into it, and next thing I know, Blaise and Ash tossed his ass."

Cambri plucked a cigarette from her bralette and pinched it to the corner of her mouth, talking around it.

"It was *glorious.*'Bout time someone put that bastard in his place. And good *God* is he delicious."

The image of an unfamiliar man stitched itself into my thoughts. While we had our regulars, remembering every patron was impossible...but even through the shadows and flashing lights, forgetting a face like that would be downright tragic. We'd locked eyes from across the room just long enough for me to know he wasn't simply another horny client hiding his wedding ring and spending a small fortune on ass and tits. Call it intuition or paranoia, but I felt his presence here tonight meant something.

And clearly, I'd been spot on.

Not that I cared. I'd stopped giving a damn about men a long time ago. If I hadn't, maybe I would've stuck around for a little extra cash. But tonight had already been lucrative. What I wanted now was a hot shower, a warm bed, and a good book

"What's that look for?" I asked, eyeing Cambri's smug little grin.

"When that man saw you on stage?" She lit her cigarette, exhaling a curl of smoke. "He damn near threw me across the bar, Amara. He was *mesmerized.*"

Rolling my eyes, I wiped the last specks of glitter and stood.

"You know that means nothing to me. He's just another swinging dick getting hard to a half-naked woman putting on a show."

Cambri trailed behind as I slung my bag and headed for the door.

"I *know*, girl. But getting in good with the boss has its perks. You know that better than anyone. Lorenzo spoiled you, even gave you your own dressing room, while the rest of us peasants still fight for a corner of the mirror."

"Cambri, you know you're welcome to share with me," I said, laughing at her theatrics and throwing my arm around her shoulder.

She leaned into me with a mock sigh. "Fine. I'll move my stuff over tonight."

"Perfect."

"Can I have this fabulous vanity, though?"

"Don't push it..." I trailed off, tugging the door open and freezing when I found myself face-to-face with our new boss.

The glare of the stage lights hadn't done him justice. From a distance, sure, he was handsome. But up close, I wasn't ready. Something twisted low in my belly. Not butterflies. Not heat. None that shit women feel when they see an attractive man.

I felt...*sadness*.

I didn't know what it was about him that stirred the ghosts of my brothers, but suddenly the room felt too small, too loud, too *much*.

And I needed air.

I took a step back and nodded a greeting, planning to skirt around him until he shifted, his broad shoulders squaring, body filling the space like he *owned* it.

Technically, he did.

I sucked in a breath and clenched my fingers, nails digging into my palms to suppress the urge to reach for my knife.

"You must be Amara," he said, extending his hand. His accent reminded me of Lorenzo's.

"I am." I didn't take it.

His dark eyes held mine for a breath too long before sliding past me. "And you and I already met. Cambri, was it?"

"Yes, sir," she answered, perky as ever, reaching for the hand he never offered her, but shaking it with gusto anyway.

He chuckled, low and amused. "Call me Santino."

The invitation was meant for her, but his gaze was fixed back on me.

"Santino Leone. I'm taking over now that my uncle, Lorenzo, is no longer with us. And Luca is on a permanent leave."

"Welcome," I said flatly.

I caught the twitch in his eye at my indifference. If he thought I was one of those women impressed by angled jawlines, a pretty face, and a little status, he'd learn soon enough how far off the mark that assumption was.

I let my eyes drag down his towering frame, taking in the crisp, tailored suit before returning to his face, just in time to catch the flick of his tongue as he wet his lips.

And maybe, just maybe, that small act made me swallow a little harder than I meant to.

I took another step back.

"Amara, I'll grab my stuff and meet you outside!" Cambri slipped between us, grinning as she passed. "It was great to meet you, sir—Santino," she corrected, practically giggling before vanishing down the corridor.

I made a mental note to murder her in her sleep.

Santino leaned against the doorframe, one hand lazily rubbing the perfectly trimmed scruff along his jaw. It was all it took not to roll my eyes. Sure, he looked smooth and better than any man had a right to at 2 a.m. Meanwhile, I'd scrubbed off my makeup, twisted my hair into a bun, and thrown on bike shorts and an oversized T-shirt.

If I gave a damn, maybe I'd feel self-conscious. But the part of me that cared about a man's opinion died a long time ago.

"You were great out there."

This time, the eye roll was inevitable. "I'm sure I was," I said, letting out a dry laugh as I pushed past him into the hallway.

Santino followed—of course—matching my pace.

"No, I didn't mean it like that. I meant that it was a great performance. I can see why this place is such a success."

"I don't carry this club on my own, *Santino*. All the dancers here keep a loyal roster of Miami's wealthiest clientèle."

"Gorgeous and humble. Impressive."

I came to an abrupt stop. It took him two more steps before he noticed and backtracked.

"Look, I'm not the one. You may be Lorenzo's nephew and the new owner, but don't think just because I dance here I'm going to drop to my knees and suck your dick because of your last name."

Fuck. Forgot my filter. Not exactly the most innovative way to start this working relationship.

I was half-expecting him to lash out, maybe even fire me on the spot, until the most aggravating, unexpected grin crawled across his face.

"Noted."

His voice was smooth as velvet, and his stare held so much weight I nearly looked away.

Nearly.

But pride's a bitch, and I wasn't about to let him win a staring contest I didn't agree to.

I could have apologized, but that wasn't something I did anymore.

"So you kicked out your own cousin, huh?" I finally said, attempting to break the ice, but instantly regretted initiating more small talk. The last thing I wanted was to invite more dialogue, to let this man think he could worm his way into familiarity. Because he couldn't. And I wouldn't let him try.

"Irreconcilable differences."

I kept walking toward the exit, and again he followed. Didn't surprise me.

"I can see that."

"You think he'll be missed?"

"I guess it depends on who you ask."

He caught the crook of my elbow, and although his touch was gentle, it was enough to tug me to a stop. Glaring at where we were joined, I lifted my eyes to meet the audacity on his face, but his focus was on the silk band wrapped around my wrist.

"I'm asking *you*," he rasped.

I pulled my arm free and kept moving, heels clicking across the pavement. "I preferred Lorenzo, if that's what you're asking."

"Good to know. And I hope to take his place soon enough."

I stopped abruptly a second time. "Mr. Leone, did you ask all the girls the same question?"

"Only you."

Maybe that pretty grin and those dark, hooded eyes worked on other women, but I wasn't them. I knew men like him. Powerful. Handsome. Dangerous. The kind who viewed me as either an easy fuck or a shiny new toy to break in.

I sighed, ready to put him in his place, hoping not to get fired, but willing to take the risk.

"Listen—"

"Your eyes," he said softly, cutting in. "They're gorgeous. I don't think I've ever seen anything like them."

My whole life, people either complimented or ridiculed my heterochromia. I'd grown numb to both. But there was something different in his tone. And damn it, it stirred something feather-light in the pit of my stomach.

"*Bastardo! Ti ucciderò!*" Luca stormed through the lot, gun raised and pointed at Santino. "I open my doors to you, and you humiliate me in front of *my* patrons."

Without hesitation, Santino stepped in front of me, shielding me from my former boss's line of fire.

"You were dismissed and caused a scene. And I put an end to it."

"You just want to fuck me over because you think you're the better man. *Come sempre.*"

I wasn't sure how to feel. On the one hand, I was in the middle of a familial dispute I had no interest in, and second, this man I met less than fifteen minutes ago put himself between me and his cousin's eager trigger finger. Men like him didn't protect women like me.

There went another flutter.

"I don't think this is the time or place," I said, peering around Santino's broad chest, trying to step out from behind him. But he swiveled, his back to the threat, and held me in place.

"Amara, get back inside. I'll handle Luca."

"You're either brave or incredibly foolish. What's stopping him from shooting you in the back?"

"My cousin knows better," Santino said with a chuckle, completely unfazed.

"Definitely option two."

His eyes lit with amusement, but before either of us could say more, Blaise and Ash cocked their weapons, and a third man swiftly disarmed Luca.

"*Cuginetto,*" Santino said, turning back as he lit a cigar, voice deadly serious. "I'm going to overlook what happened here tonight because I know you're upset. But I won't forget. If you ever come by here again, I promise you'll regret it."

Luca's teeth clenched when Santino clapped his jaw.

By the time a disgraced Luca was marched to his car, I was already halfway to mine.

"I'll see you tomorrow, Amara," Santino called after me.

I didn't bother to turn around. Not because I was angry. No, the stupid grin tugging at my lips told me otherwise.

TEN

Am...

Every floor number that lit up on the elevator panel blurred more than the last the harder I stared into the void of my thoughts. Eventually, I leaned back against the metal railing and let out a long breath, my brain in overdrive after tonight's events.

Santino represented a change at Illusion, one that hadn't fully revealed itself, but the shift was coming. I could feel it in my bones.

And my vibes were rarely ever wrong.

Unless he was a master deceiver, it was already clear he and Luca were nothing alike. Where Luca barked orders and wore his authority like a weapon, Santino's power came with a smile and quiet calculation. Somehow, that made him even more dangerous.

I brushed slow fingers over the spot where he'd grabbed me, and maybe it was insane, but I could still feel the prickle of his touch crawling beneath my skin. It had been so unexpected that I had to commend myself for keeping it together and not sinking my knife into his throat.

The man was charismatic, brave as he was reckless, and cocky as hell. But none of that mattered. His good looks wouldn't save him from my wrath if he so much as thought about crossing the line.

When the elevator came to a stop, I pushed off the railing as the doors slid open, but instead of stepping onto my floor, I froze. A small figure stood just outside.

A boy, no older than three, clutched a stuffed dog beneath his arm. Big brown eyes watched me as I started toward him cautiously. A child alone at this ungodly hour was either a horror movie coming to life or an ambush. Slipping a hand into my bag, I wrapped my fingers around my gun, keeping it out of sight as I cleared the floor on either side of him.

"Hey," I said, kneeling to his level. "What are you doing out here alone?"

The toddler blinked but said nothing. Not having been around children since I was one myself, I wasn't even sure if kids his age spoke, let alone understood language.

"Where's your mom? Where did you come from?"

He shrugged and pointed down the hall, which told me absolutely nothing, considering there were four units, none of which had an open door or signs of children.

"This is not happening."

The boy smiled, all wide-eyed and baby teeth, and began trotting down the hall opposite, where he'd pointed, toward a stairwell whose door was propped open by a maintenance cone.

"Hey, get back here." The last thing I needed was this kid trying to climb down and eventually tumbling eight stories' worth of stairs. But as if on purpose, the little shit ran, giggling the moment he heard me coming after him. "Stop!"

Fisting the scruff of his green pajamas just as he reached the threshold, I yanked him back toward me and knelt again, tipping his chin.

"Listen, kid, it's late. You and I should be in bed, not playing Tag out here. I need you to tell me where your people are."

His eyes fell on the bands around my wrists. Small fingers reached up and tugged one gently.

"Boo-boo," he said, finally speaking. "Ouch."

I nodded slowly, a slight smile cracking through at his compassion. "Yeah, ouch."

Hyper-focused now, he grabbed my arm and tugged back down the corridor. I let him, hoping he knew where he was going.

Unit 804.

The black door budged when he pushed, but closed again under its own weight, the hinge too strong for his tiny hands.

"Is this where you live?"

"Ouch," he repeated, groaning as he attempted the door a second time. "*Ajuda*."

Portuguese.

Something in my chest tightened when he spoke what had been my first language.

"*Você fala português?*"

His smile lit up his entire face, but he didn't have a chance to answer before the door wrenched open, and an older man looked at us with wide, confused eyes.

"What the hell? Thiago?" He scooped the boy in a flash and stepped back, suspicion twisting his expression as he stared me down. "Why do you have my son?"

"I think the better question is, why is your *son* wandering the halls at three in the morning?"

The man's gaze flickered to a chair left by the entryway.

He was either still half asleep or stunned into silence. But it was too late to care.

"I would probably secure that door a little better."

I turned and finally made my way to my own unit, two doors down from the tiny escape artist.

———

Scalding water poured over my head as I braced my hands against the shower wall, letting tears I hadn't shed in years slip down my cheeks. Something about Santino's presence brought forth a host of emotions and memories. I wasn't sure why he reminded me so much of Kai and Derek, and that period of my life that ultimately destroyed everything I was. But there I stood, my soul torn open, letting grief consume me as I mourned their absence. But it was better this way. Safer. For them. For me.

I'd always have a reason to run from my past and look over my shoulder, until the day Ronan lay dead at my feet.

Raking nails across my skin, I released a sob when the echoes of screams thundered in my ears and visions of unforgiving cruelty flashed behind my eyes.

Powerless, vulnerable...*nothing*.

"Never again," I whispered, scrubbing harder against my reddened flesh.

I knew no matter how much blood I shed, those deaths meant nothing as long as Ronan Cain was still breathing. I had to sever the head to kill the snake.

Like I did with my brothers, I'd kept tabs on him and clocked his location from afar, biding my time until I was ready to take him on. But four years ago, he fell off my radar. It was as if he'd vanished into thin air. No funeral. No mention of his death. Ronan was just gone.

I knew better.

He was still out there, and he was mine. In the meantime, I'd reap the city of men with a taste for depravity and pain. They made it easy. These sick assholes and the women who supported their vices came flocking the moment they thought they'd found their next victim.

I cut the shower spray and rested my forehead on the hot tiles.

"They made me this way. Broken inside, but never weak."

ELEVEN

Amara

Loud vibrations against wood pulled me from a dream as my eyes opened against the rays of light filtering from the window above my head. I glanced at the device and saw Cambri's messages and missed calls. Panic jolted me upright. I snatched the phone, heart lurching. Only to exhale when I realized there wasn't a life-or-death emergency.

"Talk about a heart attack for breakfast," I huffed, scratching behind Phoenix's ear. My Bengal cat purred and nuzzled my neck as I settled my nerves.

I'd promised myself I'd always be there for Cambri the way she'd been there for me. She saved me that night. And I swore I'd always have her back. She didn't know it, but I'd killed twice for her. And I'd do it a million times over. Sometimes, I wish I could tell her how beautiful her bastard ex-husband had screamed for me. Or how her stalker cried like the pussy he was when I gutted him. But none of that mattered, as long as she was safe.

> CAMBRI: I called you five times. You better not be dead in a ditch. Call me back as soon as you get this message. Santino called a meeting. Gotta be at work two hours early.

> CAMBRI: AMARA CARVALHO, I'm calling the FBI if you don't answer me.

Just as I reached to hit the callback button, an unknown number flashed on my screen with an area code I didn't recognize. I wasn't in the habit of answering calls from strangers, but something made me pause.

I said nothing, waiting for the other end to break the silence first.

"Amara?"

Santino.

A strange current swept through me at the sound of my name on his lips.

"How did you get my number?"

"Good morning to you, too," he said with a chuckle. "And you're in the club's database."

Of course.

"Is this about the meeting?"

There was a pause before he replied. "Cambri assured me she'd let you know, but I wanted to see to it you got the message personally."

"Message received."

Another chuckle. Santino's indifference to my shit attitude irritated the hell out of me.

"I won't take up any more of your time. I look forward to

seeing you again, Amara. And I hope last night's incident didn't give you the wrong impression of me."

"No, you're exactly who I thought you'd be."

I said nothing else and ended the call.

Maybe I'd come off as a bitch. But lines needed to be drawn, like I had with Luca. While Santino didn't give off the same perverse vibes as his cousin, I knew what the extra attention and the flirty smiles could lead to. He'd quickly learn I wasn't a woman interested in romance or one-night stands.

And I never would be.

By the time I'd eaten breakfast, I'd forgotten about Cambri until another series of messages popped up where she threatened my life. But almost comically, soft knocks at my door diverted my attention again.

When I brought up the footage of my unexpected guest, I was surprised to see my negligent neighbor on the other side of my door. Despite the warm weather, he was dressed in a blazer.

I briefly debated whether to pretend I wasn't home, but living two units away from each other would make avoiding him forever an impossibility. And I refused to be uncomfortable and on alert in my own home.

"Good morning," he said, sporting a cordial smile.

I nodded a greeting, my door open just enough so that we made eye contact, hoping he'd get the hint that I wasn't one for neighborly small talk.

"I want to apologize for last night and thank you for saving my boy. I'd had a long shift, picked him up from the sitter, and didn't secure the safety lock when I got home. I'd hate to think what could have happened if you hadn't found him when you did."

"He was at the elevator and nearly ran into the stairwell."

Fuck, Amara, can't you just say you're welcome and get this shit over with?

"I know, I know." He hung his head and sighed. "I've been reeling over the what-ifs all night. Thiago is all I have left."

Send him away. This was getting too personal.

"Well, nothing serious came of it. Glad I could help," I said in a rush, stepping back as I motioned to close the door.

His hand shot out. "Wait."

Heat surged through my veins at the intrusion. Without thinking, my fingers moved to the blade tucked in my back pocket, while he slid his free hand inside his blazer.

Just as the steel edge of my knife threatened to flash, I caught sight of the silver detective badge clipped to his waistband, and the small white business card pinched between his fingers.

"I'm Raymond Braga. Your neighbor." He chuckled. "Also, lead homicide detective at the 10th precinct. You can reach me here if you ever need anything—anything at all."

His mouth was still moving, but nothing was processing beyond *homicide detective.* My neighbor, whose attention I had inadvertently garnered, specialized in imprisoning people like me.

The fucking irony.

"Your...name?" he prompted, and I snapped back to his face, where the crinkled corners of his eyes narrowed, friendly smile fading. "Is everything okay?"

Nodding, I put on my best good girl act and returned the smile. "Yeah...yeah. I'm Amara. I'll be sure to take you up on that," I lied.

"Good. And I hope I didn't overstep by coming by. I just wanted to give my thanks and apologize in case I came off like a jerk."

Another fake smile. "You're fine."

"I'll see you around then."

With a nod of his chin, Detective Braga was gone.

I closed the door and leaned against it, pulse slowing as Phoenix padded over and nudged my leg. She had this way of sensing my distress. Maybe it was her way of looking out for me, repaying me for having saved her life. I bent down and cupped her little face.

"You're thinking what I'm thinking, huh? A homicide detective as a neighbor. We're fucked."

TWELVE

Santino

Amara Carvalho.

I flipped through her file for the tenth time, hunting for a possible piece of information I might have overlooked. But nothing out of the ordinary jumped out. And maybe that was precisely the problem. Her past employment and places of residency were too damn cookie-cutter, as if someone had chosen the most generic shit to cut and paste together. My years of reading people told me this woman held a vault of secrets. Her eyes, those fucking incredible eyes, were layered with stories and experiences I craved to uncover.

There was something strangely different about her. The women in this industry didn't often reject men in positions of power and wealth. Most coveted even the most minute scraps of attention, with the hopes they'd be lifted from a lifestyle usually forced on them by life's circumstances or the absence of choice. But while the other dancers lined up to introduce themselves, Amara couldn't have been more disinterested.

I leaned back in my chair, scoffing around my cigar as the live feed from the lot played out. Amara was a different breed. In the face of death, she remained uncharacteristically calm and fearless. Nonchalant, even.

Secrets.

And just like that, this woman—this stranger—had piqued my absolute interest.

The vibrations from my desk drawer snapped me out of my thoughts. I smirked when I saw Silas's name.

"Brother, what kind of shit do you need me to bail you out of now?"

We shared a laugh, remembering old times. While I was glad he had settled down and found his place in the world and someone special to share it with, I couldn't help but feel the nostalgia tightening my chest. We'd been close friends for nearly two decades. My family and I had worked alongside Hades. And when the organization turned its back on Silas, my loyalty never wavered.

He was my brother, and I'd never begrudge his happiness, but I did miss the bastard.

"Leni and I landed in Philly a few hours ago. She's already off running errands with Maksim, so I thought I'd check in. I saw your message about staying in Miami, and I wanted to ensure you hadn't suffered a head injury."

I was still getting used to the idea of Silas as a father figure. But from what I knew, he and Leni had fallen into their roles as caretakers for the orphaned teenager.

Setting down the cigar, I lost myself in billows of smoke as I tried to conjure an excuse that wouldn't make me sound like I'd lost my sanity. However, if anyone understood how bewitching the right woman could be, it was Silas.

"A business venture, Si. I came here convinced of one decision and stayed once I saw its potential. Illusion is just off the marina, with the yacht club out back, the beach, an unrivaled view. Like a precious gem among stones."

Silas cleared his throat. "Okay...that sounds like you're saying a lot without saying much."

We'd never felt the need to keep secrets; now would have been no different. But was there even anything to tell?

Not yet.

Several minutes later, the image of a familiar black car pulled into the property.

"Si, it was great to hear from you, but I've got to run. Give my regards to Leni and that boy of yours. Hope he's still doing well. And call whenever you need me to save your ass again."

His barking laughter filtered through my speaker before he said his goodbyes and ended the call.

I hadn't taken my eyes off the parked sedan since its arrival five minutes prior. She'd yet to emerge, and I wondered what was keeping her. No sooner had the thought crossed my mind than the driver-side door pushed open. A wave of long brown curls spilled into the breeze, catching the sunlight just right. I couldn't help envisioning my fist tangled in that hair and my name, a whispered moan on her lips.

My feet carried me to the door before I realized I was even moving.

"Good evening, Mr. Leone," a woman's voice called from an adjacent hallway. I bid her a nod, my eyes fixed on the back door, where Amara was only seconds from breaching. "Can I get you anything to drink?"

Again, the same voice.

Whirling around, I found myself far too close to a young brunette in heels almost as tall as one of her calves, and even then, she barely made it to my shoulders. Her height wasn't the problem; It was the flushed cheeks and wide doe eyes of a girl who looked a few years too young to be working here.

She flashed a flirtatious smile and moved in closer. "Is that...a yes?"

"How old are you?"

Her smile twitched, trying to hold.

"Twenty-one." The bravado from moments ago was gone.

"I'm only going to ask you once more. And if you're lying, there will be consequences."

Tears welled over her blue contact lenses, and she began to

fidget, looking away and probably regretting her decision to speak to me.

"Nineteen," she murmured.

"I gave you one chance."

When I reached into my pocket and retrieved my cell, she grabbed at my arm in a panic. "Okay, please. Don't call anyone. I can't go back home."

"Age," I demanded, not moved in the least by her begging.

"Six...sixteen."

"Get the fuck out of my club."

The girl flinched and shuffled backward before turning and running as fast as her ridiculous heels would permit.

A fucking child.

Luca was a son of a bitch. I wouldn't deny the fact that some of my faction had dealings involving the trafficking of women and young girls, but I always kept my distance and never received a dime of those profits.

Maybe because I had three younger sisters.

"I always knew she was hiding something."

I whipped around at the sound of Amara's voice, my mood shifting the second I saw her.

"I don't employ children."

A faint smile played at her lips as she nodded. "I have a feeling Luca was aware."

She didn't break eye contact, and I didn't look away.

"If I knew my cousin, I'd wager you're right."

Amara said nothing more on the subject and pushed off the wall. I followed like a goddamn puppy.

"I'm sorry to make you come in early tonight. I promise I won't be long."

"Oh, so it's one of those could-have-been-an-email type meetings?"

A joke? Had she just cracked a joke?

"Maybe," I said with a laugh. "But the last time I was here, this place was just a foreclosed building by the beach. I signed the paperwork and flew back to Naples the next day."

"I'm assuming you mean Italy."

"Correct." Our steps had synchronized, and the fact she wasn't running off like she had last night was progress. "It would be good to touch base with everyone and cull the staff if need be."

She nodded once and came to a stop in front of her dressing room, then turned to face me.

A woman's lips had always been my biggest draw, but as enticing as hers were, I couldn't pull my gaze away from her unique eyes. The left was a warm shade of honey, and the right was primarily bright blue, apart from a sliver of brown bleeding from the pupil to the edge of her iris.

I'd gone home last night and googled the condition.

Heterochromia.

"I'm going to drop off my things and be in the lounge in a moment."

My hand twitched to catch her elbow, but I remembered her hesitancy and decided against it, stuffing both hands in my pants pockets as insurance.

"Amara, is there anything I should know before I address them?"

That earned me an eyebrow lift. "You don't exactly strike me as the kind of man who needs direction, let alone one who cares much what strangers think."

She read me like an open book.

"Maybe. But I don't want to come off like the asshole they expect. Can't just, as they say, show my hand."

Amara eyed me curiously. "Is that what you're doing with me? Pretending you're interested in my opinion. Hiding your ace."

"Do you think that's my objective?"

She folded her arms across her chest and wet her lips. I was sure the movement was an innocent one because the woman was barely lukewarm. But my eyes fell on her fleshy mouth all the same.

"All I know is that you have a knack for answering questions with a question."

I couldn't help the laugh that bubbled out. "Do I? Fuck."

A whisper of a smile touched her lips again. Had I blinked, I would have missed it.

"See you in a few, Mr. Leone."

Without so much as another glance, she disappeared into her dressing room and shut the door behind her. I'd never had to work this hard for a woman's attention. Hell, I never cared to. But Amara had snared me from the moment those first notes caressed my senses. Whatever game she'd unknowingly started was the most exhilarating thing I'd tasted in years. With scores of dead men on my roster, I wasn't one to back down or lose.

THIRTEEN

Am

"You're on in ten."

Cambri stuck her head into my dressing room.

"Wait—What?"

"Star caught some stomach bug and was puking in the bathroom. She insisted on going on stage anyway, but Boss said no. Sent her home. So you're up."

I turned back to the mirror and slipped in a contact lens. "I don't know that I'll be ready in time. You can have her slot. I don't mind."

"Not tonight, babe."

Cambri pushed the door open the rest of the way and twirled in a 360, showing off her barely-there outfit. A hot pink G-string, the thickness of dental floss clung to her skin, leaving nothing to the imagination, front or back, while clusters of jewels served as pasties.

She often danced fully nude. The woman was smoking, so it was no surprise when some of the most elite patrons vied for her attention and showered her with cash.

That said, she never turned down extra earnings. Judging by her chipper demeanor, it was obvious she'd been booked for a second floor private.

Wealthy men from around the country, and even overseas, spent an ungodly amount for one hour with the girl of their choosing. Depending on the package, one involved touch, while the other strictly forbade it.

I'd never accepted a request. I knew my limits. Alone in a room where a man was too drunk or high to accept the word no was too great a temptation—a disaster waiting to happen.

"A rich Russian prick has summoned me," she said, leaning in and touching up her liner. "But I have a few minutes if you need my help."

I nodded, letting the silky white robe slide off my shoulders. "Please."

"Of course."

Cambri pressed a gentle kiss to my temple and swept the hair from my back. I twisted it into a tight bun as she readied the airbrush kit. Moments later, the soft hiss and cool puffs of concealer danced across my skin, masking the scars beneath her skilled touch.

———

The music's bass thumped deep in my chest as I cast one last sweeping glance at the crowd gathered around the angular stage. Closing my eyes, I slipped away to the one place in my mind where nothing could touch me. Where I was the only one in control.

Their voices echoed just beyond reach as I kicked up and circled the pole, legs soaring overhead, one knee hooked around the cold metal. Cheers threatened to shatter my walls when I straddled my legs, giving the sea of patrons exactly what they wanted.

Just enough.

Lorenzo hadn't pushed the subject of dancing fully nude, but Luca had all but demanded it. I managed to stave him off long enough for Santino to take over, though I wondered if he'd also attempt to force my hand. Something told me his views were more in line with his uncle's way of running a business—happy employees are loyal ones—but maybe that was wishful thinking. Deep down, I suspected Santino was no different than the swath of horny men in this room.

Slipping through the haze of my concentration, a strange charge pulled at me like an invisible spark of electricity. Beneath the veil of the dark venue, my eyes connected with the man I'd conjured in my thoughts. The mask over my eyes shadowed my line of sight, so he likely remained unaware of my scrutiny from afar. But as I moved through my routine, I realized I was no longer lost in my head.

Santino's face became my new focal point.

The world slipped away again, and it was just him and me in a room thick with smoke and flashing lights. Tingling energy buzzed beneath my skin as I crafted each movement, curating my dance for the steel features fixed intently on me from across the room.

Every twirl and twist around the pole, every swing and undulation of my hips, was guided by the heat in his gaze.

I felt it, breathed it, burned it to memory.

For the first time, I didn't have to hide in the pockets of my mind...and the feeling was exhilarating.

When the last note closed, I was on my knees, chest heaving, surrounded by silence for the next two breaths until a chorus of whistles, hollers, and claps rang out from the crowd of patrons I'd forgotten were even there.

Bills rained down around me like confetti at a Times Square ball drop.

I realized I was smiling, the dull ache in my cheeks growing nearly unbearable. But the moment fizzled the second our eyes locked again.

There wasn't a trace of pride, or a smile, or even a fucking job well done on the hard lines of his face.

Humiliation prickled at my neck as I rose and backed into a shadowed hallway.

What the fuck was wrong with him?

Hugging my body, I stalked toward my dressing room, so disoriented that I walked into a wall.

Only the wall had arms, but it was Santino's hands that caught me, steadying me before I stumbled back onto my ass.

"You okay?"

His voice was low, but those fingertips burned like fire against my skin.

I jerked free, stepping out of reach. "Watch where you're going."

He chuckled, sharp and cynical. "Me? You're the one plowing through here."

"So you saw me coming?" I asked, squaring my shoulders while the memory of his reaction to my performance fueled my rage. "You let me bump into you on purpose?"

"No. You came around that corner like you stole something." A flash of red from the lounge glittered across his dark eyes, highlighting the intensity behind them. "But maybe you did."

He stepped forward.

And his jugular suddenly begged to be drained. Every instinct inside me screamed to react with violence or back away, but for unknown reasons, I stood firm, facing off with the man who had my emotions in a whirlwind.

"Excuse you?"

The corner of his mouth tipped to a grin. "The show, *preziosa*... You stole the show. Hear them calling for more?"

It was then the chants for an encore reached me, but I couldn't focus on their voices.

What had he called me?

"You did good."

I noted the strained look on his face. Was he lying?

"Yeah? Well, you didn't seem all that thrilled from where I was standing."

Another cheeky smirk.

"Were you looking for me?"

"It's a little hard to miss that inflated head of yours."

Santino's laugh shook his chest. "I won't even argue with that one."

"Figures," I said, trying desperately to hold back the smile creeping across my lips. As much as I wanted to detest his arrogance, I found myself strangely amused. "I'm heading home for the night."

"I'll have your winnings sent to your room," he assured me as I started down the hall. "And I'll see you tomorrow, Amara."

I kept moving without a second glance, but much like our moment on stage, I felt his eyes on me...and maybe, for the first time in a long time, I didn't experience the usual pricks of anxiety that came with the presence of a man at my back.

FOURTEEN

Santino

I couldn't deny the disappointment that settled in my chest every time I watched her leave. Always through the grainy live feed flickering in my office. If I had even an ounce of a moral compass, I'd feel guilty, maybe even disgusted, at my growing obsession with this woman. But I couldn't be bothered. I'd indulge in her beauty when I saw fit, whether from the comfort of my space, stage-side, or our purposeful interactions.

Inflated head, I repeated in my thoughts with a chuckle. It was the second time she'd let her guard down with me.

But I needed more.

We'd had a moment, she and I, when eye contact wasn't necessary because I felt her passion from across the room. No one else existed at that moment. Amara had performed for me.

Slamming my glass of scotch against the wooden desk, I stormed to my feet.

Watching her dance for a room full of men was becoming increasingly difficult the stronger my obsession grew. Knowing they coveted her the way I did, were mesmerized by her the way I was, it made me want to lock her up and keep her for myself.

Although something told me, Amara Carvalho wouldn't be kept.

Movement from the corner of my eye shifted my attention back to the monitors as she emerged from the back door. The knot she usually wore in her hair at the end of her shifts was missing. Tonight, she'd left her curls loose. Black dress pants and a sleeveless top also replaced the more casual outfits she'd changed into.

"Where are you going, *preziosa?*" I whispered to myself.

She reached her car, but without losing her stride, continued past the small Audi and headed toward the sidewalk.

Drawing in a strained breath, I gripped the edge of the desk and warred with the overwhelming urge to follow her.

1 a.m.

The streets of Miami were no place for her at this hour. I snatched my key fob from the drawer and bolted for the exit, the door slamming behind me.

I probably looked unhinged, sprinting through the lot like a man possessed. But I didn't give a fuck. I hit the curb just in time to catch a glimpse of her turning the corner.

People stumbling out of clubs, bars, and the pier still littered the street. I didn't give a damn who I shoved past—groups split, curses flew, but I didn't slow for anyone. When I reached the corner she'd disappeared behind, I thought I saw the back of her hair, but before I could confirm, a young man, probably too young to drink, slammed into me and landed on his ass.

"What the fuck! Watch where you're fucking go—"

He cut himself off the second he saw my face.

Without wasting another second, I dusted my suit sleeve and pressed forward. I hadn't felt the heat of a Miami summer night until then. Cursing, I slipped off my jacket and tossed it. My cuff links were next.

"Thank you!" shouted a homeless man perched against a brick building. I gave the poor bastard a subtle nod and kept moving, rolling my sleeves as I walked.

At the next crosswalk, I scanned the crowd for familiar curls. Nothing.

"*Cazzo!*" I muttered, coming to a stop once I realized I'd lost her.

"Do you make it a habit to follow all your employees?"

I spun around at the sound of her voice. There she was, like a goddess, leaning against the glass of a storefront, eyes trained on me. But something in her had shifted. Her eyes leveled with mine like we were strangers again.

I couldn't blame her.

Clearing my throat, I sifted through excuses that wouldn't make me sound like some perverse stalker. But then I realized...I didn't care.

"Well?" she pressed, stepping away from the wall. I noted the tension in her posture, and if I hadn't known better, I'd probably be worried she'd put a bullet through my face.

"No. Only you, *preziosa*."

Her blue eye twitched. "Don't call me that."

I slid my hands into my pockets. "I saw you leave, and it's late. I thought maybe—"

"Do you hear yourself? You went out of your way to follow me because—*it's late?*"

"I know what that sounds like—"

"Yeah, like you're overstepping boundaries." Amara was just inches from me now, fire in her eyes and an accusatory finger pointed at my chest. "First, I'm a grown woman—what I do, where I go, and when is none of your business. Two, don't *ever* follow me. Outside of Illusion's walls, I don't answer to you."

We remained locked in a stare-down. Where I would have lashed out at anyone attempting to berate and disrespect me, a tongue-lashing from Amara was rather enjoyable. Against my better judgment, I cracked a smile and put my hands up defensively.

"I didn't mean to intrude or overstep any boundaries, as you say. Those weren't my intentions. But these streets can be brutal, especially to a beautiful woman walking alone."

A counterargument was brewing on her lips, but I spoke first.

"And you're right, outside of the club, I'm not your boss. But your car is still on my lot, so technically, you're still under my supervision. And part of the job is ensuring my dancers are always safe."

She scoffed. "That's bullshit."

"Maybe. But it's the best I've got."

With a shake of her head and what I could have sworn was the hint of a smile, Amara looked up and down the street, scanning the sidewalk, and something twisted in my gut.

Was she meeting someone?

"Listen, not that I need to explain myself to you, but I just wanted to get some air. And, as you can see, I'm fine."

"This air sucks," I said, shoving my sleeves farther into the crook of my elbows, seeking every ounce of relief before it came down to ripping my shirt off.

She couldn't hold back her smile this time.

"You better hurry back then."

With one last sweeping glance at my inked forearms, she turned toward the crosswalk.

"Amara, wait."

Her name left my mouth before I could stop it. She faltered just for a second. Barely a hitch in her step, but I caught it. And then she kept walking.

I should have gone back, kept my distance, and stopped trying to forge a friendship she clearly did not want. But when I spotted the small cafe ahead, open to the beach, passing up the opportunity wasn't an option.

"Can I buy you a mango smoothie as a peace offering?" I asked, catching up with her.

She didn't acknowledge me right away, too focused on whatever message she was furiously punching into her phone.

With a small, resigned breath, she stopped short.

"You must not be used to hearing the word no, huh?"

Her eyes flicked to mine, and the way she broke contact set

off quiet alarms. Still, I waited. The patience I had for this woman unnerved even me.

"I didn't mean it…like that."

I reached out, daring to tip her chin up. As expected, she pulled away before I could touch her. But despite having followed her and persisting to remain in her company, I had a feeling that whatever message she'd received had been the thing responsible for souring her mood.

"My offer still stands."

Amara peered down the street, then back at me, deliberating.

"Fine. Lead the way," she finally said, falling in step beside me as I crossed the intersection.

"Were you meeting a friend?"

"Something like that."

Apart from Cambri, she seemed to keep to herself, so a night out with one of the other girls was unlikely, which left the possibility of a date. The thought of Amara meeting with some random man at this late hour made my blood burn a little hotter.

So I decided to pry.

"You don't seem too torn about it?"

She focused on the path ahead, but I noted her brief side-eye.

"Why don't you ask what you really want to know?"

The way this woman made me smile more than I ever had in anyone's company besides Silas's was uncanny. "And according to you, what do I wish to know?"

Everything was the correct answer. But I'd take the scraps of whatever she was willing to give, pathetic as it was.

"It was only coffee. Cambri set us up—something about not getting out often enough." Again, her gaze slid toward me, accompanied by a cunning little grin. "Or getting laid."

Fire. My blood blazed at the thought of another man touching her. My only consolation was that, somehow, I knew she was fucking with me.

"It's a good thing he canceled then."

Amara's grin stretched. "Is it?"

"Yeah, very much."

Her brow arched, and the edges of her white teeth caught her bottom lip. She said nothing more about the subject and kept walking until we reached a small cafe with outdoor seating just off the beach. I led her to a corner table with a view of the ocean. Despite the darkness, the streetlights and those from the various vendors lining the strip were enough to illuminate the shore, where soft waves crashed against white sand.

I'd never visited this cafe, but I prayed they had mango smoothies, as it was the first thing that had come to mind in my desperate attempt to remain in her company.

"Looks like we have to order at the desk after hours. Mango?"

"Surprise me."

I placed our order with the cashier, a smoothie for her and a water for me, turning around in time to catch a man approaching Amara. I wondered briefly if he'd been her date, who'd decided to show, after all. But her indifference told me otherwise. She shook her head and folded her arms, resting against the back of her chair. But instead of moving along, the bastard leaned a hand on the table and into her personal space. I was at her side before my next breath, close enough to the foolish stranger that his face nearly brushed me as he straightened.

"Are you lost?"

"No, I was just—"

"Leaving," I gritted out, stepping closer.

The man's eyes flitted to Amara, and I almost thought he wanted to get brave. But it turned out he rather enjoyed his life, and retreated.

"He didn't disrespect you, did he?"

"No, but if he had, what makes you think I'd let it slide?"

I took a seat. "That's not the point. I'd have handled him whether or not you sent him to hell."

"Is that what you do, Mr. Leone?"

Her question was vague, but I knew exactly what she was asking. My family was well-known in the area when Uncle Lorenzo established his connections and business dealings years ago, before expanding with the construction of Illusion. It was an unspoken truth among the patrons and employees. But our reputation preceded us. The opinions or assumptions of the masses had never interested me before now.

What would Amara think of me as a man in the business of murder for hire? And why did that suddenly matter?

"Defend women against disrespectful assholes?"

"Sure," she said, voice laced with sarcasm.

"No. Again, only you."

"Well, at least you're consistent."

She had to feel how the air between us ignited with every glance, every word, every time I let my gaze linger too long on her mouth or eyes.

The cashier called our number, slicing straight through the current between us.

Moment lost. For now.

"How about we take those to go?"

We took off down the street, drinks in hand. I allowed her a slight head start as we reached the crosswalk, indulging in her perfect curves and sweet ass.

"You and Cambri are close, yeah?"

"We are. She's like a sister to me."

"I have someone like that in my life. He doesn't live here, but we're as close to brothers as it gets. And you, do you have family close by?"

"No."

Always with the vague responses. "They live out of state?"

"I don't have family," she said, very matter-of fact, eyes still focused ahead.

Everyone has or *had* somebody, but it was evident the subject wasn't up for discussion. I'd respect her privacy—for now. In the meantime, I'd enjoy watching her lips wrapped around that straw.

"How'd you end up at Illusion?"

It was a loaded question. I knew that. I was willing to risk her wrath if it meant gaining even the slightest knowledge of her life.

Her eyebrow twitched, and she gripped her cup a little tighter. "The same way you did," she said with a slightly taunting lilt.

"How so?"

"I walked through the front door, Mr. Leone."

"Fair enough," I replied with a chuckle. "Amara, please call me Santino."

We reached the club's lot. Not yet ready to leave her company, I dreaded every step closer to her black Audi.

"That sounds a bit too personal. I wouldn't want you to get the wrong idea. To assume that you and I are...friends. Especially after tonight."

"Or just friendly."

"Maybe I'm not the friendly type."

"Even better."

Perhaps she thought keeping me at arm's length would put me off, but everything about Amara drew me in. Not only was she stunning, but she was the most intriguing mystery. Maybe I was biased, as she had struck me from the moment I saw her on that stage, but something told me she didn't belong in a place like this.

Her phone vibrated, and she glanced down at the message, smile faltering despite her best effort at a poker face.

"I have to go," she said abruptly, tearing open her car door and practically throwing herself into the driver's seat.

I caught the door before she could slam it shut. She froze, startled by the sudden block, eyes wide, but I didn't give a damn. Not when her hands were trembling slightly. Not when something had clearly shaken her.

"Wait—" I said, softer now. "Is everything okay?"

"Everything is fine." Her voice was even, almost too calm. But beneath the surface was an edge.

"Then why are you racing off like this?"

"Goodbye, Mr. Leone," she said, tugging the door closed with finality.

Without another glance, Amara pulled off, tires screeching against the blacktop as she recklessly merged into traffic.

FIFTEEN

Amara

Blood surged through my throat and ears so hard I could damn near taste it. Once I'd left Illusion's parking lot, I blew up Cambri's phone, but call after call was sent straight to voicemail, rattling my nerves even further. Without a word, she pinned her location. Either something had happened to her, or she was dodging me.

I decided then that if she wasn't already dead, I'd kill her myself for worrying me to the point of panic.

HELP.

That one word had me breaking every traffic law as I raced to find my friend. The text was sent with no explanation, but I knew she'd never be intentionally vague about something so dire.

My foot slammed the gas harder, engine roaring as I tore down the blacked-out stretch of highway, flying blind into whatever hell waited on the other end.

But I was fully prepared.

With a trunk and glove compartment stocked with guns, ammo, and all my favorite sharp things, I was ready to fight or die for the woman who'd risked it all to save me years ago.

As I rounded the bend, tires shrieking against asphalt, my high beams cut through the dark and caught the silhouette of a woman staggering along the shoulder. I slammed the brakes and pulled up behind her. One stiletto dangled from two fingers, the other still strapped to a scraped, swollen foot. I recognized the tattered outfit and her long, dark hair.

If she was aware of my vehicle rolling up behind her, she didn't acknowledge it.

"Cambri!" I shoved the door open and sprinted toward her. "Cambri, oh my god! What happened?"

When I grabbed her shoulders and gently turned her to face me, nothing could have prepared me for what I saw. My blood chilled. One of her eyes was swollen shut, lips bloodied and split in several places. The right side of her face was grotesquely enlarged, as if she'd been repeatedly struck with a fist or blunt object. There wasn't an inch on her body that wasn't covered in bruises, scratches, and lacerations.

The sight of her took me back to the night she'd found me, broken and near death.

"Baby, look at me." My voice was brittle as rage steeped in my veins. "Tell me right now, who did this to you?"

She crumbled to the ground and sobbed, gripping my arms, "I'm sorry...I was...so stupid."

"No, this isn't your fault. No one deserves this."

She shook her head violently, eyes wild. "I knew it. I knew I shouldn't have gone." Her words slurred—whether from alcohol, drugs, or the injuries on her mouth, I couldn't tell.

"Cambri, we have to get you to a hospital." I cupped her face gently, trying not to hurt her. "This looks really bad. You could have a brain bleed."

Again, she shook her head, panic creeping into her voice.

"They're looking for me." Her eyes darted like she expected someone to appear any second. "They'll kill me," she whispered.

"No one's going to touch you. But I need names."

We'd promised to always look out for one another. And I had every intention of following through.

Cambri tried to protest, but I hooked her arm around my shoulder and helped her to her feet, steadying her wobbling legs.

"I'll drop you off at a hospital just outside the city. And on our way there, I need every last detail."

———

I gave the bastard three nights and, like clockwork, he walked through the door, his goons in tow as they scanned the lounge. There wasn't a doubt in my mind he was searching for signs of Cambri. While stupid enough to accept an invitation back to his home, by some saving grace, she'd left her purse and identification behind. All they knew was that she was a dancer at Illusion.

And here they were, coming to collect and silence the woman who got away. Luckily for him, I was feeling particularly stabby tonight.

"How's Cambri doing?"

Santino's voice cut through the dark behind me, sharp and unexpected. I'd been actively avoiding him since the night he'd followed me after my shift—when he'd almost caught me meeting up with a client who deserved to watch the sunrise with a blade to the dick. As much as I wanted to send that fucker to meet his maker, relief had washed over me when he'd texted to say our little date had been canceled, saving me the trouble of coming up with excuses to get rid of my boss.

"She's still sick. Tested positive for the flu," I said, eyes still fixed on Ivan. "Cambri said she'd keep you posted. Did she forget to call?"

"I spoke to her earlier today."

I turned fully to face him, confusion tightening my brow. "Then why ask when you already know?"

His smile deepened as he closed the gap between us.

"I needed an excuse to talk to you. You've been avoiding me."

"I've been working."

"And avoiding me."

Santino was a distraction and a weakness. The last time I let myself get swept up by a man, I missed all the red flags and lost everything. I refused to let that happen again.

The more time we spent being friendly, the more he knocked me off my game and made me second-guess my motives. I'd spent years chasing the high of my first revenge kill. Mr. H's death had given my life a new purpose. Instead of withering away, letting my trauma consume me, I'd made it my mission to seek out sadist men like him.

I didn't need to bleed on a contract anymore. I'd bled on enough perverse dick for a lifetime.

"Mr. Leone, I don't know what you expect, but whatever that is, I assure you I'm not your girl."

My eyes flickered to a blonde at the bar. She'd come in on the arm of a man twice her age but had yet to take her eyes off Santino.

I convinced myself that I'd only noticed because I'd been on high alert in search of Ivan.

"Try your luck with the lady in the green dress over there. She's been eyeing you for the past hour. You might just get lucky," I teased, clapping his chest.

"Tell me now." His accented voice vibrated against my ear just as I turned, intent on shifting my attention back to Ivan, only to find myself completely consumed by the man at my back. "How would you know that?"

Maybe it was the sudden intrusion, the proximity, or the fact that he'd just called me out—but I swear my heart stuttered to a stop for a full five seconds.

That's new.

"If anyone asks for a private tonight, I'm open."

I turned to head for the dressing room, but Santino caught my elbow. The teasing smile he always wore had vanished, replaced by something darker.

"I thought you didn't accept those."

"You thought wrong." His jaw ticked. "I have to get ready. I'm on in a few."

I looked down at where his hand gripped my arm, then back up into his eyes.

I wasn't in the business of asking men for permission to remove their hands from me once they lost their minds and overstepped, but Santino...

Santino confused the hell out of me.

He made me feel vulnerable in ways I didn't know how to process, stirring emotions I'd long since buried.

SIXTEEN

Amara

As the music swirled around me, building toward the climax of my performance, I dropped to my knees and crawled toward the edge of the stage, right into the crosshairs of Ivan Tarasov's lidded gaze. Leaning forward, ass in the air like a fucking lioness in heat, I pumped my hips, thighs straddling the floor.

Two.

Three times.

His hands fisted on his knees as I slid closer, my tongue teasing the corner of my lips. My mind threatened to retreat inside itself—I was too close, too open—but I had to see this through. I needed him to feel like the luckiest bastard in the building.

The only one.

Ivan needed to crave my mouth on his cock more than his next breath.

"Fuck, baby," he growled as I turned and thrust against the stage one last time. The song faded, and the club erupted into hoots and crude catcalls.

Straightening, I threw a heated stare over my shoulder, catching him as he sank deeper into his plush V.I.P. sofa and murmured something to one of his lackeys.

I slowly diverted my gaze, drawing his eyes with my own until I was out of sight, where I could finally release a steadying breath and brace for the invite.

The knob slammed into the wall as I burst into my dressing room. I snatched a water bottle from my vanity and chugged the cool liquid until it tempered the bloodlust coursing like fire through my veins.

Three days had me nearly frothing at the mouth to paint my hands red with his blood. I knew he'd be back. Men like him thought themselves gods. He'd have come here every day, chosen a different girl, violated and maimed her, all without care for repercussions. His money and power had gifted him that false sense of invincibility his whole life.

But today, he'd learn a hard truth. Pity it would be a little too late.

"Amara."

I whipped around to find Santino standing beneath the threshold. His expression was unreadable, but if the tension in his shoulders was anything to go by, something told me he wasn't too happy.

"Next time, knock."

"The door was open."

I wasn't in the mood to argue, so I waited, allowing him to say his piece. But testing my patience seemed to be his favorite pastime lately. With a huff, I turned back to the mirror, reapplying my lipstick in slow, deliberate strokes.

"Looks like you got your wish."

"Let me guess. Tarasov?" I asked with feigned innocence.

"Do you know who that man is?"

"Someone who will pay my bills. That's all the information I need."

Santino stepped inside and slammed the door shut. I froze, eyes meeting his reflection.

"Get out."

"He's Bratva—the kind in the business of selling sex, if you know what I mean."

He couldn't imagine how much.

"It's just a lap dance, *Santi*," I said, letting the nickname slide off my tongue like poison. His eyebrow twitched.

"Amara, this isn't a joke."

A sudden rush of anger set my blood on fire. I turned on him, my voice sharp.

"Is that what you told Cambri when Ivan requested a private with her three days ago?"

"I don't know anything about that."

I clenched my fists, swallowing back the scream building in my throat. I couldn't afford to blow my cover. Not yet.

"Even if you had, I doubt you would have tried to stop her."

"You're not Cambri," he shot back.

Smacking the lipstick against the vanity, I stalked forward, needing to end this—to kill whatever he thought could happen between us.

"I *am* Cambri. We're all Cambri. I take my clothes off and shake my ass for money, too, *Santino*." I swallowed the space between us, but he didn't budge or seem fazed in the slightest. "I don't need or want special treatment. So, if you'll excuse me, my client is waiting."

His fingers closed around my wrist, tugging me back. "You're not going."

"Careful," I warned. "Because maybe you're right. Maybe I'm not like Cambri."

His dark gaze narrowed, but instead of backing off, he stepped in.

"Is that a threat, *preziosa?*"

The whisper of a grin on his lips had my hands itching to reach for my blade. But I was fooling myself. And I knew it.

"Do you feel threatened?" I asked, nudging his chest.

Santino loomed over me in a way that made me question my sanity. I'd never felt the urge to climb a man the way I did at that moment unless I planned to slit his throat. God, I wanted to hate him, but I hated myself because I knew I didn't. And when the tip of his nose brushed mine, when his breath ghosted my cheek, I didn't move. I couldn't.

"You scare me. I'll admit that. But not in the way you think."

"Sounds like I've got work to do."

"Perfect."

The air simmered between us. But neither moved an inch. Santino's gaze dropped to my mouth, and my teeth caught the corner of my lip, betraying me. I couldn't even remember the last time I *wanted* to be kissed, and the thought alone was enough to make my stomach twist with shame.

"Get out," I spat from between my teeth.

His grin opened up, and he leaned in a second time, *"Cosa mi hai fatto?"*

I wasn't fluent in Italian, but whatever he'd whispered into my ear caused a traitorous flush of arousal to pulse between my thighs.

Fuck.

———

I was in Ivan Tarasov's vehicle, perched on his lap, within thirty minutes of our private. Santino would lose his shit when he found out I'd left the club with the very client he'd explicitly forbidden me to see, but my boss was at the bottom of my list of worries. So, I stuffed all thoughts of him into a safe place and focused my attention on the sack of meat in front of me.

"I'm going to take good care of you, *malyshka*."

"I'm sure you will."

His fingers combed through my hair, the other hand snaking up the back of my neck. It took over a year after my escape to lose the tremors and impending panic attack that would ensue at even the slightest hint of a sexually charged touch. I'd learned to temper my fear, internalize and lock it up, then spit it back out as raw and unfettered rage.

"You are what I call an exotic beauty. Where are you from?"

"Miami."

An unamused chuckle bubbled up his throat, and he tightened his grip a little more than I was comfortable with. "You know what I mean."

It was easy to deduce that Ivan was the type of man who got off on being in charge and loathed disrespect. One moment, he spoke in a way meant to lull me into a state of complacency, where I unquestioningly handed over my trust as easily as my body. The next, he demanded it through aggression.

Leaning close, I murmured in his ear, *"Brasil."*

"Are all the women there as gorgeous as you?"

His hand curled possessively around my throat as the car rolled to a stop inside a mostly empty parking garage. Cambri had said he lived on a gated property. But apparently, he was giving me the penthouse special—Only I wasn't stepping out of this car until he was no longer breathing.

"Are you asking me about other women while I'm grinding my pussy in your lap?"

He grazed his mouth up the length of my cheek.

"You may be in my lap, *malysh*, but you're just another whore for me to use as I please."

Just. Another. Whore.

And just like that, the facade of this night had ended.

Closing my eyes, I reached for the pendant hanging between my breasts, pulling free a short blade. With a swift motion, I drove it into the side of his neck. His eyes widened in shock, meeting mine as I struck again, basking in the red squirting between his tightly clasped fingers.

"Cambri sends her regards."

"Suka," he gruffed, sliding a hand toward his waistband.

I caught his wrist mid-reach, squeezing tight.

"Can't have you shooting me. The last thing I need is another scar."

The small blade plunged into his side three times as I wrestled to keep his weapon out of play until he was fully incapacitated. He shoved me hard, but as I fell, I grabbed onto his bloodied collar, pulling him down with me and driving the blade deeper.

The bastard fought like he had nine lives, each stab only fueling his desperation.

A single gunshot shattered the cramped space of the car. We froze, our eyes locking for a heartbeat before I slid the blade to its new home. Ivan's blue iris split with a sickening, wet squelch, his agonized howls echoing in the confined space. I wanted to savor his pain, but the sound of the passenger door ripping open snapped me back. His driver was coming. Fast.

"Sit tight, friend. I'll be right back."

Ivan's only good eye fluttered as he gurgled something unintelligible. As soon as I cracked the door, the bald driver burst out, guns blazing. I dropped and rolled behind the trunk just in time.

"Shit."

Screeching tires let me know there were more assholes incoming, so I took aim from beneath the car and fired. Two shots tore through the man's ankles, and when he collapsed, I put a bullet through his face.

I jumped over Ivan's twitching body as it hung halfway out of the door, his head twisted on the concrete in a puddle of blood.

That bastard had the nerve to still be alive.

My night had flipped on its head. I was supposed to be in his bedroom, surprising him with a few of my favorite blades on very specific parts of his anatomy, then sneak out undetected. But life didn't care about plans.

I flung Tarasov's piece of shit Beretta and reached for my own gun from inside my boot, and an extra magazine in the other.

"Get that bitch!"

Ivan's bodyguard pulled in front of the car, another man beside him, and a hail of automatic gunfire rained down on the vehicle. The noise inside the cabin was deafening, my ears ringing painfully as I ducked for cover, wondering how long the bulletproof exterior would hold.

"Damn it," I cursed, shielding my ears when the chaos suddenly gave way to an eerie silence—until two suppressed pops, followed by heavy thuds, echoed throughout the garage.

Seconds crawled by, thick with unnerving quiet.

Then I heard the most unexpected voice.

"Amara. Are you okay?"

Santino.

SEVENTEEN

Santino

Amara eased out of the car, stepping over the body beneath the opened passenger door. Her eyes fixed on me, gun drawn and aimed at my chest, as if waiting for me to make a move.

"What are you doing here?"

Not an inch of her skin was free of blood.

Despite the threat to my life, I shuffled forward. The urgency to know she was unhurt was stronger than my fear of getting shot.

"Don't," she warned, steadying her weapon

I'd stared down the barrel of a gun more times than I could ever recount. It hardly fazed me, especially when my concern lay elsewhere.

When I saw her get into Tarasov's car, I raced through the club and was out the door just in time to watch him pull onto the street. Not a second later, I trailed the vehicle, calling Amara's cell, only to get voicemail.

"Are you hurt?"

She snickered. "What's wrong with you?"

"I'm not the one covered in blood, *preziosa*."

"Stop calling me that."

There was a quiver in her hand and uncertainty burning in

her eyes. It was clear she was grappling with a decision—whether or not to take my life. I didn't blame her. One look at the carnage around us was enough. Not disposing of a witness to murder was as stupid as getting into a car with a man the likes of Ivan.

I shifted my foot, letting a thin river of blood flow past my shoe where the driver lay dead from a perfectly executed headshot.

I'd suspected Amara was hiding something, but nothing—**nothing**—could have prepared me for this. Whoever she was, this version of her didn't make any sense. She was clearly trained. Composed. The average citizen would have fled screaming, mind spiraling into panic.

I'd rubbed elbows with the darkest corners of our society's underworld. And what I saw here reeked of a blood oath. If that was the case, what kind of financial desperation—or vendetta—had brought Amara to Illusion?

"Why did you follow me?"

"Did you think I was going to just sit by and let you get in that asshole's car?"

"You should have," she said, finger still on the trigger.

I slid forward another step, expecting to get shot but hoping she wouldn't.

"Why, so those two bastards could kill you by pinning you inside this car?"

"I can handle myself."

My eyes skimmed over the bodies littering the garage floor. I nodded, daring to inch closer. "I can see that."

"Santino," she warned, voice low, "you know I have to."

"Do you?"

Another step. Her jaw clenched. I'd be lying if I said my heart wasn't thundering in my chest.

"You shouldn't have come here."

"If I hadn't, you would have died in there."

As I closed the gap between me and her weapon, titanium pressed against my chest.

"Why would you care?"

I shook my head and chuckled. "Because you've lived inside my head the moment I set eyes on you. And I can't shake you, *preziosa*. Every second of every fucking day, I think of you. So even if you kill me, at least I'll die knowing you're safe."

Her chest rose and fell with shallow breaths, the only sound between us as our eyes locked.

"You're insane," she breathed.

"I am. But I knew that the moment I refused to sign over Illusion and decided to stay...because of you."

A flicker of emotion passed through her features, thinning her irises.

I slowly lifted a hand, intending to slide the gun from hers, when she suddenly whipped out of my reach and fired four rounds into Tarasov's face.

"I am, too. Remember that if you're thinking of fucking me over."

Stepping on the dead bastard, she briefly climbed back into the tattered car, rustling around for several seconds before emerging with a black bag slung over her shoulder. As she walked past me, she sent another round into the driver without missing a beat.

Dannazione. Goddamn.

My cock hardened.

"We should probably vacate this garage. The whole thing might come down when the car blows."

"Oh, fuck," I said, jogging after her with a grin stretching across my face.

Penso di essere innamorato. I think I'm in love.

EIGHTEEN

Santino

"Who are you?"

I glanced at her still figure in my passenger seat. She sat silently, eyes glued to the window, as if watching the city roll by —though we both knew she wasn't sightseeing.

Amara was lost in her head, probably still debating whether she should put a bullet through my temple. Maybe I was desensitized to violence and death, or maybe I'd simply lost my damn mind. Because seeing her tonight, covered in blood and handling business, awakened something primal in me.

I was never one to believe in fate, but I never imagined I'd come across anyone as perfect as the woman sitting beside me—even if, moments ago, she had her finger on the trigger and my chest in her sights.

I leaned my elbow against the door and bit down on my fist to hide the smile splitting my face, doing my best not to provoke her any further.

For now.

"You know who I am," she finally said, still searing a hole through the window.

"I know who I thought you were, but what happened back there—"

"*Nothing* happened back there."

"Right. But between us, I feel like that conversation needs to be had."

She shifted toward me. "You mean the one where you're stalking me? Watching me? Following me. *That* conversation?"

The car rolled to a stop at a red light, and I met her fiery gaze. "It's my job to look after my dancers."

"Bullshit, Santino. If that were true, you would have followed Cambri the night she left with that bastard—the night he almost killed her."

"What are you talking about?"

"Yeah, Cambri doesn't have the fucking flu. She's in the hospital recovering from a concussion and multiple fractures, courtesy of Tarasov."

Her words reeled in my gut—not because I felt guilt over what happened to her friend, but because I felt like I'd somehow failed her. And she'd hold that over my head, perceive it as a weakness.

"Why didn't you tell me?"

"What difference would it have made?"

Amara was right. I wouldn't have lifted a single finger to avenge Cambri. But I would've torn Tarasov's head from his body before he ever stepped foot inside my club—before he set his sights on her.

"Is that why you did what you did? Was your goal to kill him tonight?"

Her narrowed eyes cut into me, hands clutching the hem of her skirt as if debating whether to answer.

"He deserved it."

"Agreed. But one doesn't kill a man on a whim, Amara. Not the way you did. That takes training, sharp instincts, and reflexes, and a stomach made of steel to empty a mag into someone's face."

She looked away as I pulled into traffic.

"So I ask you again—who are you?"

"A woman with a lot of demons. And I don't kill men on a whim, Santino. I kill them because I like it. Men like Tarasov deserve to die like dogs."

She hadn't given me a moment to process before the barrel of her gun was pressed to my head.

Again.

"You missed the exit. Turn around and take me to my car." Her voice was tight.

"I'm not going to worry about whether or not you make it home."

"I never asked you to drive me home. And how am I not surprised you know where I live?"

I chuckled. "I hate to disappoint you, but your address is on file, too. Although that's not where we're going."

"Do you have a death wish, Mr. Leone?"

"Not particularly."

She shoved the weapon with more force, asserting the threat. "Turn. Around."

"Have you seen yourself? You look like you've slaughtered a man—or three. You're willing to risk someone seeing you the moment you step foot inside your apartment complex?"

"I'm insulted you think it's my first time."

That earned a laugh. "Maybe not. But something tells me you're not usually this—*messy*."

"You really are fucking crazy, aren't you? I have a gun to your head. I tell you that I enjoy watching men bleed; you saw what happened back there, and yet you still insist on helping me."

"*I'm* insulted you think I'm fazed by murder. I'm a Leone, *preziosa*."

"Is that supposed to mean something to me? And stop with the damn pet name."

Squeezing the steering wheel, I leaned my head back and blew out a breath. "If you trust that I won't out you to the cops about what happened to Tarasov and his men, then you can trust that you're safe with me."

"Who said I trust you?"

When I turned to face her, the hard barrel was positioned between my eyes. "Because you would have already pulled that trigger."

Annoyance pinched her face. Possibly because she realized I had a point.

"I can count on one finger the people I trust. And I'm sorry to report that you don't exactly make the cut."

"Fair. But allow me to change that." Taking a chance, I slowly reached for her hand, mindful of her quick reflexes. "We're just ten minutes away. You get cleaned up, and I'll get you home."

"Why?" she asked, finally lowering the weapon, the hard edges of her face and tone softening.

"What I said about you being stuck in my head—I meant it."

She inhaled, ready to counter my confession, but I beat her to it.

"I have my demons, too. And maybe we're more alike than you think."

———

The remainder of the car ride to my property was quiet. I let her have her peace, unwilling to agitate her further. Amara might have seemed like a pillar of steel and ice, but I was well-versed in trauma and the layers one needed to pile on to keep the darkness at bay.

"You brought me to your home?" she asked, sliding out of the car, gun still in hand. I followed and climbed the steps to the front entryway, a sense of victory filling my chest when I felt her presence close behind.

"Just to get cleaned up."

"Right."

Keeping her in my periphery, I went through my routine of disarming and re-engaging the security system, powering on the monitors that fed footage from every vantage point of my property. I'd admit I'd paid well over the home's worth, but choices were slim when making a last-minute impulse purchase.

Amara's eyes tracked me, assessing, hyper-aware of every move I made

Trained.

"Are you hungry?"

"No," she replied dryly.

I acknowledged her vigilance with a nod and dared to step closer. The recessed lighting above us was dimmed, but enough to highlight the parts of her the darkness had obscured. Red spatters stained her skin, deepening as they spread across her forearms and hands, where the color nearly blackened.

Pushing the boundary between us, I reached for her hand, and her tentative eyes shot up to meet mine.

"Are you okay?" I asked, flipping her hand over and scanning the stained flesh, finding only minor defensive wounds.

"It's not my blood."

"Good."

A strange spark of pride rolled through me.

Neither of us spoke for several beats, her hand still firmly in mine. I counted that as a small victory.

"Where's that cleaning up you promised me?"

Her voice held a hint of amusement, and she surprised me when she slipped her gun into the bag strapped across her body. She wouldn't admit it, and maybe her trust only stretched so far, but she'd let her guard down just enough. That was progress, however small.

"Down that hall. My bedroom has the ensuite."

Her eyes tightened as they met mine. "Your bedroom?"

"Lock the door. And help yourself to my closet. Nothing will fit quite right, but anything's better than being soaked in that son of a bitch's blood."

She shrugged and started down the hall. "It's like a trophy."

The door closed behind her, but I heard no click of the lock. In any other situation with any other woman, I'd have taken that as an invitation. But with Amara, I was learning her silence was more of a dare.

I wasn't the type to chase or court—never had to—yet here I was, inviting a near stranger into my home. A woman who'd been ready to kill me just moments ago in a desolate parking garage alongside four other men. If anything, I should have ripped her apart for even considering pointing a gun at me with intent.

Letting out a slow huff, I sank onto the couch, drink in hand, scoffing at my own predicament. Everything I stood for—the code I lived and breathed—was unraveling. Damn it all to hell, I'd been fucked from the moment I laid eyes on her.

My obsession only deepened now that I knew her heart was just as black as mine.

NINETEEN

Amara

I tied off Santino's sweatpants at my waist, tucked in the oversized tee, then lifted my gaze to the mirror, silently asking myself what the actual fuck I was doing. I'd only known this man for two weeks, yet he'd stumbled upon my darkest secret, somehow convinced me not to kill him, and now he'd brought me to his home. Here I was, in his bathroom, drenched in his clothes and the scent of his body wash.

Trust wasn't something I granted easily.

Especially not to a man like Santino, now privy to my taste for blood. He was a liability. Who was to say he wouldn't use what he knew against me, blackmailing me in exchange for silence? Despite being an accomplice, Santino Leone had sway, money, power—everything he needed to clean his slate. Meanwhile, I was just a stripper.

My eyes drifted to the bag I'd dropped by the vanity. The Glock called to me, begging to end his life and avoid the fallout of his inevitable betrayal.

"He wouldn't see it coming. Not if I play my cards right."

But what if I was wrong? He'd helped me tonight, risked his life when he could have just kept driving. My eyes slid to the unlocked bathroom door—one I'd purposely left ajar as a test.

I shook my head, pushing aside the traitorous thoughts clouding my judgment, and gripped the sink.

He'd followed me.

Again.

And I didn't know how to feel or what his intentions were.

"Because you've lived inside my head the moment I set eyes on you. And I can't shake you, preziosa. Every second of every fucking day, I think of you. So even if you kill me, at least I'll die knowing you're safe."

Men lusting after me wasn't new, but his words, given the circumstances, felt genuine, cutting deeper than they should. Or maybe he said them out of self-preservation.

Before I could spiral, I grabbed my bag and headed toward the man in question. As I moved through his spacious bedroom, I noted how every piece of furniture, the decorative pillows on his bed, the artwork on his walls, and every crease and fold in his sheets were meticulously arranged and clean. Unlike the rest of the home, which was sparse—just enough furniture to seem lived in—this space radiated warmth, even boasting a few live plants I didn't recognize.

A woman's touch, no doubt.

The thought sparked a strange flutter in my stomach as I wondered who she might be.

Santino rose when he heard me approaching, making no effort to hide his gaze lingering on my borrowed clothes.

A foreign wave of insecurity rippled through me. My hair was damp, and without any products to tame my curls, so I'd twisted it into a high bun.

Why did I care what he thought?

"That's better," he said, motioning for me to sit.

"I should get going."

"We have a conversation pending."

"Do we?"

He set down his glass and closed the distance with confident steps. Too fast for me to react, he covered the gun tucked at my waist. I slammed my hand down over his.

I gritted my teeth.

"Let go."

"I'm not going to hurt you."

My nails dug into his skin, but he didn't flinch. "*Not going to hurt me?* That's the most overused and abused phrase that ever existed."

The corners of Santino's dark eyes creased as he studied me.

"Tell me, who hurt you, *preziosa?*"

His words carried the weight of a thousand knives and just as many tears.

The answer hovered on my lips. It was a piece of my soul, my past, that he hadn't earned yet.

Surprise flickered as the word *yet* burned in my mind.

"What are we going to do here?" I asked, pushing past his probing gaze.

"What you saw back there with Tarasov—"

"I saw nothing," he replied with a grin, loosening his grip. "If I let go, will you promise not to shoot me?"

"As long as you don't do anything to make me shoot you."

"Fair. But can I make a request?" His hand slid away, slipping into his pocket.

The motion made his shirt stretch over the muscles in his arms and chest, and for the first time, I was drawn to his masculinity in a way I hadn't felt since...

Since...

Ezra.

The name hit me like a punch. My heart thundered, and I stumbled back, swallowing down the sudden wave of anguish. The back of my knees collided with the coffee table, and I started to fall—until Santino's arms caught me, lifting my feet off the floor and pulling me close to his chest.

"Easy," he crooned. "That son of a bitch has caught my knee more times than I'm proud to admit. And now it tries to get you?" His eyes dropped to my lips. "Seems to me it needs a new home."

"You watched me kill a man today, yet you're worried about a coffee table?" I murmured, breathless at how close he was.

An amused laugh bubbled from his lips, and despite myself, a smile crested mine.

He set me down without waiting for a request, which I was thankful for, and motioned toward the sofa. I fought against his silent plea but found myself yielding when I realized the demons I'd been trying to keep locked away had momentarily vanished in the cradle of his arms.

———

Warm, bright light soothed my skin, and the aroma of a delicious meal filled my senses, pulling me gently from sleep. I drew in a deep breath, but then awareness gripped me suddenly. I snapped my eyes open in a panic, unable to remember when or how I'd fallen asleep.

Most importantly, I realized I wasn't in my bed, my room, or even my apartment.

"Breathe," I whispered, feeling the first stirrings of a spiral as memories of those dark days when I was put to sleep against my will resurfaced.

He's not like them.

I wanted to believe that with every fiber of my being because, as much as I'd tried, I didn't hate Santino's company.

I shot up from the couch, surprised to see my gun and blade resting on a side table. The coffee table that once sat in the middle of Santino's living room was nowhere in sight—a strange detail, but not my priority. Clutching both weapons, one in each hand, I followed the low thrum of music and the scent of cooked pork down the hallway toward the kitchen.

When I entered the bright space, I wasn't sure what to

expect, but Santino, shirtless and holding an oven mitt by the stove, caught me off guard even more than waking on his couch.

"I haven't done anything yet that would warrant a shot in the back," he said with a teasing smile as he spooned scrambled eggs from a skillet onto a plate.

"Why did I just wake up on your couch instead of my bed?" I asked.

"You fell asleep, *preziosa*," he said, casual as ever, adding two strips of bacon to the plate before twisting around. "You looked exhausted. Why would I wake you?"

"Why *wouldn't* you?" I bit out.

I tried to focus on his face and not the gray sweatpants hanging low on his tapered hips as he rounded the large island separating us and set a beautifully plated breakfast in front of me.

"Coffee? Giada, my housekeeper and chef, makes the best cup. But she has the morning off—"

"Santino! Don't play dumb. We barely know each other. I can't just spend the night."

"I'll remember that next time."

I shook my head and snorted an incredulous laugh. "Next time, huh? Your delusion knows no bounds."

"You're coming off a little ungrateful."

"Better than crazy."

He leaned against the counter, arms folded over his heavily inked chest. Saliva thickened in my throat, and I swallowed harder than I expected, caught between taut muscle and that cocky smirk.

"Elaborate."

I set down my weapons, mirrored his stance, and schooled my expression. "I tried to kill you three times last night, and you made me bacon and eggs."

"Would you prefer pancakes?"

I opened and closed my mouth, suddenly at a loss for words.

"What exactly are you looking for, Santino?" I finally asked with a huff.

"You and I have a lot in common. And we share a secret."

Was this the part where he tried to blackmail me?

"Careful. You're sounding more and more like a loose end."

Santino chuckled and pushed off the counter. As he stepped closer, I had to tip my chin to meet his eyes. With a hand against his hard torso, I stepped back and perched on the edge of the island.

"What happened to your coffee table?"

His grin widened, eyes flicking past me toward the living room.

"Well, I wasn't sure how you'd take waking up on my sofa, and I didn't want you hurting yourself in case you decided to spring up and attack me."

I didn't know what to make of this man. He'd risked his life to help me. And even after I'd threatened him, he still insisted on these small, thoughtful gestures, without a shred of resentment.

I was wary. Men weren't often kind without a twisted, vested interest driving their motives. But something about Santino told me he was sincere.

Letting my guard down wasn't an option. But neither was killing him.

And then there were the feelings fluttering inside me—unfamiliar, disarming. As a woman in the business of sex, I'd entertained a revolving door of men, many of them beautiful by society's standards. But I never saw them beyond the payday. I didn't notice anything except what I could exploit—and the size of their bank accounts.

He made me aware of things I otherwise wouldn't have thought twice about—like how my hair probably looked like a family of birds had taken up residence, how I didn't have a toothbrush, and that I was barefoot.

I found myself instinctively tugging the sleeves of Santino's borrowed shirt past my knuckles, hiding the scars etched around my wrists. Not just because my past was mine alone, and opening that door wasn't an option right now, but because...

I lifted my eyes to where he stood, watching me, waiting for me to speak.

Santino brought out insecurities I thought I'd buried long ago. I didn't want him to see the broken parts of me, to notice my flaws. The ugly pieces that lived inside me... and the ones inked into my skin.

"I have to go," I blurted, rising to my feet.

The smile he wore vanished as I stormed past him.

"Wait."

By the time he caught up, I was already booking a ride. "I'm sorry you went through all this trouble."

Sorry?

Had I just...apologized?

"Amara, at least let me take you home," he said, tugging gently on my elbow.

I whirled around, jaw tight.

"Look, whatever you think could happen between us—it can't. And it won't. One, you're my boss. And two...I—"

I faltered, the words catching in my throat as my heart thudded harder against my chest.

He tilted his head slightly, gaze thinning as he searched mine. "You what?"

"I strip and shake my ass for money. I'm a whore, Santino," I snapped, venom dripping from every word. "And every now and then, I like to spill the blood of the men who think I'm nothing more than entertainment."

But the grin spreading across his face was *not* the reaction I expected—or needed.

He stepped in, slow and steady, until his breath ghosted over my ear, lips brushing the shell.

"I think your attempts at scaring me away are... cute."

He twirled a curl around his finger, intrusive, brazen. And yet, my knife wasn't in his gut.

"I know what you do. That ass is what caught my eye in the first place. And maybe there's nothing sexier than a woman who knows her way around a gun...and doesn't mind a little blood."

He dared to tuck a loose strand behind my ear. And I let him.

"I don't mind a lot of blood either."

"Even better."

I rolled my lips between my teeth. "You're broken."

"Aren't we all?"

You have no idea.

Santino's dark eyes roamed my face, settling on my mouth. I knew that look—knew the fire that lit up in a man's eyes when desire took hold. When all they saw was a hole to fill. Santino was no different. Not entirely.

But beneath the heat in his gaze...there was something else.

"Santino," I whispered. "What do you want from me?"

"I want to earn everything you give me." He stepped closer. "Your smile." His thumb brushed my lips. "Your friendship." Another strand of hair tucked gently behind my ear. "But most importantly—your trust."

"I trust no one." The words came out softer than I wanted, more breath than sound.

"I'm up for the challenge."

His closeness. His voice. His certainty.

That flutter in my stomach returned.

Oh, hell.

"Fuck, fuck, fuck…"

I whispered into the void as Santino buried his face between my breasts, his hands splayed against my back, guiding my rhythm as I rode him hard—thighs burning, head thrown back, his name slipping off my tongue like a ragged plea.

"*Preziosa*," he rasped into my ear, nipping my lobe..

I moaned a barely audible "What?"

"Wake up."

I jolted upright, heart pounding.

Pheonix scrambled off the foot of my bed and padded down the hallway.

A dream.

A fucking *wet* dream.

Groaning, I collapsed back against the pillow, yanked the white comforter over my face, and screamed into the fabric.

I didn't know what was worse—that I dreamed about fucking Santino…Or that I'd woken up before the orgasm.

I'd made peace with celibacy, embraced it.

At least, I *thought* I had.

Goosebumps crawled across my skin. Flashes of the last time my body had climaxed—

Unwelcome.

Unwanted.

My mind fought, but my body betrayed me.

And afterward, the shame swallowed me whole. I'd doubled over, retching the filth and self-loathing.

It doesn't matter now.

That girl is dead.

I shoved her back into the pit where she belonged, then wiped the sweat slicking my brow.

Santino Leone.

As much as I wanted to pretend the dream meant nothing, that it was just a byproduct of last night's chaos and sleeping in his home...I knew better. The sexual tension still smoldered between us.

One moment, I was threatening his life. The next, I let him into my space. Let him touch me. Let myself soften at his gestures. Swooned at his words.

Trust?

He said he wanted to earn my trust. But if I was being honest with myself...he already had it.

Otherwise, he'd be on his way to the morgue beside Tarasov. Instead, I spent the night on his couch. Ate his damn breakfast. Let him drive me home.

With a long breath, I covered my face with my hands.

And now I was dreaming of his cock...and liking it.

My pussy still throbbed. And as terrifying as it was to admit, I'd give anything to fall back asleep and meet him in a world where I was safe, where I could taste even a drop of bliss.

Just for a night.

Just *one* night.

Before I could overthink it, my hand slid beneath the sheet, fingers brushing the waistband of my panties. He may have been a product of my fucked-up dreams, but my body didn't know the difference. It responded like he was real. Tentative touches quickened the beat of my heart.

"Santi," I whined into the dark, fingertips gliding in slow strokes, imagining his hand instead of mine, his lips on my neck.

He'd whisper *preziosa* against my ear...not just telling me I was beautiful, but making me feel it, kissing every inch—even my scars.

"Just like that."

My hips thrust up, fingers slick with arousal as I circled my clit, groaning,

"Fuck..."

My thighs spread wider. I bit down on my lip, chasing that sharp, aching high. Pleasure surged, and the urge to scream overtook me. I grabbed a pillow, muffling my cries as I tumbled over the edge with Santino's name on my tongue.

For five minutes, I just lay there, staring at the ceiling, mind blank and racing all at once. I didn't want to think. Didn't want to dwell on what it meant.

So I shot up and headed for the bathroom.

Ten minutes later, I was dressed, slipping out the door past a half-sleeping Phoenix. She lifted her head as I grabbed my black bag.

"Don't look at me like that. I'll be back."

———

Bells jingled overhead as I crossed the threshold of *The Veil*, a bar just two blocks from my building. For a Friday night in Miami, it was surprisingly quiet. Maybe two dozen patrons in total. Most clustered near the bar, while a few lingered around the pool tables and flat-screens.

I settled in a far corner, back to the wall, and ordered a water.

The bartender, a woman in her fifties with a blonde bob and a warm, easy smile, raised a brow at my drink of choice but didn't question it. She slid the glass toward me, condensation trailing behind.

"Let me know if you want something with a little more kick," she said. "You look like you could use the good kind of amnesia."

I narrowed my eyes. "What's that supposed to mean?"

She shrugged, wiping down a water ring on the bar before tucking the rag into her back pocket. "Just means you look like you've got a lot on your mind."

"Don't we all?" I replied with a sigh.

"True. But I know that look. Relationship trouble."

Was it that obvious? Was my face still flushed from earlier?

"I'm not in a relationship."

"Break-up?"

"No, I—"

"You want to be in one?"

I blinked, thrown by her barrage of questions. "That's... not it."

"Sure," she said with a knowing wink. "You know, a girl as pretty as you shouldn't stress over a man...or a woman."

If she knew the full extent of the shit I was stressing over, she'd be vaulting over the bar and sprinting out the door. I raised the glass to my lips and chugged my water, hoping to shut down the conversation. But Stacia—her badge clipped to her belt loop —was relentless.

"I've never seen you around here before. And I don't forget a face, especially one like yours, with those pretty eyes. You live in the city?"

She suddenly reminded me of one of my mother's neighbors back in Rio—a kind woman with too much time on her hands and just as many stories. As Stacia began rambling on, I noticed a man across the room. His hands were slick, like a magician's. Unfortunately for him, he wasn't fast enough.

I caught the moment he dropped a powdery substance into the drink in front of him. I didn't see his companion, but I assumed he'd waited until they were out of sight.

Adding another waste of skin to my tally hadn't been part of my plans tonight. Still, I was always prepared. Squeezing the strap of my bag, I rose to my feet. Stacia paused mid-monologue, her eyes fixed on me as I approached the man whose cock would harden for the last time tonight—well, unless you counted rigor mortis.

As clumsily as I could manage, I tripped over my own feet and crashed into his table, deliberately tipping the drink in his direction. The special cocktail spilled onto his lap, and he snapped upright.

"Oh my God, I'm so sorry!" I cried, slipping into my best damsel act.

"Shit." He shook off his pant leg as droplets splattered onto the floor.

In a flash, Stacia moved with a rag, but I snatched it from her and began wiping the man's wet crotch. Of course, he let me.

"Let me get that." I grabbed his waistband and pulled his hips toward my face, looking up through lowered lashes. "Just a little dab, and it should dry in no time."

The corner of his mouth twitched into a slight grin. I returned it, adding a wink for good measure.

"It's...okay," he said, twisting a curl around his finger.

I leaned close to his ear. "There's an alley around the corner. I'll wait fifteen minutes. How about you let me make it up to you?"

The bell chimed as the door swung open behind me. I stepped into the warm night, adrenaline flooding my veins with every step.

Turning the corner into the empty strip, I smiled as I slipped on my mask, and savored the familiar tingle of an impending kill. It had taken years to nurse my wounds, not just the physical ones, but the scars carved deep into my soul. I never forgot the look of horror in Mr. H's eyes as I drained his life, just like he had mine.

For months, I'd dream of all the men lined up to violate and destroy everything I was. The only way to silence their voices was with violence and death. Finding the worst of society was easy. They didn't just lurk in the darkest corners of the internet or some underground club.

Monsters lived among us.

"There you are." His dark shadow lurked at the end of the alley.

He'd pulled a hoodie over his head, hiding his face. But I imagined the smug grin, the hard cock in his pants, ready to take his fill.

"Here I am."

Despite my invitation, like the scum I knew he was, his hand wrapped around my throat, pushing me against the brick wall.

"You cost me a fun night. But I'm a forgiving man...for the right price."

I brought my mouth to his jaw and cupped his balls. "Who says the fun's over, pretty boy? The night is still young."

The smile on his face lasted a breath—just long enough for my knife to slide into his gut. Twice. Quick and clean before he even realized what was happening.

His eyes widened. Lips parted. He stumbled back, staring at his bloodied hands, then at me, like I'd betrayed some unspoken contract.

When I returned home, my thoughts would be overrun by Santino and all the ways he fucked with my head.

But for now I'd quench my thirst for revenge and silence the screaming in my skull with the pathetic whimpers of Mr. Douchebag Rapist.

TWENTY-ONE

As the elevator doors slid open, I glanced at my hands, checking for any blood beneath my nails or stray spatters I might've missed.

Clean.

He hadn't put up much of a fight...though I supposed it was hard to struggle when your intestines were spilling onto the pavement.

Disembowelment hadn't been on the agenda tonight—too messy, too crude—but he forced my hand.

"Good evening, Miss Carvalho."

I froze, key mid-air, his voice yanking me out of the slow-motion replay of tonight's kill.

After weeks of avoiding him, timing my comings and goings to sidestep any contact, Detective Braga had finally caught up to me. And in a weak moment, no less.

If I ignored him and ducked inside without a word, I risked drawing more attention...more inconvenient encounters like this one.

But what snagged me, what made the blade at my waist feel a little less idle, was *how* he addressed me.

Miss Carvalho.

The name sat heavy in the air. I might've shared my first name that night, but I'd never given him my last. Of that, I was certain.

Which meant only one thing.

Detective Braga had researched me.

And that begged a more pressing question:

Why?

"Detective," I said coolly, turning to face him.

I was instantly irritated, mostly with myself. I'd been so deep in thought, I hadn't even noticed him approach. That lapse unnerved me.

He seemed like a good man. A decent father. The idea of disposing of him, and orphaning his son, didn't exactly thrill me.

But if it came down to protecting my secret?

Detective Braga would have no one to blame but himself.

"I'm glad I ran into you this morning," he said, voice easy. "My boy still remembers that night, you know?"

That struck me as unlikely, considering the kid could barely string three words together.

"Does he?"

The smile that stretched across Detective Braga's face—one that neither confirmed nor denied his claim—told me everything I needed to know.

Bullshit.

He just wanted a reason to talk to me.

I could read men and their intentions like a book. But this one confused me. When he looked at me, his eyes never strayed from mine. His grin wasn't seedy, and he never encroached on my personal space the way most men did—especially those at Illusion. Or life, for that matter.

Raymond Braga had ulterior motives.

And suddenly, I was intrigued.

"I'm sorry to be blunt," he said, "but I have to ask—have you been avoiding me?"

There it was.

"Should I be avoiding you, Detective?"

His jaw ticked, just slightly. Eyes narrowed. Barely noticeable, but I caught it.

"Absolutely not..."

A pause.

"But?"

"Amara, these streets aren't kind to pretty girls alone at night. I've responded to one too many scenes where luck didn't fall in their favor. I've noticed you coming and going at odd hours, and—"

"Detective," I cut in. "With all due respect, you're not my father. I've been taking care of myself for a long time."

His gaze dropped, lips pressed into a hard line. He was biting back something, concern, frustration, maybe both.

"I'll see you around," I said, turning to end the conversation.

"Amara..."

Or not.

"Are you hurt?"

I followed his eyes to the back of my leg where dried blood streaked down my skin.

Shit.

"Yeah, I caught myself on some metal at the park, Must've missed it when I cleaned up."

Raymond glanced at his watch. "You were at Hyde Park this late?"

Questions, questions. What was it with everyone and their damn interrogations?

"Sometimes I can't sleep. That's all," I bit out, harsher than I meant.

"What keeps you up at night?"

Something about Detective Braga made me hold back my sharp tongue. Maybe it was the way he reminded me of home— kind eyes that crinkled at the corners like my father's, and the gentle cadence of our native language. Apart from Lorenzo, he was the only man who expected nothing from me but conversation.

"Life." The word left my mouth laced with grief. "That's what keeps me up."

His expression softened.

"Amara, my wife was murdered on her way home from work two years ago. You remind me of her...when we first met. I'm not trying to pry. I just—I'd hate to see something bad happen to you."

Everything bad already had.

His eyes misted unexpectedly. His throat bobbed.

"I appreciate your concern. I really do. And I'm sorry about your wife."

He tipped my chin, gentle, almost paternal, and I let him. Maybe I was losing my edge. Maybe Santino had chipped too far into the walls I built.

"*Não consegui salvá-la.*"

He couldn't save her.

I shook my head. "*Você também não pode me salvar.*"

He can't save me either.

Silence settled between us, heavy and final. He nodded, the worry lines etched deep into his face.

"You've still got a few hours before sunrise. I hope you get some sleep."

"Me too," I murmured, slipping inside my apartment.

Phoenix greeted me like she hadn't moved from the door since I left. I scooped her up, pressing her close to my chest.

Tossing my keys on the counter, I stood in the stillness of my empty living room. My stomach hollowed at the thought of the dead man bleeding out in the alley.

The high was gone.

Something was changing.

TWENTY-TWO

Santino

The cut glass gave under the pressure of my grip, collapsing inward until the shards pierced my skin. But the pain barely registered, just a pinprick compared to the aggravation burning up my spine as I watched her dance on the live feed.

Her number had ended ten minutes ago. Still, my eyes stayed glued to the screen while the last of her winnings was collected.

Amara had been magnificent, as always, leaving me torn between losing myself in her performance and hurling the goddamn bottle of scotch at the screen to blot out the way other men lusted after what was mine.

And she was mine.

Even if our relationship still tiptoed around this power dynamic, I'd give her the time she needed.

For a man used to taking what he wanted, my patience with her was...unprecedented. Over the last few weeks, we'd grown closer. But still, there was a wall between us. She was careful with her words, guarded in her gestures, keeping just enough distance to drive me mad. But I was nothing if not determined.

Two soft raps on the door pulled my attention away, like I'd conjured her with my thoughts. I didn't need to guess who it was. Amara always brought a jolt of electric energy that stirred something deep in my chest.

"Come in," I said, rounding the desk with hasty steps, eager to see her face in person.

The scent of her perfume hit me before she fully stepped into the room.

"To what do I owe the pleasure of your company, *preziosa?*"

She tilted her head, feigning exasperation at the nickname. Maybe it was unprofessional, but the word slipped from my mouth without thought. Decorum be damned.

"I need time off. In about two weeks," she said, leaning against the back of a chair.

My heart staggered—not at the request, but at the way she said it. Her voice was clipped, her eyes avoiding mine. I didn't need more than that to know this wasn't a vacation.

No, this was connected to her very interesting extracurriculars.

"And may I ask what for?"

"No."

Why did that answer not surprise me?

"How long?"

"A week."

"A week?" I grimaced.

A fucking week without eyes on my girl. Without knowing if she was all right.

Fuck no.

"Where?"

"Out of state."

A resounding *fuck no*.

"We're still down a dancer. Maybe when Cambri gets back," I lied.

I knew how capable she was—*deadly* even. But I also knew her. Knew the way she could act on impulse when it came to matters that cut too deep. The Tarasov shitshow came to mind. And something about a flight out of state, paired with the stiffness in her shoulders and the way she refused to meet my eyes, told me this trip was personal. Dangerous. And that made my blood run colder than I liked.

She pursed her lips, a move that only made me want to bite them.

"I'm not exactly asking. Just giving you a courtesy heads-up."

I chuckled, folding my arms. "Is that how this works?"

Her mouth parted, then closed again. Whatever comeback she had died when her gaze dropped to the smear of blood on my sleeve.

"You're bleeding," she said softly, placing her hand over mine and gently flipping it over to examine my palm.

"It's just a small cut."

She eyed the shards still scattered across my desk. "How does that happen?"

"Flimsy glass."

Her eyes flicked back to mine, a grin tugging at her red lips. "You're a bad liar."

"Almost as bad as you."

"Wrong. I'm a great one."

She moved without hesitation, retrieving the first aid kit from the bottom drawer of my desk—she didn't need to ask where it was.

"Sit," she commanded, nudging me toward the chair.

I obliged, if only to soak in the feel of her hands on me. Her closeness. Her care.

"Where are you flying to?"

"Pennsylvania."

My brows lifted slightly, surprised she answered. "What's in Pennsylvania?"

"Loose ends," she said, dabbing at the blood with a wipe.

"I'll go with you."

"Santino, we're not a team. I don't need your help. And you wouldn't understand."

I reached for her wrist, gently tracing the black bands that wrapped around them—markings I knew covered scars beneath. Someone had hurt her. Deeply. And I needed to know whose heart I was going to rip out.

"I can try."

She shook her head, a softness blooming in her expression. "Two weeks," she murmured, sidestepping what I'd just offered her.

"I'll make arrangements. Have an aircraft ready for us both. Just say the word."

It was time I paid Silas and Leni a visit anyway. And maybe I'd finally meet Maksim. But more than that, it would mean time alone with her. Uninterrupted.

Whatever she was about to say died on her lips when her eyes lifted to the monitors behind me. A flicker of confusion crossed her face, and I turned.

Luca sat beside the stage, a familiar man posted to his right.

That son of a bitch.

I shot to my feet, fist slamming into the desk before I stormed toward the door. Blaise and Ash moved to follow, but a sharp wave of my hand told them to fall back.

I wouldn't tolerate outright disrespect, especially from my disgraced cousin. Luca knew damn well he was banned from my establishment for life.

As I closed in, the familiarity of his companion's face finally struck me. Gregorio Andretti—one of my father's long-standing business allies. The man lived full-time in Sorrento. What the fuck was he doing in Miami...and why the hell was he sitting next to *Luca*?

I'd run contracts for Gregorio for years, back when I worked alongside Hades and The Six. Which only made his presence here, with a family fuck-up, even more suspicious.

"Santi, wait. He's not alone."

Amara's voice was low and urgent, cutting through my rage. Her hand slid over mine, grounding it against the grip of my gun.

But it wasn't just the warning that stopped me. It was the *nick-name*. Santi.

She tilted her chin to ten and two o'clock. Two men—stoic, all business—stood just inside the shadows, pretending there weren't tits on stage while their eyes scanned the room for threats.

I hadn't noticed them.

"I thought you said we weren't a team," I murmured, brushing my thumb across the soft skin beneath her mask. She must've pulled it on before following me from the office. I hadn't even realized she'd come.

"You promised me a private jet, Mr. Leone. Just making sure you follow through."

Jesus. Even now, with blood pounding in my ears and a gun drawn at my thigh, she had the power to reroute my focus with a single sentence.

"So...that's a yes?"

"He sees you coming," she replied, ignoring the question, and squeezing my hand once.

I moved in front of her, shielding her body with mine. My gun remained low, out of view of the patrons, but steady in my grip.

"You will leave in one of two ways, Luca," I said coolly. "Walking...or in a bag. This is the only time I'll give you the choice."

Luca chuckled and leaned back, chin tipping toward the bar.

I resisted the urge to glance that way. I liked my bartender. I'd hate to paint the walls with his brains just to remind people how loyalty works.

"Santino, is that any way to treat family?" Gregorio clapped a hand on Luca's shoulder, stretching his arms along the back of the booth. His eyes brushed mine, just briefly, before sliding to Amara.

I stepped directly into his line of sight.

"Blood means nothing without loyalty and trust," I said. "And even that expires the second lines are crossed."

His mouth tightened. Message received.

"Oh, come on, *cugino*. Let's talk this out and put what happened behind us. Tensions were high. No hard feelings, yeah?" Luca leaned in, eyes darting past me to catch sight of a silent Amara. His grin widened. "There's my best girl. Told you you'd like her. *Bellissima!*"

"Get out. And take your men."

His cynical laughter shook his chest. "Every man has a price." He slid out of the booth, smoothing the front of his suit as he stood. "And every man has a breaking point. Remember that, Santino."

The threat wrapped in his words snapped something in me. I reached instinctively for my waistband—until Amara's hand settled over mine again. Our eyes locked.

This was a moment: despite the miles of distrust between us, she was slowly sharing pieces of herself I'd only seen reserved for Cambri.

"It was nice seeing you again, Gregorio." Luca tipped his chin as he headed for the door, throwing a last glance my way and signaling his men to follow.

"Well, that was interesting." Gregorio sat up straighter, eyebrows knitting with amusement as he lit a cigarette, a cloud of smoke billowing above him. "I remember you and Luca as boys, and I see not much has changed." He flicked ash with a smirk. "But family is family, no? Maybe you should hear him out. This *was* his father's place."

"Respectfully, whatever he's told you is probably true. But none of it's your business."

Gregorio's lips thinned, but he nodded. His gaze slid back to Amara, a bastard grin spreading.

"Come on." I placed a firm hand on the small of Amara's back. She tensed briefly but let me lead her away, toward my office, where Blaise and Ash waited, eyes glued to the monitors.

"Who's the bouncer on shift?"

"Alec, sir."

"Take him downstairs."

Everyone knew the rules: Luca was not welcome here. His brazen entrance with his own security was unforgivable. Incompetence wouldn't be tolerated. There would be an example made tonight.

I closed the door behind my men and turned to Amara. "What was that about?"

Amara pushed back her mask, a corner catching in her curls. I was at her side instantly, carefully loosening the tangled strands.

"What was what?" she asked, her tone softer than usual. Less sarcasm, more something unreadable.

As I freed the last strand, my gaze locked with hers, faces just inches apart. I expected her to pull back, but she stayed still, waiting for an answer she didn't need. Still, I humored her.

"Twice you stepped in for me."

"Well, you were barging in there, guns blazing, making a scene. Not the smartest move. You were outnumbered."

"And you were worried?"

Her blue eye narrowed—a quirk she wore when hiding discomfort or annoyance. I smiled, ghosting my fingers over her cheek. Again, she didn't pull away.

"Maybe I still need this job. A dead boss and a shot-up club wouldn't help much. Plus, the private jet."

"Is that all?" I laughed.

Her lashes fluttered when my thumb brushed her bottom lip. Maybe it was wishful thinking, but I swore she leaned into the touch.

"Yeah," she whispered, lifting her eyes to mine.

Without breaking eye contact, I looped my arm around her waist, drawing her closer. My lips against her ear. "*Sei una terribile bugiarda.*" You're a terrible liar.

I felt her shudder.

"Santino."

There was vulnerability in her voice, but before I could unravel it, a knock shattered the moment, and she pulled away.

Paris, the woman with the blonde pixie cut, appeared on the small screen above Amara's head, fidgeting nervously.

"Come in," I said, eyes never leaving Amara.

"Sir, I—*Oh!* There you are." A flicker of confusion crossed her face as she spotted me. "Amara, a client requested a private. Says he'll pay double for the mysterious woman in the mask. That's you!"

She gestured for Amara to approach, and a wave of sickening déjà vu clenched my gut. I stepped between them.

"She's not available."

Paris's eyes widened, darting between me and Amara. "But Mr. Andretti already paid. What should I tell him?"

"That she can't—"

"That I'll see him in fifteen."

I whirled just as Amara slipped her mask back into place. Suddenly, the roar of blood pounding in my ears drowned out everything else.

The fuck she would.

TWENTY-THREE

Amara

"Amara, wait."

Santino grabbed my hand and spun me around just as I reached my dressing room.

It had been years since a man stirred fear in my heart—but this wasn't that kind of fear. This was worse.

He'd broken through my defenses. Against every warning bell screaming in my head, I trusted him. Trusted this man, even though I'd been conditioned not to.

My gaze dropped to where his hand held mine. If it had been anyone else, I'd have fought back and tried to end them. Instead, I relaxed. With a mock sigh, I motioned for him to speak.

"Refuse."

"No."

He gritted his teeth. "Why?"

"Santino, I don't have the luxury to say no. Rent's always due."

It wasn't a lie, but it wasn't the whole truth. Contract killing for Ares had its perks, but those days and that money were long gone. Revenge jobs? The pay sucked.

But this was more than money. Andretti was scum. Exactly

the kind of scum I hunted. The way he moved with Luca, the way he looked at Santi...

Santi.

I could use his moment of weakness to extract what I needed—or kill him. Both were solutions.

"I'll give you whatever you need, *preziosa*."

"I won't take your money."

He rolled his eyes. "You're not going. Not him. He's a slimy son of a bitch who respects no one. And if he touches you—"

Santino sucked in a harsh breath, looking away as if holding back his temper. I didn't know whether to be annoyed or...whatever this strange tingle was stirring in my gut.

"That's not how this works. He can't touch me. You know that."

"Oh, I know he won't."

Santino pulled a blade from his pocket and headed for the door.

"Where are you going with that?"

"To remove the temptation."

I never thought I'd feel flutters at a man's possessive streak, but Santino made me want to be claimed and taken care of.

Did I want that?

"Santi," I called, knowing my voice would make him stop.

He froze, stiffened slightly when I placed a hand on his back.

"I've disemboweled a man. I can handle Andretti."

"Is that what you think I'm worried about?" He turned around, gently tilting my chin up as he closed the space between us. "I saw the way he looked at you. And I don't appreciate him thinking he can have what's..."

He paused, wetting his lips, breaking eye contact as if wrestling with whether to finish the sentence.

"What?" I whispered, silently begging him to meet my eyes again, to say the words I needed to hear. But he didn't. Giving nothing else, he slipped out the door.

I hated that I'd upset him. But I hated even more that I

cared—and now I was debating whether or not to accept just to keep the peace with my boss.

My cell buzzed against the vanity.

CAMBRI: I've been cleared to return to work in two days.

ME: Bullshit. You have a broken arm. And healing cracked ribs and nose. Absolutely not.

CAMBRI: It could be my gimmick.

ME: No. Bye, Cambri.

CAMBRI: Amara, I have bills. I can't afford to sit on my ass another week.

Fuck. It looked like I'd be shaking *my* ass for Andretti, after all.

———

Before my private, I went searching for Santino, hoping to smooth things over and explain my motives. But his office was empty. The disappointment hit harder than I expected. We'd been teetering on the edge of something, dancing around each other, or maybe just me doing the dancing in more ways than one.

What had I really expected?

It had been so long since I'd felt drawn to a man, especially after everything I'd survived. Even Ezra—our time was so brief, and I was so young, so naive then.

Leaning against the doorframe, I traced the scarred skin

beneath the black silk wrapped around my wrist. Santino had no idea what hell I'd clawed my way out of.

What if I told him?

A petulant voice inside warned, *He won't want you.* But that thought wasn't just intrusive—it was real. I was tainted. Ruined.

Over and over.

Still, maybe I wanted him to say I was his. Not just for one night or a fleeting thrill.

But *his.*

I gripped my chest as the truth I'd been denying slammed into me. I liked him. A lot. It was terrifying, thrilling...and unbearably sad. Because even though our worlds felt close, Santino and I might as well be galaxies apart.

I had nothing left to give anyone. And that was how it would always be.

A tear slipped beneath my mask before I could wipe it away.

"Breathe," I whispered. "Pull it together. Survive another night."

———

The elevator climbed slower than usual, stretching the moment I dreaded. When the doors parted on the second floor, Blaise was there, catching me off guard because the red rooms weren't his usual posts. Santino had taken him and Ash on as private security.

Maybe my boss was gone for the night, disappointed by my choice. Or maybe the truth of who I was had finally settled in.

A stripper. Not exactly the kind of woman you bring home to your mother.

Blaise offered a slow, reassuring smile and reached for the door handle.

"You know what to do if there's trouble. I'll be right outside."

I nodded, exhaled, and slid the second mask into place—the

one I wore when I stepped into my own world, where nothing could touch me.

Shadows pooled around the room, streaked with red lights cutting through the darkness just enough. I traced the scarlet glow until it landed on a pair of expensive leather shoes.

Italian, I was sure.

Italian.

My eyes traveled up the length of the man's long legs to a crisp white dress shirt, perfectly tailored. The first three buttons were undone, revealing a sculpted chest etched with a maze of tattoos.

Panic flushed hot up my neck as I realized I'd stepped into the wrong room—until I recognized the man staring back at me.

"Santino? W-what are you doing here?"

That's when I noticed his arms pinned behind him, the clinking of metal confirming he was cuffed or chained.

My blood thrummed. Instinct kicked in, and my body shifted into a defensive stance. "Who did this to you?"

"You did."

My brows furrowed. "What are you talking about?"

"*Mi stai facendo impazzire,*" he said, tugging at the restraints. "You're driving me crazy."

"That explains nothing." I hugged myself, as if holding together the pieces that were unraveling for him.

"You have no idea how many times I've wanted to drag you off that fucking stage." His jaw tightened. "Those men—they don't deserve you, Amara."

Ruined. Tainted.

I sighed, shaking my head. "And you think you do?"

A faint smirk ghosted across his lips.

"No. But I'm a selfish man. And that's why I'm here."

My pulse pounded like a drum in my ears.

"What do you want, Santino?" I stepped closer, unable to resist the pull.

His chest rose and fell with quick breaths; our eyes locked in the darkness.

"I want you to dance for me, *preziosa*. Only for me."

I closed my eyes, swallowing down the pangs of doubt and uncertainty.

"And why are you tied down?" My voice was breathy, hopeful.

"No touching the dancers. That's the rule, right? But I don't trust myself to be good. Not with you."

Conflicted didn't begin to cover it. Part of me wanted to run, knowing there was no turning back from what would happen next. But another part ached to live every sensation—to relive the sweet pleasure from this morning, when I'd come undone with Santino's face in my mind and his name barely whispered on my lips...like I had every day since that first night.

Stop thinking. Stop feeling, I told myself. Take what you want.

A wicked grin curled my lips as my eyes flew open.

"You're going to regret those," I whispered.

"I don't doubt it. I'm already on the verge of chewing my own goddamn hands off just to get to you."

My breath hitched, heat pooling deep in my belly.

Music flooded the room, the lights pulsing with the soft rhythm that stirred through me. My hips swayed on their own accord—I didn't have to think, didn't have to force it.

Santino was always the perfect motivation.

His hungry eyes never left me, his mouth slightly parted as I stalked forward. Each strike of my heel on the tile echoed the rapid beat of my heart. Just a few inches more, and I'd close the gap between us, crossing into something new. But even if tonight was only a beginning, the next thirty minutes promised to be worth every second.

"What did you do to Andretti?" I asked, sliding a leg over his thighs.

Santino groaned low, the sound vibrating through his throat as my pelvis brushed over the bulge in his pants.

"No, don't ask me about that bastard. Not now."

Leaning close to his ear, the urge to bite him nearly overwhelmed me, but I swallowed hard.

"Why did you come here?"

One hand snaked up the back of his neck while the other glided over his cock, making him curse in Italian.

"You want to know why?" His voice was strained, lips trailing a featherlight kiss across my bare shoulder.

Wet and aching for a man was nearly foreign to me, but every dip against him sent me soaring, craving more friction.

Our eyes locked.

"Tell me," I practically begged, my pussy grinding firmly into his lap.

"Isn't it obvious?" He leaned forward, pressing a slow kiss to the corner of my lips. "You're mine, *preziosa*."

"Yours?"

"From the day I laid eyes on you, I was fucking gone."

Digging my nails into the back of his neck, I bit down on a moan as pleasure rocketed straight from my core.

"I don't belong to anyone," I half-whined, breath catching when he thrust upward to meet my hips.

"Wrong."

"Santi..." I exhaled his name like a prayer.

"Fuck, baby...say that again."

His breath seared against my neck, every word an accelerant to the fire already consuming me.

"You don't understand," I whispered, even though my body betrayed me, clinging to every bit of contact.

"I don't," he rasped. "I fucking swear I don't know what you've done to me, Amara. But I want it. God, I want it so badly."

The metal around his wrists clinked violently as he fought against the restraints, knowing damn well they wouldn't give.

"Sometimes," I said, pushing off his lap, my voice trembling, "we don't know what we're asking for."

I needed space, needed to breathe, but the second I lifted off him, I regretted it. My body screamed at the loss, the absence of his heat.

I turned and bent over, letting him indulge his eyes before dropping to a split and whipping my hair.

Another vicious tug on the cuffs.

"I'm not asking," he growled. "I'm begging."

Arching off the floor, I slid the zipper of my suit down, slow and deliberate.

"Santino Leone, begging me?" I bit my lip, teasing him with a sultry grin.

"Would you like me on my knees, *preziosa?*"

"And what would you do for me on your knees?"

I slipped my arms free of the suit and ran a finger down the center of my chest, circling the pink pasties covering my nipples.

"The things I *wouldn't* do is a much shorter list."

A shiver danced down my spine at the thought. Santino unbound, on his knees, crawling over my body like a man possessed.

No.

"Oh fuck, sweetheart...look at you. That's the prettiest fucking shade of red I've ever seen."

Squeezing my eyes shut, I forced those memories down and locked Athena away again, sealing her behind the mental door where she couldn't hurt me.

"Amara," he called, voice lower now, gentler. Like he sensed something was wrong.

But I shut the door on my emotions and rose to my feet, sauntering behind him, letting my hands glide along the ropes of muscle in his arms.

He tilted his head to follow my movements, but I avoided his eyes, circling him like prey.

"What do you want from me?" I asked.

"Everything."

"You don't know me." I shook my head, the weight of his

words too much to carry. "You don't know what you're asking for."

"Let me in."

God, how I wanted to.

Feeling reckless, I slid back into his lap, arms wrapping around his neck as if they belonged there.

He wouldn't want you.

That voice again, familiar and cruel, My resolve cracked, but I held myself together.

"I can't," I whispered, more to myself than to him, but his expression shifted. He'd heard me through the pulse of the music and the war in my head.

"Tell me."

Our eyes locked, and in that instant, something broke.

I rolled my hips against him, igniting the burn in my belly.

Again and again.

I ground down on the hard length of him, riding the edge between anguish and sweet ecstasy.

I needed this, to lose myself while taking control.

For once, I held the reins.

My nails bit into his skin and I threw my head back, chasing the rush.

"That's it," he rasped, jaw clenched. "Use me, *preziosa,* I'm yours."

His words cut me deep. No man had ever said that to me.

Men took and used, drained until there was nothing left.

But Santino was different. Even when tied down, even when he had nothing to gain but me...*especially* me.

I hated that he made me *hope.* But I couldn't stop. Because gaining control meant surrendering too. And I was already falling.

"Fuck...*fuck,*" I whined, climbing higher, every movement more frantic than the last. My hips ground down hard, chasing the high I'd been holding back for far so long.

Santino hissed when my fingers curled in his hair, nails

scraping against his scalp. But I didn't let up. If anything, my grip tightened as I teetered on the edge.

"Come for me, Amara," he rasped, voice rough with restraint. "Hurt me if you need to. Show me how fucking beautiful you are when you let go."

He was holding on for me.

Let go.

I bit into his shoulder, teeth sinking in as the cry built in my throat. And then I shattered. Hard.

My body trembled, unraveling against him as I rode out every aftershock.

But still, something stayed buried. Locked up deep.

And maybe it always would be.

I didn't know when the music had stopped, or when my hands had curled into fists in the fabric of his shirt. But I felt it now.

The wetness.

Droplets fell from my lashes, soaking the back of my knuckles.

Tears.

"Amara," he said gently, voice no longer ragged but soft. "The key's in my breast pocket."

My entire body went still. I couldn't let him see me like this.

Not broken. Not *weak*.

If I moved fast enough, I could still run. Blaise wouldn't free him in time.

I shifted, weight easing from his lap, preparing to bolt—

"Amara," he warned, firmer now. "Don't you dare run."

A pause. Then a kiss, featherlight, pressed to my temple.

"Let me out of these cuffs." Softer. "Please."

TWENTY-FOUR

Amara

I squeezed the slim key between my fingers, weighing the urge to flee against the pull to stay. But when he kissed along my hairline, I slipped to the floor, compelled by something deeper than lust, and knelt before his bound hands. With a sharp breath, I unlocked the cuffs.

Even if I still meant to run, to escape before I had to face any of this, Santino didn't give me the chance. Before the thought could fully take hold, he tugged me back into his lap.

"Why are you crying?" he asked.

"I'm not," I lied.

He caught a tear with his thumb, smiling like he saw right through me. "Okay. But either way, I need to know we're good."

I nodded stiffly. "Yeah. I know how this works. What happens in these rooms stays here."

"That's not what I meant." He shook his head, then let out a quiet, disbelieving laugh. "I don't know how else to say it. I paid off a guy, twice what he was offering, and cuffed myself to a fucking chair *for you*, Amara." His hands framed my face. "I want you. I want *this*. You and me. I want a chance."

His words knocked the air from my lungs, and fresh tears rolled down my cheeks.

"Stop." I blinked up at him, his face framed in a wash of red light. "I can't give you what you're asking for."

"And what is it you think I want, *preziosa?*"

My face dropped. "The parts of me that died a long time ago." My voice barely held. "I have nothing left for you...for anyone."

Goosebumps skated across my skin when he gently moved my hair aside and pressed a kiss to my shoulder.

"You're right," he murmured. "You have nothing for anyone else. Because I already told you—I'm a selfish bastard. And I don't want just pieces of you, Amara. I want it *all.*"

I shook my head, trying to find air in the space between us. If he *knew*...if he had any idea of the horrors I'd seen, the things done to me, the pieces of myself I'd lost, he'd run.

"If you knew..." I started.

"There isn't a single damn thing you can say," he interrupted, "that would make me walk out that door the same way I walked in—without you."

Then, slowly, Santino slid the black silk from my wrist and turned my hand over in his palm.

"This doesn't scare me," he said, eyes on the jagged scars. "It makes me furious."

"Me too," I whispered.

He traced the lines with a reverence that made my heart ache.

"Let me take you out," he said, tipping my chin until I had to look at him.

"A date?" I asked, biting the corner of my lip despite myself.

"How about the marina? Tomorrow night."

"I work."

He smirked. "It's a good thing I own this place."

A smile threatened to break through until reality slapped me. I'd just dry-humped my boss and came on his lap.

"Oh, shit."

I braced my hands against his chest, ready to push off and follow through on my plan to run. But Santino was quicker. His arms tightened around me before I could move an inch. Panic flared, sharp and breathless, until he murmured soft words against my ear.

"I don't regret what happened," he said gently, "and neither should you. I don't want to go back to the way things were."

His hand pressed between my shoulder blades, holding me against him.

"I'll take however much you want to give, *preziosa*."

My eyes fluttered closed as I leaned into him, the weight of his arms anchoring me, the warmth of his body easing the last threads of my anxiety. I couldn't remember the last time I'd felt so...safe.

Kai's name flickered in my mind. Then Derek's.

But I shoved their ghosts back into the vault where they belonged.

———

Slinging my bag over my shoulder, I opened my dressing room door at the exact moment Santino raised his hand to knock.

I didn't bother hiding my smile this time. Leaning against the frame, I said, "I'm heading home."

"Can I walk you to your car?"

"You're not going to start getting all overprotective on me, are you?"

He stepped in closer, and my stomach sparked with heat.

"You have to know by now, that's just part of who I am when it comes to you."

I grabbed the front of his shirt and pulled him in. "It's not like you can't watch me from your office."

He chuckled. "You know about that?"

"Camera angle number three is always set on my car," I murmured, brushing the corner of his mouth with mine.

A kiss seemed so simple, just lips and breath, but it meant more than either of us said aloud.

Trust.

The last time I kissed anyone by choice, I was seventeen.

And strangely, it wasn't my past that made me nervous now, it was the fear that I'd forgotten how.

"Easy, baby," he whispered, his hand covering mine where it trembled against his chest.

"Mr. Leone!"

Ash.

Santino sighed and rested his forehead against mine. "What is it?"

"Some drunk assholes started shit with Rome. Jumped the counter. Broke a bunch of stuff. Rome stabbed one of 'em in the neck with a bottle of Patrón. Guy's bleeding out on the floor. Give me the word, boss, and I'll toss his ass off the pier."

Santino met my eyes. "Don't leave. I'll handle this and I'll be right back."

Ash gave me a curious look but said nothing as he followed Santino down the hallway.

I rested against the doorframe, feeling weightless and hopeful for the first time in a long time. And when my phone buzzed in my back pocket, not even the sudden jolt could wipe the grin from my face, no matter how hot my cheeks burned.

Cambri had called and texted for the third time that night, ever since I told her I was picking up a private to help cover some of her costs. She knew it wasn't my usual, and she just wanted to check in.

Loud music still thumped from the lounge, so I waited near my car. Santino would know where to find me.

Camera number three.

The parking lot was mostly empty, aside from a small group of guys stumbling toward a white pickup. Part of a bachelor party, too young for marriage, in my opinion, and likely broke after blowing every dime they walked in with. Another alert lit up my screen, and I started to answer until a voice I didn't expect stopped me cold.

"I believe you owe me a dance."

Andretti.

"I don't owe you shit."

He was so close, his laughter vibrated in my ear.

"Amara? Who is that? Are you okay?" Cambri's voice shouted through the speaker, right before one of Andretti's men slapped the phone from my hand and crushed it beneath his boot.

Great. One of those nights.

"Get in the car, *bella*."

"You know," I said, yawning dramatically, "I was hoping for a low-key evening."

Andretti shoved me against the car, pressing cold steel into my ribs.

"Well, we can't always get what we want now, can we?"

He didn't seem like the type to get his hands dirty.

No.

He was a fucking coward who needed two of his men to corner little ol' me in a dark parking lot, force me into my own car, and drive me to some remote location so he could try to empty his non-existent ball sack.

Little did he know, I'd rather die than be a victim.

Never again.

I reached for the knife at my waistband and drove it into his chest, but not before my foot caught on a shard of my broken phone, causing me to miss his heart by a hair.

Gunfire cracked from the right.

I spun, yanked the knife free, and hurled it into the face of the man who'd fired. He screamed, crumpling backward.

More shots whizzed by. Two slammed into my car door, and another shattered the rear window.

"Asshole! Do you have any idea what the deductible is on that?"

With a snarl, I grabbed his gun and slammed it into the

knife's hilt, driving the blade deeper into his upper lip. He wailed like a little bitch before choking on blood and shards of broken teeth.

Another bullet sliced across my shoulder.

"Fuck!"

Just what I needed. Another fucking scar.

Gritting my teeth, I turned and raised the weapon. But a barrage of bullets suddenly lit up the night around my car.

"I thought I told you not to leave."

Santino stood over the twitching body and shot a quick look at me, eyes locking on the blood soaking through my pink sweatshirt. He exhaled sharply, raised his gun, and emptied the rest of the magazine into the man's face until there was nothing left.

In an instant, he was on me, eyes scanning my wound.

"It's just a graze. I'm fine."

"Are you sure?"

"Nothing a bandage won't fix."

"Fuck, Amara." He holstered the gun and held my face gently between his hands. "I'd just walked into my office. Cambri called. I looked at the cameras..." His voice dropped. "I just got you, *preziosa*. You're not going anywhere."

Butterflies after killing two men was a bit unorthodox. But Santino made me feel things.

"I wasn't planning on it."

I'd never wanted to be kissed more. But, as if cursed, our moment was stolen again. This time by Andretti's pained groans as he tried to drag himself away. I raised my gun, but Santino covered my hand and shook his head.

"Leave him. I have a message to deliver. Blaise will take you home—if that's okay with you."

I nodded. "Yeah—"

Santino's lips crashed into mine. One hand gripped my waist, the other tangled in my hair. Stunned, I hesitated. Then melted. He tasted exactly how I imagined. Whiskey, mint, and Sin.

He pressed me back against the hood, tongue sliding into my

mouth, guiding me, consuming me. I chased his lips until our teeth clashed and a moan spilled from my throat.

I hadn't done this since I was teenager. My insecurities lasted maybe half a second because Santino kissed me like I was his favorite fucking meal.

And I savored every growl, every possessive scrape of his mouth on mine.

I was soaked. Desperate. Fuck, I wanted this man.

My eyes were still closed when he whispered, "*Mia preziosa,* don't get into any more trouble tonight."

TWENTY-FIVE

Santino

"I know you're still there."

Andretti's hoarse voice carried a tremor. I'd let him stew in his own anguish for ten minutes now, testing my patience more than his. The urge to rip him apart, to watch his ragged lungs haul their final breath, had me crawling out of my skin.

After what he tried with Amara, the fact that he wasn't already chained to an anchor at the bottom of the Atlantic made me deserving of a fucking medal.

"Where else would I be but here with you?"

"Santino...*Nipote*, you know it's just business. Nothing personal."

"I'm not your nephew. And you made it very personal."

I circled his chair, lighting my cigar. The flame flared bright, casting warped shadows across the blood-slick tile.

"You followed my dancer to her car."

"She owed me."

"Did she?" I exhaled smoke through my nose. "Because I recall Blaise paying you nearly double to settle that debt. Am I wrong?"

Andretti doubled over, breath wheezing as blood dripped from the legs of the wooden chair, pooling beneath him.

"Luca hyped her up..." He spat thick clots into his lap. "Wanted to see what all the fuss was about. Didn't think..." More bloodied spit oozed from the corners of his mouth. "You'd miss a random whore."

I grabbed a fistful of his greasy hair and yanked his head back.

"You mean the one who nearly took out your heart?"

"That bitch," he seethed, sucking in air.

His eye socket suddenly struck me as the perfect placeholder for my cigar. I pressed it in, soft flesh sizzled, and his shrieks filled the air.

"You can keep that," I taunted. "I've got another."

"Oh, you son of a... bitch!" He thrashed, rattling the chair across the tile. "After all these years, this is how you repay me? *Per una prostituta?*"

I cocked a grin and slid brass knuckles over my gloved hand.

"Wrong answer."

The cigar dislodged on the second right hook, but I didn't stop until his jaw was mangled and he could barely stay upright. The noises coming from him weren't even words anymore. Just gurgles and groans.

I uncorked a bottle of my favorite bourbon, shoved it between his ruined lips, and tilted it down his throat. He coughed and choked, sputtering when I yanked it away, then I emptied the rest over his head.

"Wrong girl."

"No... no..." Gregorio knew what came next.

From my suit pocket, I pulled a fresh cigar. I let the moment hang in the air as I lit it, savoring the scent of tobacco over blood and alcohol.

"I've no doubt my cousin Luca put you up to this," I said coolly. "So I'll make sure he understands the weight of his mistake—and what's waiting for him too."

I flicked the cigar into the puddle at his feet. His pant leg caught fire first. The flames climbed fast, swallowing him. He screamed until his throat scorched shut and the room filled with the stench of burning flesh.

"Ci vediamo all'inferno."

———

The elevator doors broke open on her floor. I followed the ascending numbers, searching for the one listed in her file. I'd stared at my phone countless times, debating whether to call or text—ask for her permission before stopping by. But I chose neither, afraid she'd say no.

Blaise had assured me she seemed fine, but no amount of convincing would mean anything unless I confirmed it myself.

"Can I help you?"

I turned to find a man approaching with a sleeping toddler slumped against his shoulder. His eyes narrowed with suspicion as he looked me over from head to toe. Sure, it was late, but I could've been visiting a friend or relative, for all he knew.

"Just here for a visit," I said, deciding to play nice.

"Is that right? And your friend lives here?"

Andretti had drained the last of my patience and humanity. This man's questions weren't going to end well for him.

"I'm sorry. Are you security?"

"You could say that. But considering you're at my door, I think I have every right to ask who the fuck you are."

My gaze flicked to the black numbers on the metal door, certain I had the correct address, then back to the man and the child.

Blood thundered in my ears as a devastating thought passed through me. Was this man someone important to her? Was the kid hers and *his?*

There were similarities. The boy's complexion, the soft curls falling over his forehead.

"Are you... okay?" the man asked, taking a cautious step back.

His eyes dropped to my shirt, where flecks of Andretti's blood painted the fabric.

Our eyes locked—and in that split second, we both saw the other as a threat. He reached behind him.

So did I.

"Santino?"

Amara's voice broke the standoff.

He turned first, looking past me. I followed his line of sight and saw her step into the hallway.

"Amara, you know this man?"

I didn't like how he said her name—too familiar. Too protective.

"*Sua camisa está ensanguentada.*"

The blood on my shirt had riled him.

I gritted my teeth.

Who the fuck did he think he was?

"It's okay. He's a friend," she said, catching my elbow and pulling me toward the door she'd just stepped out of.

The bastard narrowed his eyes again, giving me another slow once-over. Only when the child stirred in his arms did he ease up.

"I'll be right here if you need me," he told her, like a promise, before turning back to his unit.

Neither of us broke eye contact until both doors had closed.

"What are you doing here?" she asked. "Why didn't you tell me you were coming? I would have..."

"Told me not to?" I raised a brow.

"Well...for starters, I would've given you the right address..." She looked down at her striped socks and let out a soft laugh. "And probably changed into something more appropriate."

I'd seen her in nothing but pasties and a thong, but something about this, socks pulled up to her knees, an oversized sweater hanging mid-thigh, made me want to wrap her in my arms and never let her go.

She's yours now.

I hooked a finger into the front of her sweater and gave it a gentle tug. She rose to her toes.

"You're perfect."

A flash of discomfort moved across her face, and she stiffened. But before she could shut down or say otherwise, I leaned in and kissed her. Relief hit like a drug when she melted into me.

She tasted sweet—maple syrup. And I wanted more. I swept my tongue along hers until she gave in, meeting me with soft moans that spilled into my mouth. I swallowed every single one.

"I knew I should've made you pancakes that day," I teased, brushing my mouth against hers.

She giggled. "I wasn't expecting company. I couldn't sleep and...Would you like some?"

"Yes."

With one hand at the nape of her neck, I pulled her in and kissed her again, deeper.

That taste on her lips was my new favorite flavor.

"That's not what I meant," she said, her eyes still closed, a smile tugging at her pretty lips.

"*Preziosa,* who's your neighbor?" I asked, that protective, territorial streak rising again.

The image of him warning her in Portuguese still lingered in my mind, like I hadn't nearly taken him out with his own son in his arms. I suppose he'd been right to be wary.

"He's just that—a neighbor. But he's also a homicide detective, Santino. Which means I'll have to do some damage control." Her gaze dropped to the blood on my shirt.

"I should've gone home and changed. But I needed to see you."

I gently touched her wounded shoulder, fingers grazing the bandage beneath her sleeve.

"You don't owe him anything," I added.

"I know. But he's...persistent."

I stilled. My eyes narrowed. "What the fuck does that mean?"

I hadn't noticed I was backing toward the door, or that my hand had drifted to my holster. She grabbed my collar and pulled me back.

"No, Santi, not like that," she said quickly. "He wouldn't still be breathing if that were the case."

I believed her, but the instinct to end him didn't subside.

"Elaborate," I said flatly.

"I came home one night and found his little boy wandering the floor. The kid had escaped while the detective was asleep, exhausted from a tough shift, or so he claimed." She sighed, then led me into her living room.

A striking cat lounged on the windowsill, its coat like a miniature leopard, fur patterned in golds and blacks. It stared at me with eerie green eyes as I sank onto the couch.

"So now you're friends with a homicide detective," I muttered, dry and humorless.

"No. But he shows up sometimes. Thinks he owes me something for saving his kid. And..."

She paused, looking toward the cat.

"And what?" My fingers twitched, itching for steel.

"He reminds me of...home. In a way."

"Home?"

She nodded. "Back in Rio. A long time ago."

Brazil.

I'd suspected it from her name, but hearing it from her now felt like something sacred. A small opening in the wall she always kept so high.

As if sensing her shift in mood, the cat padded over to her feet, curling around her legs before leaping onto her lap.

"He's from your hometown?" I asked.

"Not exactly," she said, stroking the animal's head. "But close enough. And the language...there was a time I was terrified to forget. But now...sometimes I think it'd be easier not knowing."

I brushed my fingers along her cheek, and her eyes fluttered shut. God, I wanted to know every shadow in her soul, every break the world had carved into her. I wasn't a man deserving of redemption—but if I could, I'd fill her cracks with mine until she held no pain I didn't share.

"One day," I said softly, "when you're ready... I want you to know you can trust me."

She studied me for a beat, silently turning the words over in her mind, before looking back down at her pet.

"That's an interesting looking cat."

"She's a Bengal. Poor thing was near death when I found her. I was never much of a cat person, but her owner had the misfortune of swallowing my blade. After that, I couldn't leave her behind."

She glanced up at me with mischief in her eyes, watching my reaction.

"What's her name?"

"Phoenix," she said, resting her forehead gently against the cat's. It purred loud enough for me to hear. "I thought it was fitting."

Rising from the ashes.

That name wasn't just for the cat. It was her, too.

"One day, *preziosa*," I said, tilting her chin until I was drowning in the storm behind her eyes, "you'll let me in. And I'll burn it all down for you."

TWENTY-SIX

Santino

Amara had nodded off, her head resting against my shoulder, and her soft breaths the only sound in the room. I lay back, staring at the ceiling while my fingers absently worked through the fur of the sleeping cat curled in my lap. Phoenix had warmed up to me over the last hour, though I suspected it had more to do with the piece of pancake I'd slipped her when Amara wasn't looking.

A quiet laugh rumbled from my chest, jostling them both. I froze, worried I'd wake her.

God, I hardly recognized myself around this woman. With anyone else, if I hadn't fucked in forty-eight hours max, I'd have been out. Gone. But with her…I knew she needed time. And the craziest part? I was willing to give it. A month ago, just that thought would've been enough to make me sign over my soul and run back to Italy.

Che tragedia.

Tragedy indeed.

The image of her in my lap, falling apart as she used me, played on an endless loop in my mind. I'd give anything to hear those sweet, broken sounds again, her voice laced with my name.

Carefully, I slid the cat off my lap, then shifted Amara's

weight into my arms as I stood. I laid her down gently on the sofa. I'd return her key tomorrow—well, later tonight.

But as I stepped away, her fingers wrapped around mine.

"Don't go," she whispered, gazing up at me. "Take me to my room, Santino."

Right then, I knew there was nothing she could ask of me that I wouldn't give.

Without hesitation, I scooped her up and started down the hallway.

"Which way?"

"Last door on the left."

I kicked the bedroom door closed behind us, leaving Phoenix to guard the living room.

The space was dim, lit only by the soft glow of the balcony light bleeding through fluttering curtains. Even in the dark, I could tell her room was simple. Sparse. The only color came from the vanity—a scatter of perfume bottles, lipsticks, and small, delicate things I wanted to know more about.

The bed stood at the center, upholstered and soft-looking. I sat her at the edge, and she reached up, untucked my shirt, and began working at the buttons.

Her fingers shook.

She was nervous.

"Amara—"

"Can I ask you something?" she said, rising to her knees as she continued undoing my shirt.

"Anything."

"Please don't ask me if I'm sure...because I'm not. I won't ever be. And that's the honest answer."

I wanted her to open up, but only when she was ready. However fast or slow, I'd follow her lead.

With her eyes on mine, Amara grabbed the hem of her sweater and pulled it over her head, letting it fall to the floor at my feet. My gaze dropped to the swell of her breasts, nipples drawn tight.

"Bellissima," I whispered into her ear, pressing my thumb gently over one hardened peak. She tensed under my touch for a breath before opening my shirt and pushing it down my arms with more force than I expected.

"So many," she breathed, tracing a single finger across the ink on my chest.

"They tell a story. Every chapter of my life is painted on my skin." I pulled her closer and kissed her shoulder. "I thought I was done...but maybe I was wrong."

As I worked my lips along her throat, Amara tilted her head back, closing her eyes.

"Yeah?"

I climbed into bed, hovering above her as she lay back beneath me. "Yeah," I murmured, pressing a kiss to her stomach and pausing to breathe her in. Her skin was warm. Soft. Clean. But as I dipped lower, I noticed something—she was trembling.

At first, I thought it was the breeze from the balcony, but the night was warm, and there wasn't a single goosebump on her skin.

Then I saw her hands, clenched tight in the sheets, her eyes shut hard, like she was trying to control her breath.

Everything sharpened.

"Preziosa," I said softly, brushing my knuckles over her ribs, "you're shaking. What's wrong?"

She drew in a shuddering breath, loosened her fists, and reached for my hand.

"I'm sorry...I—I've never been with anyone..." Her voice wavered as her eyes fluttered open and met mine. "By choice."

For a second, the world dropped out from under me.

By choice.

I shifted off her, sitting at the edge of the bed. My blood churned—caught somewhere between ice and hellfire.

"Who?" The word came out low, guttural.

She didn't answer.

Amara sat up, hugging her knees to her chest. "All of them."

"Amara, what does that mean?"

The first tear slipped down her cheek, carving a path through the silence.

"He said he'd break me...and he did. They all did."

I gently took her hands in mine.

"Sometimes I still feel them inside me," she whispered, eyes distant. "In my head. They won't die, Santino. So I have to kill them."

"Oh, baby..."

My chest caved as I lifted her hands to my lips. I kissed every knuckle, every scar I couldn't see. Begging her silently to look at me. To stay here, with me, in this moment.

But she didn't move.

Tears streamed silently, catching the corners of her mouth and falling off her chin.

"I won't stop until he's dead."

"Who? Who did this to you? Tell me, and they'll be dead by sunrise."

My looked to her wrist, where my thumb brushed across a faint scar.

Fuck.

My mind couldn't begin to grasp the full magnitude of what she'd endured. Every second I spent trying to process her words landed like a blow to the chest.

I shifted beside her, pulling the sheet over our bodies. My first instinct was to gather her in my arms, to protect her from the world, but I hesitated, afraid even that closeness might push her away.

She felt it.

Amara turned toward me, pressing both palms to my chest. Her voice was small but steady.

"I'm not afraid of you, Santi."

That was all I needed. I pulled her flush against me, one arm cradling her waist while the other traced the curve of her spine.

That's when I noticed it, subtle disruptions in the smoothness of her skin. Raised ridges. Scars I hadn't seen in the dark.

"He still owes me for those."

"Name," I growled, my voice rough. The rage in me had teeth now, gnashing at the edges of my restraint.

"Sasha. But he's just one more dead man walking." Her voice faltered. "Because it was someone else..."

She paused, her eyes haunted.

"I-I've never said his name out loud. I can't."

"He's the one who started it?"

She nodded. "Yeah. He set everything in motion. And it spiraled so badly. But it was also because of him that I survived."

I frowned, confusion cutting through the firestorm in my head. "How? I thought you said he—"

"He did." Her voice hardened. "And that's exactly why I can't let him walk away from everything he caused...from everything I lived through."

I crushed her tighter against me, the space between us obliterated. I needed to feel her.

"Where is he now? Does he know you're here?"

She exhaled slowly, resting her cheek over my heart. "He probably thinks I'm dead. I've kept hidden. Kept tabs on him. And on—" Her voice broke, then steadied. "I wasn't ready to face him then. But he disappeared a little over four years ago."

"Maybe he's the one who's dead."

"No." She shook her head. "People like him don't just vanish. He's part of something bigger, Santi."

Her voice dimmed to a whisper as she closed her eyes. "He's still out there. And I'm going to find him."

I tightened my hold, kissed the crown of her head, and let her breathe against me. Whatever it took, blood, fire, or vengeance. I'd give it to her. Because Amara was mine. And she would never be alone again.

TWENTY-SEVEN

Give – Sleep Token

"I lied."

Santino stopped stroking my arm and waited for me to continue.

"When I said I wasn't afraid of you...I lied."

The sun's rays peeked through the curtains, and I realized I'd lost track of time. Hours had rolled by since I revealed my past, but Santino didn't seem to mind. He listened. Held me when a memory became too painful. Yet despite his compassion, the fear of his judgment had a vise grip on my heart.

"I've been through things that some people don't come back from. And if they do, they're never the same. I was violated and left for dead. I might've been breathing the day I woke up in that hospital room, but they'd already killed everything inside me that mattered."

"That's bullshit, preziosa."

A frail laugh left my lips. "No, I'm tainted, Santino." My voice shook, eyes filling with tears I thought had long run dry.

"Look at me."

Sitting up, he took me with him, positioning me over his lap.

"The only one of us ruined here is me," he said, swiping at my wet cheeks. "I don't know what you did or how you did it, but fuck, baby, I'm gone for you. You're mine."

My heart thundered, beating out of my chest at a pace I was sure would render me unconscious when I came crashing down from this high. But I was willing to fall...for him. I finally had a taste of happiness—something I hadn't felt in so long—and I wanted more. The world had taken everything from me, and it was finally my turn to steal my life back.

For tonight...or however long we had.

Fuck it.

There would be plenty of time for regret tomorrow, but this moment was mine.

"Make me," I murmured against his mouth. "Make me yours."

His eyes darkened, and he flipped us over, burying his face in my neck. I bit down on my lip, swallowing the sounds threatening to escape.

Maybe I was crazy, but I needed this, no matter the emotional toll that came after. I'd deal with the fallout later...or not. But there wasn't anyone else I would've chosen to share this moment with, to take this risk.

"I want you to tell me if and when to stop."

Nodding, I pulled him in for a kiss. Santino couldn't understand what his words meant to me. My past was muddied with men—no, monsters—who treated me like I wasn't even human. Like I was worthless. But in his eyes, I saw pieces of that girl I used to know.

"Don't stop," I begged as his mouth covered my nipple. His licks were cautious at first, as if gauging my response, but when a rolling moan slipped from my mouth, he went all in, alternating between deep pulls and slow tongue swipes.

"I'm going to touch you. Can I do that?"

Clutching the sides of his hair, I grinned and warned, "I'll stab you if you don't."

My bravado wavered as he slid a hand over my hip, coaxing my thighs open and dipping his fingers between them. I jerked slightly at the contact, and he snapped his attention to my face.

A silent exchange drifted between us, and I arched my back when his thumb rolled over my clit in tight circles.

"Open up for me."

I relaxed and rocked against him as pleasure guided my thrusts.

"More," I whispered, throwing one leg over his back.

Santino popped my nipple out of his mouth and gazed into my eyes as he pushed two fingers inside me. A gasp filled my lungs, but instead of looking at me for reassurance, he pressed his lips to my trembling belly and sank deeper.

"That's it, baby. Just let go. Let me make you feel good," he murmured, nipping at my earlobe. "Let me show you how you deserve to be worshiped."

I didn't trust my voice as his curved fingers slid in and out, so I grabbed him by the back of the neck and kissed him. He swallowed every moan and every cry of his name until my body shivered on the brink of an orgasm.

"Come for me, *preziosa*. I'll never forget the way you looked when you came apart in my lap."

I kissed him harder, smothering a whimper when he slipped in a third finger. The stretch was painful, but I pushed through, rocking my hips and letting myself get lost in that fleeting glimpse of euphoria before intrusive thoughts could slip through the cracks.

I felt their suffocating weight clawing at the doors to the vault in my mind. But I refused to let them win.

Where pain had always meant violence and revenge, this moment belonged to me.

Maybe that was my vengeance. And I was finally freed from their shackles.

I ran a hand down my face and huffed a shaky sigh, rising to my elbows just in time to catch Santino licking his fingers.

"So fucking sweet."

Nerves buzzed in my belly, but there was no turning back. I reached for his waistband, and we locked eyes as I worked his belt.

Words weren't necessary. We knew what would happen here.

Santino's cock sprang free, and I found myself momentarily frozen. This was the first one I'd actually seen.

I expected to feel a rise of panic, but curiosity took over when I noticed a piece of jewelry piercing the tip.

"Did that hurt?" I asked, almost impulsively.

"Of course."

"Will it...hurt?"

His smile faltered, and he tipped my chin. "It shouldn't. But if it's been a while..." Santino trailed off, a crease of uncertainty forming between his brows. "I'm sorry."

I lifted up and kissed him softly. "Don't be. It *has* been a while. But I need this. I want *you*," I said, wrapping my fingers around his erection. "I'm done being afraid. This is the last bit of power they still have over me—and I'm taking it back."

He slid his hand over mine, guiding my strokes, quiet encouragement in every movement. For how hard he was, I appreciated his patience.

"Thank you."

"You're thanking me?" he asked, somewhere between amused and bewildered.

"I am. Now shut up and follow through on your promise."

He chuckled, one arm around my waist as he lowered us onto the mattress. Feeling a little bold, I let my thighs fall open and watched the hunger light up his eyes.

"You're beautiful."

Men had always paid me compliments, but they were just words laced with desire and the hopes that I'd let them fuck me. But Santino made me feel beautiful again despite my scars, my past, and the broken woman I saw staring back at me in the mirror.

"So are you."

I reached for his cock and stroked the thick length, each pump coaxing a bead of pre-cum from the tip. Nerves twisted in my belly, but curiosity won out. He wasn't just big—he was *pretty*. And pierced.

It should've made me hesitate. Instead, I ached for him even more.

With another chuckle, he pressed his lips to my inner thigh.

"Come here."

He took my hand and pulled me into his lap. I straddled him, arms wrapped behind his neck, his erection hard between us.

"You're dripping down your thighs. And as much as I want to run my tongue through every fucking drop, I want this to be on *your* terms. Sit up."

I rose onto my knees as Santino guided his cock between my legs, sliding the piercing over my clit and along my soaked seam.

"I want you to feel good. And when you're ready, you're going to sit that sweet little cunt down."

Tingles bloomed in my core. I nodded, lashes heavy as the cool metal teased over my swollen flesh again and again.

"Santi...so good," I breathed, rocking my pussy harder against him, my hands gripping his shoulders.

"Just like that, baby. This is all you."

The gravel in his voice dragged me closer to the edge. He'd given me control, but the strain in his tone—the way he held back—only made me want him more.

"I need you. All of you."

My lips brushed his ear as I wrapped my arms behind his neck.

"I'm yours."

Our eyes met, and I stilled my hips as he positioned himself at my entrance.

"All you, *preziosa*."

My mouth parted as I slowly sank down on him, the stretch sharper than I'd expected.

"Take your time," he whispered, rubbing soothing circles into my thigh with his thumb.

I bit my lip and eased a little farther. "You're too goddamn big," I said, laughing through a breathy moan.

Santino reached up and fisted my hair, the sharp tug sending a pulse straight to my core and dragging me down another inch.

"You can take me, baby," he growled against my neck, his mouth warm as he kissed and sucked. "I *know* you can. You know why?"

I tossed my head back, panting. "Why?"

"Because you were *made* for me." Another inch. "Your pussy? *Mine*." Deeper. "You're everything I never knew I was looking for."

"*Fuck*," I whimpered, finally taking every last thick inch until he bottomed out.

He filled me to the brim, and the delicious ache pulled a smile from my lips.

"I did it."

"You did."

He kissed me hard, his grip tightening in my hair.

"Now...ride what's yours."

"Like that?" I teased, rolling my hips in a slow grind.

Santino tugged my head back, groaning against my nipple. The vibration sent a thrill straight through me.

"Just like that."

"How about like this?"

I rose and fell over his thick cock, the ache melting into waves of pure pleasure.

"*Sii mia per sempre, Amara.* Always mine."

"Santi," I whined, my pace quickening. "Fuck me, please."

With a growl ripped from his chest, he grabbed my hips and drove into me, matching every descent with a punishing thrust. I was bouncing in his lap, chasing the sharp edge of orgasm, my cries louder each time the piercing dragged over a sweet, sensitive spot.

The G-spot. That was a real thing. *Definitely* real.

His hands gripped my ass cheeks, hard. I'd probably see the imprint of his fingers in bruises tomorrow, and I fucking loved it.

"You feel so good. So fucking good."

"Fuck, Santi...I'm—"

One more stroke. One more perfect drag of metal over nerves, and I shattered.

My body clamped around him as I cried out, teeth catching on his shoulder. Every pulse of my orgasm had him pounding deeper, chasing his own release.

He wrapped his arms around me, grunting through his finish until we both collapsed. Sweaty, breathless, and completely undone.

Morning sunlight warmed our damp skin. We still hadn't slept, but neither of us moved. He tucked me close to his side, lips soft against my hairline.

"We didn't use protection. Should we be worried?"

"No. We shouldn't be."

He didn't press. The trust in his silence sent heat to my belly.

If there was one predictable thing in my life, it was my cycle. As a dancer, tracking it was non-negotiable. Still, we had to be more careful next time.

Next time, I thought with a smile.

All those fears about how it would feel seemed almost silly now. Valid, but distant. My trauma would never fully vanish, but this morning, I felt lighter.

A little freer than yesterday.

"How do you feel?" he asked, like he'd read my thoughts.

I grinned. "Who knew something so small could bring so much pleasure?"

Santino froze—then burst into laughter.

It was the kind of laugh that was contagious. Fuck, he was so handsome. I would absolutely risk it all for another orgasm.

"You know I'm talking about your piercing," I said, trailing my fingers up his abs to his chest—That's when I felt it.

A scar. Small, faint, but familiar beneath my palm.

His smile faded as he cupped my hand over it.

"What happened?"

"I had surgery as a boy. Collapsed one day at nursery. They found a defect in my heart."

My own chest clenched. "Are you okay?"

His thumb smoothed the worry from my brow.

"I am. There are scars on my heart, *preziosa*. But maybe it was always meant to be that way."

I rested my head over his chest, listening to the steady rhythm for reassurance.

"We're all a little broken."

"Maybe," he murmured, pressing a kiss to the discolored skin on my wrist. "But I've never felt more whole than in this moment with you."

TWENTY-EIGHT

Santino

The elevator doors slid shut, only to bounce back open a second later.

I wasn't surprised to see Amara's neighbor standing there.

He stepped in without a word and leaned into the far corner rail, alone this time and looking slightly less...paranoid.

I watched him, already anticipating the conversation he'd clearly been planning. Something told me he'd been waiting for me to leave her apartment. That alone set my nerves on edge.

She'd said he was insistent, asked too many questions, poked his nose where it didn't belong. Friendly or not, having a cop next door was dangerous enough.

A curious one was worse.

"So," he said as the elevator began to descend. "You're a friend of hers."

"I am."

Silence stretched between us. Then he shifted my way, eyes dropping again to the blood on the front of my shirt.

"Everything okay?"

"Do you always interrogate strangers?"

He gave a dry chuckle.

"Just making small talk. You caught me off guard, is all. It was a late night...or early morning, depending how you see it. Last thing I expected was a bloodied stranger standing outside my door."

"Understandable. Got the unit number wrong. My apologies."

"First time visiting?"

I leaned back against the wall, hands in my pockets, and met the steel in his eyes.

"Might I remind you, Detective Braga—we're not at the precinct."

He pressed a button as the elevator hit the lobby, keeping the doors closed. That got my attention.

Bold.

And stupid.

"I'm very aware, Santino Leone," he said, voice flat. "Like I said—just a friendly conversation. Amara seems like a nice girl. Her job's a bit...questionable, sure. But I'm sure she has her reasons. I just hope they don't include being coerced by her boss. Or stalked."

My eyes flicked to the camera in the corner.

Today was his lucky day.

"I have two pieces of advice for you."

"Oh yeah?" he said, tilting his head, trying to look relaxed. But the twitch of his hand near his hip told a different story.

"One: learn to mind your business. Two: open that door."

The air between us tightened. We were both rocking on the balls of our feet, poised for the wrong move.

"Have a nice day, Mr. Leone," he said at last, releasing the button.

I stepped past him, turning as I exited. "Oh, and by the way? Cute kid."

His jaw clenched, hand curling into a fist just as the elevator doors sealed shut.

I pulled out my phone. "Ash," I clipped. "I'm sending over

some info once I get to the office. I want everything you can dig up on this guy."

Without waiting for a response, I hung up and ripped open my car door, dialing another number as I peeled out of Amara's parking garage.

"Si, I need a favor, brother."

"I'm not Silas."

The voice was unfamiliar, but I knew who the boy was.

"Maksim? I'm a friend of Silas and Helena. Is either one of them around? Can you hand Silas his the phone?" Silence. "Maksim?"

"He's outside. She's upstairs with the baby."

"Baby?"

"Valentina."

The detective's daughter. Ironic.

My patience was already paper-thin, and this kid was old enough to understand what *hand the damn phone to Silas* meant.

"I'll wait while you bring Silas his cell."

I could've sworn he muttered something under his breath.

Teenagers.

The line stayed quiet long enough for me to check if we were still connected. Then, muffled voices filtered through, followed by the low rumble of Silas's laughter.

"Santino."

"It's good to hear from you. Wasn't sure I'd get through."

"Maksim is still working on his people skills," Silas said with a chuckle. "Sorry, Leni's got me out here putting together a castle playhouse for Valentina."

"I'm looking forward to meeting them both. Partly why I'm calling. I'm traveling to Philly in about two weeks...with a friend."

"There it is. The thing you didn't want to tell me that day. I knew it."

"There was nothing to tell."

"But now there is."

"Are you going to listen, or keep talking out of your ass?"

He barked a laugh. "What the fuck are you waiting for then?"

"This girl. She's from Pennsylvania. That's all I know. She's using an alias and running from someone important. This has Six and Ares written all over it."

"Is she someone's mark?" Silas's tone lost all humor—maybe memories of his own past as a target resurfacing.

"I don't know. She's only confided so much. But whoever she's running from is still out there."

"Santino, you know I'll help any way I can. But if I run her name through our system, alias or not, there's a chance someone will spot it."

I punched the steering wheel, realizing he had a point. The organization had eyes and ears everywhere. It was a wonder she hadn't been found yet. But Amara had me now, and I had no plans of letting go.

"Fair enough. Do a local search. Separate the names Amara and Carvalho."

Silence fell between us. I knew him—this was his way of thinking things over, looking at the bigger picture. It was why he'd stood firm against my suggestions about Helena years ago. I'd never been more relieved he hadn't listened. That woman was as unhinged as they came, but those two were born for each other.

"If this is a blood oath situation, take care of yourself. Nothing else needs to be said. I know you wouldn't be calling if she weren't important."

"I appreciate you. Now finish that castle so Helena can return your ball sack."

"Fuck you," he responded with a booming laugh.

When the call ended, my mind drifted back to Amara and what we'd shared just hours ago. I'd always given Silas shit for the blind devotion he'd held for his wife—from the moment she stabbed him—but I understood it now.

There was no exact science behind a heart choosing its other half, even if both were broken or black as ash.

TWENTY-NINE

Santino

Tennessee Whiskey – Austin Giorgio

My feet couldn't carry me fast enough across Illusion's parking lot and through the side entrance. A last-minute business transaction had kept me out of the city and away from my newest addiction for forty-eight hours. Too damn long. We'd spoken on the phone, but hearing Amara's voice without being able to touch her had been a unique kind of torture.

I'd planned to stop by her flat, but she'd told me she arrived at the club earlier than usual to practice a new routine.

My jaw clenched at the thought of her on that stage, in a room full of bastards lusting after what was mine. She would never accept financial help, and asking her not to perform—or cutting the heads off every patron in attendance—probably wouldn't go over well.

"*Preziosa*, are you in there?" I knocked on her dressing room door several times. No answer.

Faint music drifted through the corridors from the main lounge. Illusion wouldn't be open to the public for another three hours, and if she wasn't here, she had to be on stage already. Over the last several weeks, I'd memorized every song she danced to. But this melody was new, hypnotic.

I followed the music like a siren's call, and found her moving like a vision from a dream. Despite all the times I'd watched her, I was utterly mesmerized, as if it were the first.

Our eyes connected across the room. She faltered just slightly at the sight of me but recovered with grace, spinning up the pole and kicking her legs into a controlled, breathtaking twist.

I stepped onto the stage and dropped to my knees as she arched backward from the top, her hair cascading like a curtain of dark curls before me.

"*Sei fottutamente squisita,*" I said, hands threading into her hair, mouth brushing over hers.

So fucking exquisite.

She grinned, playful and bold, and snaked out her tongue to lick my lips. "Like what you see?"

The groan that rattled loose from my chest was answer enough. I stood, peeled her off the damn pole, and carried her to the bar, laying her across the polished counter.

"Don't you dare move."

I caught the protest forming on her lips and silenced it with a rough kiss, leaving her breathless as I took off to lock every entry point in the club.

"What are you doing?" she called out, amusement dancing in her voice as I rounded back behind the bar.

"I think you meant to say you missed me the same way I missed you."

Amara reached for my hand and threaded her fingers through mine. "No one's ever missed me before."

"Good." I kissed her knuckles, trailing slowly down her arm until I reached the black band around her wrist. "You don't have to hide from me."

I slipped it off and pressed a reverent kiss to the discolored skin beneath.

She touched my cheek, offering a small smile. "I'm getting there. And I did miss you. But you also owe me a date."

I laughed, hooking my thumb under the thin red strap on her shoulder. "The trip to Philadelphia is booked," I said, swiping my thumb across her nipple.

She arched toward me, eyes fluttering closed. "So you're following through on that private jet after all."

"I'll take you anywhere. Just say the word and we're there the next day."

Her expression shifted, ecstasy fading into something softer, deeper. Nostalgia. She had a place in mind.

"Tell me where."

Biting her lip, she tugged me back down to her nipple. "I'd love to visit my hometown someday."

"Done." I caught the underside of her breast with my teeth, making her jerk and laugh. God, how far gone did you have to be to love the sound of someone's laugh?

"No, someday," she said more seriously. "But not yet." Gripping my hair, she brought my focus back to her eyes. "What are we doing?"

It wasn't just about lying on the bar, skin against skin. She was asking about us, whatever the fuck this was. We were making plans. Shared ones. That thought was both terrifying and...hopeful. I knew too well what it cost to give your heart away. I'd seen what love could destroy, what it could demand.

Love wasn't for the weak.

"Whatever we want," I told her, sliding off her matching red shorts and thong. I didn't need to say more; I simply indulged in everything I'd missed these last two days.

"Santi," she whispered, "touch me."

Taking my hand, she guided it down her abdomen. She trembled slightly beneath my touch, and though my cock ached to be inside her, it was her heart I needed to calm first.

I grabbed a bottle of Pinot, popped the cork, and took a long pull before climbing onto the bar and pulling her toward me.

"I got into town this morning, and all I could think about was being with you." My fingers slid into her hair. "You've bewitched me."

I brought the bottle to her lips and tilted it. She drank, wine slipping down her chin, and I leaned in to lick it off, stealing the rest from her mouth in a rough kiss. Teeth clashed. Tongues fought. I was too far gone to care about anything but devouring her.

"Lie back, preziosa," I murmured against her lips. "I'm going to taste you again."

"Right here?" she asked, breath hitching.

"Right fucking here."

The corner of Amara's mouth tugged into a shy grin, and she did as she was told.

Spreading her thighs, I nearly groaned. That pretty little cunt was soaked. I'd only had a taste, a tease, and it had been enough to hook me. But I needed more.

"Up here," I said, smoothing a hand along her calf and propping her leg on my shoulder. I tipped the bottle, watching as wine streamed down her thigh and pooled at the junction between her legs, coating her.

Fucking perfect.

I started at her ankle, laying slow kisses, my tongue chasing the taste where my fingers were already gliding across slick skin. Her hands gripped the bar's edge, breath trembling as I buried my face between her thighs and rolled my tongue over her clit.

"I always knew this is what you'd taste like."

She pressed the pointed toe of her stiletto against my chest. "And what's that?"

"Mine."

I hauled her closer, throwing her other leg over my shoulder, and feasted like a man starved. No hesitation, no mercy.

The wine bottle hit the floor, shattering. She startled at the sound, but I plunged two fingers deep, pulling a strangled moan from her lips and refocusing her on the only thing that mattered—me. Us.

"Santi...fuck," she panted, arms stretching above her head to brace against the counter.

Watching her break for me was my new addiction. Her vulnerability was a gift. She'd guarded herself for so long, but she trusted me. I couldn't erase the past, but I'd damn well be the only one she remembered.

"I don't know"—lick—"if I'll ever"—suction—"get enough of you." My grip on her hips tightened. She'd bruise. I didn't care. Neither did she. Her body shuddered against my mouth, clenching around my fingers. She was so close.

"I'm...I can't...please," she gasped, neck arched, mouth open in desperation.

"Tell me, *preziosa*." One more flick against her swollen clit, and she jolted. "Tell me what you want."

She shook her head from side to side, lips caught between her teeth, unable to speak as she clamped down and shattered.

Not a single drop.

I lifted her ass off the bar, spreading her open as she spilled onto my tongue. Her nails raked through my hair, desperate, trying to pull away. For a second, I froze, afraid she felt trapped, but then I caught the look on her face.

Blissed out. Sated. *Safe.*

That was all I needed. I dragged her back, anchoring her to my mouth until she was pounding the counter and crying out my name.

"Next time I leave, I want you with me," I murmured, kissing her trembling thighs, still savoring the taste of her. The past two days, all I could think about was Amara. Her voice. Her body. The way she felt wrapped around me. Fuck—I had it bad.

"What if... I have to work?" she asked, breathless.

Work? If that meant going back on stage, over my dead

fucking body. But that conversation could wait. Right now, my jeans were a goddamn torture device.

I scooped her off the bar, pressing her back to my chest and burying my face in her hair.

"All of that can wait. I need you."

"Take me," she whispered, dragging her nails along the back of my neck.

Her touch lit a fuse inside me.

I bent her over the counter with careful force, one hand smoothing over her ass while the other freed my cock. The red glow of a nearby lamp bathed her skin, and my gaze caught on the faint scars lining her cheeks and back—reminders of the hell she'd survived.

It haunted me. Made me pace at night, fists clenched with the need to destroy whoever had laid a hand on her. Even if I'd never known a world where death was currency, I'd still understand her taste for blood.

Hoisting her hips higher onto the bar, I got a perfect view of her slick, swollen pussy, and I was ravenous all over again. But nothing compared to the feeling of sliding into her and knowing she was mine.

Maybe I was obsessed. Infatuated, fucking mad. The agony of her absence only quieted the second I sank inside her.

Thirty

Amara

Lost.

I was lost in my own reflection, staring at the woman in the mirror in awe. There were so many nights before my turn on stage when I'd sit and question my life, and all the events that had brought me to this club. But tonight was different.

I wasn't sure I remembered what hope felt like, but maybe this weightlessness…maybe the flutters in my belly…maybe that *was* hope.

I didn't recognize her. The woman with light in her eyes. And a smile carved on her face.

I used to know her.

Soft knocks at my dressing room door pulled my gaze from the stranger in the mirror, and my smile widened when Santino walked in.

He said nothing as he lifted me from the chair, only to sit down and reposition me across his lap.

"I'm not ready yet. And I have to perform in twenty minutes."

"No," he said, shaking his head and leaning in for a kiss. "You have the night off."

"Santi, you can't just re-block. We're still down a dancer. Two, actually. Star didn't show."

He shifted my hair off my shoulders and kissed behind my ear, making me squirm and giggle. I regretted the noise instantly. But Santino wasn't fazed. He just held me.

"I don't care about any of that. I owe you a date, remember?"

"I'm off tomorrow night."

"I know. You're also off *tonight*." He stood with me in his arms. "Come on. I want to take you somewhere. Down to the beach."

He carried me out the door and through the shadowy corridor toward the back exit.

"Wait—my shoes."

"You won't need them," he said with a cunning grin.

"Okay, but you're going to have to put me down. What will people think?"

"That I'm the luckiest bastard alive."

Those butterflies had wings made of hot embers. I closed my eyes and inhaled deeply, still in disbelief over what was blooming between us.

The salty night air was breezy but warm, whipping my hair into Santino's face and catching in his mouth.

"I'm sorry," I laughed, gathering the curls into a bun. "My hair gets a little wild sometimes."

"Leave it. I love it."

I froze, slowly releasing my hair so it fell back around us. Reaching up, I cupped his cheeks, brushing my thumbs along the stubble, and flashed him a soft smile as we walked to the ocean's edge.

He sat down, and I nestled between his legs, leaning back against his chest while his arms wrapped around me.

Being with this man was strangely and unexpectedly easy. Even as fear still filled my heart.

Life had shown me not to get comfortable when things were

good, because fate always caught up, tearing me from every ounce of happiness I'd ever known.

"*Preziosa*, can I ask you something?"

I nodded.

"If I offered you another position here, would you take it?"

I shifted around to look up at him, confused. "Why would I need another position?"

"Amara, when you're on that stage, I want to commit mass murder."

I opened my mouth to argue, but he held my chin, silencing me with his thumb.

"I need you to understand something. You're mine now. I don't want to stop you if this is what you love—but I can't guarantee I'll hold back. And sooner or later, the feds will come knocking when people walk in and don't walk back out."

Despite being blindsided by his admission, I couldn't help but smile—because somehow, I knew he wasn't just being facetious.

Did I love shaking my ass on a pole for perverted bastards every night?

No. Not even a little. But I felt conflicted.

You're mine now.

His? Was I his?

Was he mine? And if I gave in to this...what else would I have to give up?

"I'm going to Philly for revenge, Santino. That won't change."

"That's not what I'm asking of you."

"Yet."

"Do I worry about you? Yes. Always. Especially after Tarasov."

I rolled my eyes, and he chuckled softly before continuing.

"I trust you know what you're doing. I'm just here to help you get there faster."

Breaking eye contact, I stared past him, tracking the couples walking along the pier.

Is that what we were?

A couple?

My thoughts drifted back to when he'd spread me open on the bar and made me come in his mouth—and the unforgettable night I'd let the walls around my heart fall. But more than that, it was the little gestures, his caring words...

My chest warmed, and I found his beautiful, dark eyes again. *Mine.*

"Are you in need of a waitress, Mr. Leone?"

He leaned in, grinning wide against my mouth. "No, but I could use an assistant."

Turning around, I swung a leg over his thighs and straddled him. "Deal."

His lips were soft, his kiss slow and tender. Flames sparked low in my stomach, and for the first time, all I could think about was being his, feeling him inside me. I craved it.

But to my disappointment, the beach was crowded tonight.

Santino's rock-hard cock pressing against me told me I wasn't alone in my misery.

"Come over tonight," I said, tipping my head back as he kissed along my collarbone.

"I'm there. But what must I do to get you in my bed?"

"Yours or mine...I don't care. I just need you."

"*Preziosa*, I'm yours."

I raked my fingers through his soft waves. "You know, I owe Luca a thank-you."

Santino's brow furrowed. I laughed, smoothing out his frown with my thumb.

"If he weren't such a fuckup, his father would've left *him* the club, and you and I would've never met."

"You think this is just by chance? You and me? *Nah.*"

The way this man cradled my face and gazed into my soul sent goosebumps across my skin.

"*Tu ed io eravamo destinati.*"

"Destined?" I whispered.

He nodded. "I nearly passed up on this trip. I'd planned to relinquish my half from the comfort of my home in Naples, but I changed my mind at the last minute. I felt a strange pull. A need to come pay my respects to Uncle Lorenzo in person, even though we hadn't seen each other in years."

A small gust of wind blew curls into his face and again into his mouth. We laughed as he tucked the loose strands behind my ear.

"I know now—I came here to find you, Amara. But this trip was never meant to be permanent. That's why...one day, I'd love for you to come back home with me."

Santino had this way of making my insides do backflips. He made me crave things that had once seemed impossible.

Maybe they still were.

But it couldn't hurt to delude myself, even just for the moment.

"Italy? But I—"

Again, he silenced me with a kiss.

"You don't have to decide now. Having you in my world is a privilege, and I don't want to pressure you. But in the meantime, when we're in Pennsylvania, I want you to meet a good friend and his wife. Silas—the one I told you about. And I must say, I never understood the love he had for his wife...especially after she tried to kill me. Twice."

I grimaced and locked my legs around him a little tighter, a spark of protectiveness flaring inside me.

"His wife tried to kill you?"

"Helena's one of the best at what she does—or the worst, if Silas is anything to go by," he said with a hearty laugh. "No hard feelings. We've moved past it. I think."

"Can't wait to meet her," I muttered, tone dripping with sarcasm as I fought down the wave of irrational hatred bubbling up for a woman I hadn't even met, especially the wife of a man Santino considered family.

I needed a distraction.

Maybe sensing my mood, Santino stood without letting go and started toward the water.

"What are you doing?" I asked.

"I thought we could go for a swim."

I gasped. "No. You wouldn't."

"It's a little warm out here." His voice was all mischief as the small waves lapped at his ankles.

"Santi, no. I'll kill you."

No matter how hard I tried to sound serious, I couldn't hide my smile.

"I'm so far gone for you, *preziosa*, I might just let you. But first..."

Water splashed my legs, climbing higher as he walked in deeper, until it was waist-high and my feet were submerged in the dark surf.

"And here I thought you wanted to get laid tonight, Mr. Leone."

He tilted his head and laughed. "That's cruel."

"I'm an expert in cruelty. Don't tempt me."

"Yeah?"

His hold tightened, and I felt the shift in his stance.

"Santino."

"I love it when you say my name. But I love it even more when you scream it."

Water swirled in my ears as he plunged us both beneath the surface, letting our bodies drift for several seconds before breaking through and bursting into laughter.

With my hair plastered over my eyes, I arched back and dipped my head again, smoothing the wet curls from my face.

"You're dead," I squeaked, scooping water into my hand and splashing him.

He trudged farther out, toward the deep, where I knew it

was well over my head. And I suddenly remembered I'd never been a strong swimmer. I clutched at his soaked shirt and buried my face in his neck.

"Santi, don't let go. Please. I can't swim."

"I'm sorry. I didn't know."

He kissed my forehead and turned back toward the shore, guilt tightening his features.

"It's okay," I assured him with a smile, right before smacking another handful of water into his face. I hadn't meant for him to swallow it and choke, but I was too busy laughing to feel torn up. I wriggled free and ran toward the shore.

He caught me easily, and we tumbled into the sand.

"I'm sorry," I said, voice soft and feigning innocence. It made him hesitate for a moment, until he grinned, flipping us over and pinning me beneath him, his muscular body warm and heavy over mine.

"I don't think you are. Not even a little."

"You're right," I murmured, pushing damp strands of hair from his forehead. "What are you going to do about it?"

Santino leaned closer, brushing his lips over mine.

"Everything."

I barely had time to catch a breath before he crushed my mouth in a heated kiss. His tongue caressed mine, teeth catching my bottom lip. Sand clung to our skin as I dragged my hands over his back and tangled my fingers in his shirt, rocking my hips up into him.

Waiting until we got home was out of the question. I wanted him right here, right now. And I knew I wasn't alone in that. He ground into me and groaned in my ear.

"Tell me to stop, Amara...or I'll take you right here on this fucking beach."

Was I capable of saying no? Or better yet—did I even want to?

"This is crazy," I whispered, ripping open his shirt.

A crooked grin curved his mouth as I leaned in, sticking out my tongue to catch a droplet of water that had rolled from his lip and trailed down over mine.

"I suddenly love crazy," he said, dipping down to kiss me again.

But before our lips could meet, a shrill scream sliced through the night, shattering the moment.

THIRTY-ONE

Amara

Two women ran past us, one crying, the other trying to console her. But both were visibly shaken by whatever they'd seen. Santino pulled me to my feet as a small group began gathering near the shoreline, several yards ahead.

"What do you think is going on?"

He shook his head, tightening his grip on my hand. "Nothing good."

Had the commotion broken out anywhere else, we would've minded our business and kept moving. But this was practically Illusion's backyard. Whatever had rattled these people into screams and tears definitely seemed worth investigating.

The closer we got, the louder the cries and unintelligible chatter. A group of young men had pulled out their phones—some snapping pictures, others recording or live-streaming.

"Santino," I gasped when I saw it: a bloody foot, skin ashen, still strapped into a six-inch heel.

I slipped from his grasp and ran toward the body, a sickening churn building in my stomach.

"Amara, wait!"

Santino called after me, but I was already halfway through

the crowd, pushing people aside. I froze when I reached the center, staring into the lifeless eyes of a familiar face.

"It's Star," I breathed as Santino caught up, throwing an arm around me and pulling me to his side. "Who could've done this?"

Star and I had never been particularly close, but not for her lack of trying. I just never cared for the shallow camaraderie that came with this kind of work. They all shared a dressing room. I had my own. It saved me the drama of petty jealousies and resentment over what they considered special treatment.

"Come on." He guided me through the growing crowd, his sharp gaze scanning our surroundings. "We don't know who's watching."

Sirens wailed in the distance as we slipped back inside the club.

"Should we tell the others?"

"Not yet. The cops will be here soon enough, asking questions and requesting the surveillance footage."

Once we crossed the threshold into his office, he locked the door behind us and motioned for me to sit while he jumped to camera angle twelve.

As he combed through footage, I caught a glimpse of us in the water. And despite the tragedy we'd just stumbled into, I couldn't help smiling. Santino's eyes flicked to me, and I knew he felt it too. That spark. Inappropriate or not.

"There!" I shot up, pointing at the screen. A dark figure appeared, dragging a limp Star across the sand. "She was alive just an hour before we walked onto the beach."

The footage was too grainy to make out a face or determine how she'd died, but judging by what I saw at the scene, it looked like she'd suffered a neck laceration and several puncture wounds to the chest.

"Star never showed up to work today," he muttered, panning the camera feed toward the parking lot. Her usual spot was empty. "Dumping her body on this beach was deliberate. Someone's sending us a message."

"Luca," we said in unison.

"I'm going to pay him a visit." He stepped around the desk and pulled me into his chest. "But maybe you should lay low, *preziosa*. Stay home. I can have Blaise watch your place. Or—" his arms tensed around me—"come with me."

The thought of going home *with* Santino was terrifying and tempting in all the best ways. But I was tired of hiding. Least of all from Luca.

My phone buzzed inside my bag. And as if the universe had heard me, the text on the screen couldn't have come at a better time.

"Is there any way your private jet can pick us up sooner than next week?"

His brows lifted. "I told you—just say the word."

"Good. Because we leave for Philly tomorrow at noon."

Santino nodded once, but when I tried to step back, his fingers clutched my wet shirt.

"Where do you think you're going?"

"Change of plans means I have to go home, pack, and drop Phoenix off at Cambri's."

He tilted my chin and kissed me. "Then come back to my place tonight."

"We almost had sex on the beach, Santi. If I do that, I won't want to leave in the morning." I brushed a bit of sand from his cheek.

His protest never made it past his lips. A knock at the office door silenced us both.

We turned to the camera feed. A man in a blazer stood outside, eyes trained directly on the lens.

"Detective Braga."

Santino moved to the door. "And the coincidences never cease."

The moment it swung open, my neighbor's eyes flicked from me to Santino and betrayed the poker face he usually wore.

"Amara?"

"Detective," Santino said, stepping in between us. "She was just leaving. I assume you're here about what happened on the beach."

His gaze swept over our soaked clothes and sand-dusted skin. "Before you go," he said, ignoring Santino and locking eyes with me, "I'd like to ask you a few questions."

"That won't be necessary," Santino interjected. "I can give my statement. That should suffice."

"That's not how this works, Mr. Leone. We may be standing in your club, but since the victim was reportedly your employee, and her body was dumped near your property, we'll need to interview all possible witnesses."

"We saw nothing."

"That may well be the truth," Braga said, eyeing our disheveled appearances once more. "But I still have to follow protocol. In any case, Miss Carvalho can speak for herself."

"Of course I can," I said, touching Santino's arm, hoping to ease the tension I felt coiling between them.

Raymond Braga already had his suspicions when it came to Santino. It was better to comply and stay off his radar.

———

Cambri threw her good arm around me the moment she opened the door. The swelling in her face had gone down, and though the bruises were still visible, they'd faded from purple and black to yellow. The final stage of healing.

"How much longer do you have with this?" I asked, pointing to her cast and running my finger along the spot where I'd signed my name with a heart.

"Two fucking weeks."

I set Phoenix's crate on the floor and let him loose. "Almost there."

"Yeah. I'm going stir-crazy."

Guilt bloomed in my chest. I hadn't been by nearly enough to see her or help out. That would change when I got back—I promised myself that.

"I won't be in Philly as long as I originally planned. We'll have slumber parties when I return."

Cambri laughed and dragged me to the sofa. "Sounds fun. But unlike me, you still have work."

I shrugged. "Maybe I don't."

Her dark eyes narrowed. "You quit or something?"

"No, but I won't be dancing anymore."

Cambri didn't say a word for a full minute after I explained everything that happened between me and Santino. Eventually, I got tired of waiting for a reaction and shook her shoulders. "Say something. When have you *ever* been speechless?"

"Not until now," she said, blinking hard before flinging herself into my arms. "Amara! I'm mad at you for keeping this from me, but I'm also so fucking happy for you, babe."

"It's only been a few days. I'm still processing it myself."

"Bullshit! You should've texted me the second it happened."

I chuckled, surprised by the strength in her one-armed hug.

"Are you okay?" she asked, her voice softer.

"I am."

This time, I was the one to pull her close. Until a few days ago, Cambri was the only person who knew what I'd been through. The only one who understood my pain. She was my best friend.

My angel.

"Amara, I want *all* the details."

I took her hands in mine and sighed, my smile fading with the weight of what I still had to share.

Her forehead creased.

"Cam, I have something else to tell you...But it's not good."

"What is it?" She squeezed my fingers, already bracing herself.

"Star was murdered today."

Her eyes widened as she gasped. They weren't close, but they'd worked together for years—even before Illusion.

Again, she was speechless, stunned by the loss of someone we both knew.

"Santino and I think Luca might be behind it."

Tears welled in her eyes. I tugged her closer and gently placed her head in my lap, combing my fingers through her hair.

THIRTY-TWO

PHILADELPHIA, PA

The wind sent a chill through my bones. Fall hadn't arrived yet, but after years in the South, my blood had grown soft, accustomed to humidity and warm nights. I wrapped my arms around myself and leaned against a storefront's glass window.

Waiting.

Santino and I landed two hours ago and settled into a penthouse he'd rented for the weekend. It never ceased to amaze me, the kind of power that came with unlimited funds and the right connections. Or maybe I'd just forgotten what that life felt like. I'd tasted it young. The perks of wealth, the illusion of invincibility.

It was all a lie.

Another gust of wind tousled my hair, and that's when I realized: the chill in my bones wasn't from the weather—it was the city itself. Every inch was haunted by memories. Sights. Sounds. Shadows of a past I'd buried deep in the blackest corners of my mind.

These streets had watched my worst nightmares come alive.

And now, they'd bear witness to the retribution I came to claim. For every piece of me they shattered.

I shut my eyes against the sting of hot tears and swallowed hard, bracing for what the night would bring. But just as I pushed off the glass, a burst of tinkling laughter made my gaze snap across the street.

And then I saw him.

I nearly stumbled, a gasp catching in my throat. Despite the years, the distance, and the extra ink on his neck and hands...I'd know my brother's face anywhere.

"Derek?" I whispered. "Derek."

He was laughing with a woman, petite, with long, dark hair. And he looked at her like she hung the moon. Like she *made* the moon.

I'd kept tabs on my brothers over the years, but I never intervened. For their safety, I disappeared. For all they knew, I was dead. At the time, it felt like the right choice. But standing there now, watching him alive, in love, *happy*, I realized just how much I'd missed.

When had he learned to love like that?

A smile crept to my lips, and a single tear slipped down my cheek as I watched their sweet exchange.

Maybe one day, I thought. *Maybe one day we'll see each other again.*

But not tonight. Tonight, I wasn't ready to face that part of my past.

I watched until they turned a corner and vanished. And with their absence came a wave of aching nostalgia that made me wonder if I'd really seen him at all—or if he was just a dream.

Then reality crashed back in. My phone went off in my pocket.

I glanced down the street one last time, where Derek had been, then turned toward the next corner. Toward the man in the dark red sedan. The one who'd soon be dead.

Opening the passenger door, I climbed in, and his hand was

already waiting, making itself at home on my lap. Bile rose in my throat at the contact, but I had to play it cool. He thought I was an escort.

There was no room for nerves or triggers here, so I let his intrusive touch linger far longer than patience allowed.

But any illusion of control vanished the moment I caught movement in the backseat.

A fucking kid.

This son of a bitch had brought a little girl on a date with an escort.

He must've seen the unfiltered shock on my face, because he patted my thigh and tried to reassure me.

"It's okay," he said casually.

The fuck it is.

"You can't be serious."

"Relax, *kroshka*. Last-minute change of plans," he replied with a grin.

Terror ripped through me at the implication. My hand flew to the knife at my side, ready to gut him right there in the front seat.

"My ex-wife's on call. Emergency surgery came in, and her usual sitter wasn't available. Don't worry. My sister's in town. Just gotta make a quick detour."

I glanced at the sleeping toddler and exhaled slowly, relief loosening the knot in my chest.

Most people might feel guilt about leaving a child without their father. But this little girl was better off without the sperm donor the universe saddled her with.

"Perfect," I chirped, releasing my grip on the knife and settling back into the seat with practiced ease.

Twenty minutes later, we were finally heading up to his condo.

"I've never seen anyone like you before," he said.

"Oh?" I asked, playing innocent, unsure what part of me he meant.

"You afraid someone'll see you?"

Ah. The mask.

"Well, this isn't exactly a line of work I flaunt in public," I said. "I have a day job, Mr. Sokolov. One I'd like to keep separate."

"Understandable. Can't let the whole world know you're a whore. I get it."

Painful. Slow. That's how he'd die.

Men made whores.

I didn't respond. Just stepped out of the elevator and followed him to his door.

"After you, whore."

Very painful.

A strange odor hit my nose as I stepped inside, but I didn't have time to process it—he shoved me forward and locked the door behind us.

"I was quite specific about what I wanted. Meek. Breakable. The last girl they sent had a mouth on her. I had to show her how to use it, if you catch my meaning."

"Did you now?"

He slid off his belt, and the noise triggered me, sending a shudder down my spine.

"Strip and get on your knees."

Familiar words sent another shock wave through my body. He spoke like his kin. All cut from the same fucking cloth.

"I'll be whoever you want me to be," I said, schooling the threat of a spiral and removing my mask.

His eyes narrowed as they locked on mine, his voice dipping. "Your eyes...that's different."

But it was *me* who recognized *him*. I knew he had ties to the trafficking ring that had held me captive. It was the reason I was here. But the night had become a hell of a lot more interesting when I caught a familiar scorpion tattoo on his neck. He didn't seem to remember me. I hadn't expected him to. He'd brutalized hundreds, maybe thousands, of girls over the years. We were just faceless dollar signs to men like him—holes to fuck and bodies to break.

"I'm different," I murmured.

He scoffed, letting his pants drop and stroking his unimpressive dick. "We'll see. But the longer you make me wait, the harder I get to fuck that sweet ass. Now turn around and strip."

"As you wish."

"*Sir.*"

The word echoed in my ears.

"Sir."

Turning my back on this sack of shit wasn't easy, but I had to play the game. He had nearly a foot on me, outweighing me more than anticipated. Sheer strength and skill wouldn't serve me well here. I needed to outsmart him, be faster, underhanded, and savage.

I let my black trench coat slide off my shoulders, pooling at my feet. Behind me, I heard him suck his teeth, strokes growing faster. Grimacing in disgust, I rolled my eyes and gripped my knife.

"I must say, you are exquisite, whore." He drew closer, his breath on my shoulder, and my hand trembled with the overwhelming urge to react. "Tell me, are you ready to play?"

Savage.

I licked the blade's edge, then turned my head just enough to smile.

"The better question is, are you?"

The knife sank deep into the side of his abdomen. He froze, shock locking his limbs while his brain played catch-up. Eyes wide, he looked down at the blood blooming across his shirt.

"Bitch..."

Three more quick stabs and a long slash across his stomach sent him stumbling back.

I could have killed him on the first hit, but I needed my fun. I hadn't come all this way for a quick death. Nothing about what I had endured was easy or fast. Maybe he wasn't the one who beat and raped me until my skin tore. But they were one and the same.

And if I could take it, so could he.

Blood dripped from the corner of his mouth. "I'll kill you."

"Try."

He lunged at me with a growl, expecting me to run.

Instead, I dropped low. Another clean slice.

Though this time, I couldn't blame his look of utter horror when he realized he was down an appendage—one he was very fond of.

"No...no!" He fell hard, ass hitting the floor, blood pooling beneath him, gushing from the stump where his cock had once been.

"You're all the same," I said, stalking forward. "You take and take, and *take* without mercy or remorse."

Tears tracked down his cheeks as he tried to scoot away.

"Fuck...you fucking psycho. What have you done?"

"Oh, Sokolov, I'm just getting started." I crouched beside him, my voice low. "Maybe you don't remember me...but we're old friends."

His shallow breaths hitched, his eyebrows knit together, and the wheels in his brain finally began to turn.

"I'm insulted you forgot. My eyes have a way of making me quite memorable."

"You..." he panted. "You shot up my garage."

"Bingo."

He grimaced and reached for a Glock on the side table, but I introduced his hand to my blade instead, driving it straight through his palm and into the flimsy wood. His scream rattled the walls, his whole body convulsing with pain.

I leaned in close, our faces nearly touching. "Hurts, doesn't it? Just breathe for me."

Circling him, I paused when I heard light tapping from another room.

"I thought you were here alone." I followed the sound. "Don't go anywhere."

With his gun in hand, I crept down a short hallway. The strange odor from earlier grew stronger and more pungent. My gut clenched, and I braced myself, then pushed open the door.

The breath punched from my lungs.

A young girl sat slumped in an empty bathtub, shackled to the faucet. She was skin and bones, filthy, with dried blood and bruises covering her body. She looked barely conscious. The tapping wasn't deliberate; it was instinct. A survival reflex.

"Hey," I whispered gently. "I'll get you help, okay?"

But the closer I got, the more unbearable it became. She sat in a pool of blood, urine, and waste. One nipple clamp lay beside her. The other still dangled halfway from raw, torn flesh.

"Fuck," I choked, squeezing my eyes shut. "I'm so sorry this happened to you."

I reached out to brush her hair back, but her head slumped forward, and she stilled.

I dropped to my knees, tears clouding my vision. I saw myself in this girl.

For a moment, the world stopped. Just her, me, and the echo of my own pain. I didn't know her name. Where she came from. How long she'd been trapped here.

"You're safe now," I whispered, fingers trembling as I stroked her hair. "Maybe now...you'll have peace."

But *he* will never know peace.

A pained groan echoed from the living room, dragging me back.

"Come here...you goddamn crazy whore!"

I met his bloodshot glare and grinned. Reaching down, I snatched his severed, flaccid cock from the carpet.

"You made me this way."

"No—oh god, no! Please!" he sobbed. Pathetic.

The ice pick holding my bun slid from my curls, letting them spill loose.

"Was she the girl you mentioned? The mouthy one?"

"Please...don't do this." Bloody drool dripped down his chin.

"Answer the damn question."

He yanked at his impaled hand, but the effort was in vain. He was too weak.

"Fuck, I don't know!"

"Let me jog your memory." I jabbed the ice pick into his urethra.

"Oh, fuck...Stop!"

"Yes or no?" His dick was halfway skewered now.

"Okay! Okay...Yes!"

His desperation almost amused me. Did he really think his favorite appendage was salvageable? As if he'd need it where he was going.

"Now we're getting somewhere. Tell me—what did you do to *teach her a lesson?*"

His fist slammed the carpet, and he sobbed when he dared to glance between his legs, like he couldn't accept that his prized possession was well and truly gone.

"I'm going to kill you," he gritted out through clenched teeth.

Squatting to his level, I laughed and grabbed a fistful of his hair. "Still the same empty threats, even when I've got you by the literal balls—or in your case, cock."

I'd seen plenty of men cry at death's door, but none had sobbed as pitifully as this bastard. His face twisted, mouth slack, as bloody drool leaked from the corners. It might've been funny if it weren't so fucking pathetic. For someone who'd handed out pain and torture so freely, he folded like wet paper.

"Since you won't talk, I'm going to assume that poor girl's final moments with you involved this sorry strip of meat. Am I right?"

"Fuck...you."

I grinned and slapped him across the face with his own dick kabob.

"The only one fucked here is you. But I'll give you a small mercy. Not for your sake—for hers. She doesn't deserve to spend another second rotting in your bathroom. But first..."

His eyes widened as I reached for his shirt and tore it open.

"What are you doing?"

"Sending a message."

Skewering his severed cock the rest of the way, I used the sharpened point to carve into his chest. He shrieked with every stroke, every tear of flesh.

"There," I said with a wink.

Maybe I'd gotten too cocky. I hadn't assessed him thoroughly enough. Because in the blink of an eye, he lunged forward and grabbed my hair, yanking me down over him.

His skin was slick with blood, and I couldn't catch my balance. Shit.

I'd fucked up.

"You're coming with me, whore," he rasped into my ear, twisting me into a chokehold. "Should've killed you when I had the chance."

He was weak from blood loss, but with my body slipping and sliding over blood and other fluids, escaping his grip was damn near impossible.

"That's it...Let's keep each other company."

Panic gripped my chest as my vision began to blur. I had seconds—maybe less. My hand slapped the wet carpet, searching blindly for the ice pick until the tips of my fingers brushed soft tissue.

Without hesitation, I grabbed the severed dick and rammed it into his face with everything I had.

He grunted, body jerking, and then his hold loosened as he slumped back.

I turned and dropped on my ass, gasping for air and then I laughed. Hard.

In my desperation, I'd stabbed him blind, and by some

twisted miracle, the ice pick had pierced straight through his mouth, shoving half his sorry dick down his throat.

"Perfect."

I scooped the gun from where it had landed and stood over him, aiming at his face.

The fucker was *still* alive.

He twitched, wrapped a shaky hand around my boot, and gurgled some ungodly sound from his very occupied throat.

"My favorite lullaby."

Two bullets to the skull and my job was done.

THIRTY-THREE

Santino

Pacing. Pacing. And more fucking pacing.

One more trip to the window, and I was sure I'd wear a hole through the carpet. It took every ounce of strength I had, and some I didn't know existed, to let her go in alone. I trusted her skills. She'd been doing this long before I came into the picture.

But fuck that. Things were different now.

She was mine to protect. Mine to watch over. And even if she'd made it this far unscathed, statistics didn't lie. Luck always ran dry. Skill could slip. In the business of death, I knew that too damn well.

Five more minutes.

That's all I'd give before I caved and went after her.

To keep the trail cold, she carried only a burner, one she'd ditch the second the job started. But I was a man not willing to deal in chance when it came to someone as important to me as my *preziosa*. So, I pulled strings and cashed in on last-minute favors, intercepting her signal and receiving all her messages, including the contact information of any incoming numbers, and pinpointed their location.

Having that information was both a blessing and a curse.

Two hours without a word was torture.

Fuck this.

I grabbed my keys and opened the front door, only to freeze when I saw Amara standing on the other side. My heart dropped at the sight of blood covering her body.

"It's not mine," she whispered, easing the worst of my fears.

I cupped her face and kissed her forehead, brushing at the dried streaks on her cheeks. Her tears had already fallen. Long before she made it back to me.

Nodding, I lifted her into my arms and cradled her close as words failed to adequately describe my relief.

"He got what he deserved," she said, her voice quiet and thick with exhaustion.

I turned on the shower and stepped beneath the stream, letting the warm water cascade over our heads.

"I was worried."

My grip was too tight. I knew it. I didn't care.

"You don't trust me?" she asked, a faint smile on her lips.

"I do, *preziosa*. But I trust no one when it comes to you."

She didn't answer. Just blinked. And the fresh tears in her eyes cracked something wide open in me.

"Talk to me."

"I found a girl. He'd chained her in the bathroom. Tortured her." Her voice hollowed out. "It was awful. That used to be me, Santino." Her eyes dropped to the scars on her wrist.

"I'm sorry, baby." I kissed her forehead, holding her tighter.

She looked up at me, eyes glassy. "She's dead."

I pressed her closer, wishing I could make the world disappear. Wishing I could be enough to make it better. But all I could do was hold her. And never let go.

Amara's fingers traced my lips, sweeping droplets as I kissed each one.

"I cut off his dick," she said almost stoically, still staring at my mouth.

"Did you?"

She nodded slowly. With the same languid pace, she blinked and lifted her gaze.

"And then I skewered it."

For several moments, only the sound of water hitting tile filled the silence. Then, deep, rumbling laughter bubbled from my throat. She followed, and we laughed until our stomachs ached and the drain below no longer streaked pink.

"Sei incredibile."

"I'm glad you think so. I scare myself sometimes."

"The feeling's mutual. Because I feel lost in you, Amara. But I don't ever want to find my way out," I whispered against her collarbone, sliding her strap down and kissing the slick skin beneath.

Our clothes hit the tile, and I pressed her against the wall.

"Let me help you put an end to this. Tell me your name."

"No."

"I have connections. Who are you looking for?"

Amara slipped beneath my arm and stepped out of the shower.

"Not yet."

"Amara." I twisted the faucet off and followed as she toweled herself dry. "You can trust me."

"I do," she countered, sounding almost offended. "But you won't find him."

"Try me."

"Santi, you don't understand. It's like he's fallen off the face of the planet. And he's not your typical low-life piece of shit like the others. We've been over this."

Dropping the towel, she began digging frantically through her suitcase.

"Tomorrow, we meet Helena and Silas. They're part of an organization." I paused, knowing the implications of what I was about to say, but I trusted her.

"Ares."

She froze, visibly jolting at the word. Suddenly, things started making sense.

"You're...Ares?" I asked, touching her shoulder and shifting her toward me. Amara didn't resist, but she refused eye contact. "You are?"

"I'm not."

"You were—otherwise, you'd be asking what the fuck I'm talking about. Look at me." I held her chin, silently begging to meet her eyes. "Amara."

"A long time ago," she finally admitted.

"Do you know them? Silas? Helena?"

"No." She shook her head, brows knitted, like she was trying to remember. I believed her.

"They can help."

Amara pulled away and walked back to her suitcase.

"No."

"*Preziosa—*"

She slammed the suitcase shut. "I said no!"

It was the first time I'd heard her raise her voice. The topic of Ares, and that part of her past, was clearly off-limits. So I let it go for now.

"Okay." Holding her gaze, I reached for her hand and tugged her toward the bed. "But I'd still like you to come with me tomorrow."

"Why?"

"Because Silas is like a brother to me. And I want him to meet the woman stealing the heart I never knew I had."

The hint of a smile formed on her lips as she followed me into bed and under the sheets. With her plump little ass pressed against my cock, hiding my erection was pointless.

"I'm sorry," she murmured, threading her fingers through mine and kissing my knuckles. "I didn't mean to react like that... It's just—"

"I understand."

She twisted to face me. "I'd love to meet your friends tomorrow."

"Good." I brushed a curl from her eye, but as I leaned in to kiss her, her smile faded. "What's wrong?"

"What will you tell them? That we met at your club?" She scoffed. "That you fell for me the second you saw me stripping on stage?"

"I assure you, they won't judge you."

Scooting closer, she shook her head.

"It's not about me. I face judgment every day, and I haven't let it faze me in a long time. But what will they think of you?"

"Poor Santino," I teased. "Stuck with a beautiful, fierce woman. Whatever will he do?"

The sound of her laughter warmed my chest, and made my cock throb.

I could listen to her forever.

THIRTY-FOUR

Amara

My heart galloped as we approached a gated driveway. After spending most of the morning racking my memory, I concluded I had never heard of or met either of Santino's friends, so I wasn't sure why nervous energy buzzed through my body. Their ties to Ares and the fact that this felt like a big step in our relationship were probably to blame.

Santino placed a hand on my jittery thigh and gave it a squeeze.

"Everything all right?"

"Of course. I just haven't done this sort of thing in a while. The whole meeting new people, playing nice, pretending I didn't just cut off some guy's dick last night."

Santino grimaced, then laughed. "I bet Helena would get a kick out of that story."

"She sounds like my kind of girl."

He pulled up to the entrance, where stone steps led to tall, black double doors.

"You and Helena. Why is that slightly terrifying?"

"Well, now I'm thoroughly intrigued," I said with a laugh.

It was easy to lose myself in his eyes and forget the rest of the world even existed. But that kind of life—twisting in my seat, I stared at the beautiful two-story home—a normal one, where I lived somewhere like this and hosted friends...that just felt out of reach.

"Come on, *preziosa*. The faster we get through this, the sooner I get you home and back in my bed."

I was convinced I'd never stop feeling flutters in my belly and throbbing between my legs. Santino made me feel beautiful, special, so many things I never thought I'd feel again, if ever.

He took my hand, rounded the hood, and led me toward the door. I waited for Santi to knock, but he simply stood there and sent me a wink. Confused, I gave him a look and motioned toward the doorbell, until I glanced up and saw the mounted camera above our heads, as well as the others strategically placed around the property.

Of course. Ares.

A teenage boy opened the door and greeted us with a half-smile and a nod. He was handsome, with dark hair and steel-blue eyes. As expected, his gaze landed on me, narrowing slightly, intrigued by the contrasting colors of mine.

"You must be Maksim," Santino said, offering his hand.

The boy nodded again but didn't speak.

Commotion from inside the house broke the awkward silence—first the sound of a toddler's giggle, then a man's voice shouting with amused exasperation.

"Valentina!"

Just then, the heavy door creaked open wider, and a little girl, no older than two, bolted through the threshold, trying to escape until the boy scooped her up into his arms.

"Where do you think you're going?"

"No, Maxy! Down!" she protested, wriggling like a worm until he nearly dropped her.

Rolling his eyes, the kid held on firmly until a man I assumed was Silas finally caught up. The baby immediately reached for him and snuggled into his chest. As small as she was, his burly size made her look even tinier.

"Maxy bad," she scolded in the cutest little rasp I'd ever heard.

Maxy threw his arms up in surrender and retreated into the house.

Santino and Silas greeted each other warmly, exchanging hugs and hard claps to the back.

Silas turned to me with an easy smile that deepened the scar over his right eye. I returned the gesture as Santino introduced us.

"This must be the baby girl who has you wrapped around her finger."

Silas laughed and tossed the girl so high into the air that I gasped and instinctively reached out in case she fell. But clearly, I was the only one worried. Her squeals of joy rivaled Silas's laughter.

"This little nugget is my niece, Valentina," he said, swinging her onto his shoulders. "Come on in. Leni should be down in a minute."

Santino grasped my hand as Silas led us into a spacious living room, where a grotesquely enormous TV was mounted on the wall. I'd never seen one that size used for cartoons.

When he set the baby down, she immediately began dancing to the catchy tune playing.

It hit me then that I'd never really been around a small child, apart from my brief encounter with Thiago.

She was beautiful. Dark brown hair tied into pigtails, each with a crooked pink bow, no doubt the result of her earlier marathon escape attempt. A frilly pink tutu bounced with every leap, while clunky little combat boots stole any sense of poise she might have had. I found myself oddly fascinated by this tiny human and the way she radiated beauty and innocence, like she knew she was untouchable.

I glanced at the two men, still deep in conversation.

The love Silas had for her was unmistakable, even in the

short exchange I'd witnessed. And Santino would kill for her by default.

Untouchable.

What would my life have been like if I'd been as loved and protected as this child?

Something about her captivated me, though I couldn't begin to explain why. Valentina twirled, then caught me staring. Without hesitation, she approached and handed me what looked like a stuffed hummingbird she'd been dancing with.

"Maxy," she said, pointing to the toy. "Mine."

I was a little confused about which Maxy she meant, since the boy had disappeared somewhere.

"She named it after my son," a woman said from the hallway.

Helena.

There's something to be said about women who can walk into a room and command attention and respect by presence alone. Helena was one of them. Regal and beautiful, she moved toward us with her eyes fixed on me, wearing a look I recognized all too well. She was assessing, sizing me up—it's what we'd all been trained to do.

The men stood, and she tipped her chin at Santino with a sly grin.

"Nice to see you again, *Santiago*."

He laughed and pulled her in for a hug. "Always a pleasure. This is Amara."

"Helena." She introduced herself to me with a smile, one she'd probably practiced to perfection. But I was good at reading people too, and I saw right through the facade. Not that I blamed her. I wouldn't trust me either.

There's something uniquely different about those who have faced and delivered death. You see it in the eyes.

"That's her favorite toy. She must like you. Children are a good judge of character."

"She's precious, and I'm honored," I said, handing the girl back her bird.

"Valentina also eats Cheerios off the floor, so her taste can be questionable."

A smile touched my lips at her quick wit and not-so-subtle dig. I wouldn't expect anything less from a woman like Helena.

"No! My boots!" the girl cried, kicking her feet when her aunt sat her on a beanbag and began trying to remove them.

"Baby, you're tripping. You can have them back when your papa picks you up." That's when her real smile appeared, genuine, warm, and reserved for this child who truly was untouchable with someone like Helena in her corner. "I promise," she added, kissing the tip of Valentina's nose.

But not even Helena held power over a toddler. Valentina scrunched her face, shut her eyes, and shook her head dramatically from side to side.

"No, no, no."

"I tried," Silas explained from behind us.

"You're such a pushover, Si." Helena slid the boots back on Valentina, and I suppressed a laugh.

Everyone had a weakness. Helena's was a three-foot toddler with dimples.

Silas chuckled. "You were saying?"

"I can't help it when her *Cain* side takes over."

Cain?

My eyes snapped back to the child, scanning every little feature. She looked up at me, as if sensing my sudden intrigue, and flashed a big, cheesy smile.

My heart dropped.

Cain.

Derek?

Kai?

I wasn't sure, but it wasn't the most common of last names. And what were the odds?

"Amara?" Santino's voice broke through my spiral. I turned to find worry etched across his face. "Are you okay, *preziosa*? You look like you're about to faint."

His arm circled my waist. Whatever breakdown was coming, I needed to have it in private.

"I'm fine. I just need to use the bathroom."

"This way." Helena motioned toward the nearest hallway, her eyes, for the first time, holding something real. Concern.

Once the door closed behind me, I braced my hands on the vanity and drew in two sharp breaths.

"She said Cain. It has to be one of them."

Derek or Kai had a daughter. Kai would've been my first guess. But that face. There was something about it. Something familiar. Traces of Derek.

Derek...a father?

It explained the pull I felt toward that little girl.

"My niece," I whispered. Maybe not by blood, but we'd been as close as siblings once. They were my boys.

The moment my eyes drifted closed, they tore back open.

"When your papa picks you up..."

Fuck.

Derek couldn't see me.

I threw open the bathroom door, ready to make a run for Santino while I cycled through excuses for why we needed to leave. But I stopped dead in my tracks, nearly colliding with Helena.

"What was that about?" she asked, straight to the point.

"Excuse me?"

"It was something I said, wasn't it?"

"And what would that be?"

"You tell me...*preziosa.*"

Helena was the kind of assassin I had once aspired to be. Confident, calculating, cold as ice. Even after eight years under Ares and a body count that would make most men flinch, eighteen-year-old me would've been both in awe and slightly intimidated by this woman.

But I'd been dragged through the darkest pits of hell. I was numb to fear.

Crossing my arms in defiance, I stared her down.

Besides Magda, the last time I'd killed a woman, I was a teenager. It was the day before my eighteenth birthday. My mark had been the thirty-four-year-old wife of a real estate mogul.

At the time, life was what it was. I hadn't cared about her past or why her name bled across my contract. My biggest gripe had been that I broke a nail in the process.

Some days, I wondered if what happened to me later was karma for the lives I'd so carelessly taken. But if that were true, then what fresh hell awaited me now?

"There's a few things I know," Helena said, her eyes sweeping over me again. "I know you're not who you say you are."

"Is that right?"

She scoffed. "You think I'd let just anyone into my home— around my husband, my son, that little girl? Granted, she wasn't supposed to be here, but her mom's a detective who got an early morning call about two bodies in some asshole's condo down-town. Awful what happened in there."

That felt like an overshare. And Helena didn't strike me as someone who spoke on impulse. No, she was far too disciplined for a slip like that. But she couldn't possibly connect that crime scene to me.

"But I digress, *Amara Carvalho*. Your paper trail is just convincing enough for the civilian population. But to me? You're a ghost. You don't exist. So that begs the question—who are you, really?"

Helena was intelligent and intuitive, but she was fishing. She had pieces, sure, but I knew as well as she did that without the vital ones, there was no connecting the dots. Speculation and suspicion wouldn't be enough. I needed to throw her off, and I knew exactly how.

Sighing, I looked away as tears welled in my eyes. Calling them fake would've been disingenuous. I had a hundred and one reasons to cry.

"That's the point," I murmured. "Hiding. Erasing my past. It's the only way I survive."

"You're going to have to be a little less vague."

There was a threat curled beneath her words.

She'd tried to kill me. Twice.

A fight with Helena wouldn't just cost me; it would cost Santino. And it would destroy his friendship with Silas.

Reaching for the hem of my shirt, I gave Helena a quick glance. Her eyes narrowed as I turned my back and pulled the fabric up and over my shoulders.

Seconds crawled by. Then, an unexpected voice shattered the silence.

"What happened to you?"

We both whipped around, startled to find the boy standing in the hallway, his gaze locked on me.

"Maksim, what are you doing here?" Helena asked, voice taut.

"Show me," he said, stepping forward, ignoring her completely.

"Maksim?"

My eyes bounced between them, suddenly feeling like I was witnessing something I shouldn't, an argument simmering just below the surface.

He shrugged off her hand.

"She's like me."

Helena's features softened as she lifted the boy's chin with a tenderness I hadn't expected from her, not even with Valentina.

"Maks." Her voice was laced with pain and the kind of empathy only a mother could feel. It seemed uncharacteristic of someone like Helena, especially considering Santino had told me they'd only had the boy for about a year.

"Someone hurt you." His words weren't a question, but a truth he recognized in me.

Helena and I met eyes. Then, with a resigned exhale, she gave a subtle nod of permission.

"They did," I admitted. "Someone hurt you, too?"

His throat bobbed as he nodded, biting back emotion.

"Does it still hurt?" he asked quietly.

"Not anymore."

"No, I mean...does it still hurt...*inside*?"

God. Real tears replaced the ones I'd forced earlier, flooding forward the moment I realized I'd judged this boy the way others had judged me, because they couldn't understand my trauma.

"Always," I said softly. I wanted to be honest. That's what he needed—understanding and compassion. Not sugar-coated bullshit.

"Yeah." He nodded again, gaze dropping to the floor.

Daring to get close, I reached out and touched his shoulder. I expected him to flinch or pull away like he had with Helena, but to my surprise, he leaned into my touch.

"What helps you get through the bad days, Maksim? When the memories won't fade and the voices refuse to quiet?"

Tears streamed down his cheeks, his shoulders shaking as he looked over at Helena.

"My...mom," he whispered.

Helena's eyes widened. She rolled her lip inward, trying to keep it from trembling.

"Good," I said, offering him a small smile.

"Maksim..." She stepped forward, her voice thick with tears and disbelief. "What did you...just call me?"

He rushed her so suddenly she stumbled back two steps before regaining her footing and wrapping him in a tight embrace.

. . .

XXX

Maksim wouldn't make some miraculous change overnight. The scars on our bodies healed, but those imprinted on our hearts and minds stayed with us until death. He was fortunate to have people who cared enough to guide him through the storms ahead.

I squeezed Santino's hand as I gazed at the little girl who'd fallen asleep on the sofa.

Derek's daughter.

The question of her paternity was answered when I came upon a framed family photograph on Helena's mantle. The woman I'd seen on his arm last night was the same one in the photo. Not only had my brooding and scarred brother become a father, but he'd also fallen in love and married. They both had. Next to Derek's was one of Kai on his wedding day with a beautiful woman in a black dress. How serendipitous that, despite life thrusting us into such distinct paths, we were all connected somehow, some way, after all these years.

Santino tugged me to his chest, and I lost myself in his eyes as I came to the hopeful conclusion that maybe we all deserved a little redemption and a sliver of happiness, whatever that might look like.

"Ready?" he asked.

Guilt pricked at my chest. My name and past with Ares were still a very big secret between us. How could we move forward while this dark cloud of deceit hung over our heads? But even thinking of speaking that name out loud made my throat constrict.

"I'm ready."

Silas walked us to the door, and as the men approached the vehicle, Helena caught my elbow.

After the exchange with Maksim, she had become friendly

and welcoming, but a rift still existed between us, something I couldn't quite put my finger on.

"Thank you," she said. "And I'm sorry. I don't know what you went through, but clearly, it was some rough shit." She arched a perfect eyebrow. "But you look like the kind of woman who knows how to handle herself."

"I'm sure you and I have quite a few stories to exchange someday," I said with a smile.

"Absolutely." She chuckled, then glanced toward where Santino and Silas were waiting in the driveway. "He's a good guy. And he's always been a loyal friend to Silas. I'll always be thankful for that." Her honey-brown eyes met mine. "I trust his judgment, and if he brought you here, that means something."

"Thank you." I started toward the car but froze. Without turning around, I said, "Oh, Helena, if you ever have questions about Maksim or need anything, I'd be glad to help."

She didn't respond, so I resumed walking.

"Amara," I stopped again. "Call me Leni."

THIRTY-FIVE

Santino

Sunlight streaked through the window, the heat pulling me from the grip of a dream I desperately tried to hold onto. She was so warm, so fucking tight as I thrust into her cunt until the pressure shot down my spine and coiled in my balls.

Fuck.

I reached behind me, grabbing the top of the headboard as the last shred of sleep slipped away. My other hand dropped to stroke my cock, only to find a fistful of long curls instead. I opened my eyes to the most beautiful fucking sight.

Amara pulled back, the head of my cock bumping her lip, and grinned before sinking down as far as she could go.

"Oh, fuck, *preziosa*."

I'd thought I was still dreaming, buried deep inside my girl, trying to stay asleep. I should've known. Nothing compared to the real thing. Gripping her hair tighter, I watched her swallow my cock over and over like it was made for her mouth.

"That's it. Just a little more."

She gagged as my piercing hit the back of her throat, and I loosened my hold to offer some reprieve. But Amara dug her nails into my thighs and pushed harder, forcing tears from the corners of her eyes.

"Look at you, baby. Your first time, and you're taking me so good."

Blinking away the moisture, she smiled around my shaft, fisting the root as she sucked and pumped in perfect rhythm. I was so fucking enthralled—her lips, her throat, the goddess she was—that I hadn't even noticed she was naked. Her breasts were bare, nipples peaked and moving in time with every swallow.

"My beautiful girl." Releasing the headboard, I reached for her and rolled a nipple between my fingers, squeezing until she groaned around my cock. "I don't know what good I did in this life to deserve you, but fuck me, I'd do it all over again, just to have you like this. Forever."

She paused, nails biting into my flesh, and let my aching dick pop from her mouth.

"Forever?" she whispered, tongue gliding along her swollen bottom lip. She crawled up my body on all fours and kissed me. "Remember when I said sometimes we don't know what we're asking for?"

I hauled her back to my mouth. "I've never been more sure of anything in my life."

Her eyes welled again, and I decided the only time I'd ever accept her tears was when she had a mouthful of my cock or when they were happy ones lighting up her gorgeous face.

"I need you, Santi," she whimpered, pulling my fingers to her lips and sliding them inside. "Fuck me."

"Then sit that sweet cunt down, *preziosa*."

A sharp hiss vibrated in her throat as she sank down and stretched around me. Every inch inside her was as close to paradise as I'd ever get.

"I could die here with you," I growled, thrusting until she pushed against my piercing. "Ride me, baby. I'm yours."

The sight of her, impaled on my cock, tits bouncing, curls wild in every direction, and my fingers deep in her throat, had me ready to bust.

"I can't get enough of you."

Slipping from her mouth, I wrapped my hand around her neck and watched her reaction as I tightened my grip. Amara closed her eyes and pressed her palms against my abs, rocking her hips in tight, desperate strokes. She was close. Her head fell back, a cry ripping from her lips when the metal hit her sweet spot.

"Fuck...Yes, Santi," she panted, collapsing over me.

I tangled my fist in her hair and caught her hooded gaze.

"I'm a greedy bastard, and I want more. Again."

She let out a breath, and a slow smile curved her lips. "I'm yours."

"I know." Flipping us over, I swept her hair to the side, kissing down her spine until I reached her ass—and bit.

She let out a playful yelp and twisted to look at me.

"Do it again," she demanded.

There wasn't a damn thing in this world I'd deny her. Whatever Amara wanted was hers. If it was within my power to give, steal, kill, or burn, she'd have it. Something as simple as biting her plump little ass was a fucking privilege. Hell, I'd kiss it, and one day, I'd fuck it, too.

My teeth sank into her with a touch more pressure, and she moaned, rocking forward onto her hands and knees. I reveled in the sight of her, dripping, desperate, and perfectly wrecked. My girl. My addiction.

Running a knuckle along her swollen clit, I grinned when she jerked.

"I want to try something," I said, sliding two fingers inside her.

She whimpered into the sheets.

"What? Anything." Her voice was strangled, breathless, her hips chasing my hand.

I fisted her hair, lifting her face from the mattress.

"I want to hear you." Another finger joined the others, curling up inside. "Tell me how hard." I gave her cunt a light slap, and she sang for me. "How fast." Two more taps.

She shook her head, whispering my name. "How good it feels."

Lowering my mouth, I licked from her clit to where she dripped, letting my tongue linger, then kissed the dimples above her ass.

"Are we clear?"

Amara nodded.

"Words, *preziosa*."

"Crystal. Now hurry up and fuck me, Santi."

I chuckled and wrapped my fist around my aching cock, painting my initials on one of her ass cheeks with the pre-cum leaking from my slit.

"Perfect. Mine."

When I slid inside her, I tipped my head back and closed my eyes as the heat of her walls swallowed me inch by inch.

"More," she moaned, easing back. "Deeper. I want to feel you damn near in my throat."

A hearty laugh rumbled in my chest, and I obliged my girl, pushing until her body took as much as it could handle. I pulled back and drove into her again. Amara gripped the sheets and arched her spine, letting me sink deeper.

"God, just like that. Faster."

Grinning, I leaned forward, lips brushing her shoulder.

"Touch yourself. Feel how wet that sweet cunt is for me, Amara."

Her teeth parted against her knuckle as the other hand drifted between her thighs, fingers grazing the underside of my cock.

"So wet...so fucking good," she murmured. "Harder."

Her knees slid forward with every thrust, body giving out little by little beneath me.

"I wish you could see how beautiful we look together."

"Deeper," she whined.

My fingers dug into her hips as the pressure in my balls

blazed up my spine. I felt myself unraveling with every clench of her pussy.

"You were made for me, *preziosa*."

"Show me. Fuck me like I'm yours and only yours."

My pace slowed, but the power behind each stroke surged, knocking her hands off the edge of the bed. Amara groaned my name, scrambling to regain her hold, but I didn't need her help. I drove her down onto my cock, her cunt sucking me in deep, my piercing knocking inside until she cried out in Portuguese, then went limp, head hanging over the side.

Growling, I emptied every last drop, filling her to the brim until I was slick with us both.

———

After the first ten minutes of admiring her sated smile and how her wild hair framed her face, fanned out like an angel's halo against the sheets, I knew I was gone. But after twenty, there was no question.

Signed, sealed, and fucking delivered.

I loved her.

Amore.

Love.

I should've been terrified, running out the door, trying to convince myself I was wrong. Amara was beautiful, and of course, I wanted to spend time with her, fuck her, put her on my arm and show her off to the world. I did. I wanted all those things.

But I also never wanted to let her go.

"What are you thinking about?" she asked, touching my face.

You.

I love you.

"About how much I'd love to stay here with you and forget that the world, the club, and my cousin still exist." I tucked her into my chest. "Thank you for yesterday. Leni can be a little hot and cold—unpredictable—but deep down, she has a good heart for the people she cares about. I think you two could be good friends."

Amara seemed pensive for a moment. "She was...nice."

I let out a burst of laughter. Taking advantage of my momentary vulnerability, she flipped us over and sat on my abdomen, arms folded across my chest as her curls fell around us like a veil.

"I'm sorry," she said, attempting to push the sex-tangled mess over her shoulders.

I caught her wrist and smiled.

"Leave it. This hair is one of my favorite things about you. One of many."

As much as I wanted to scream it to the four corners of the world, to tell her how much I loved her, I knew she wasn't ready yet. She might think I was crazy. And maybe I was. It had only been just over a month since that night she bewitched me. But I didn't need a calendar to dictate my heart. Not when it had come back to life with the sole purpose of loving her.

"Santino, can I ask you something?"

I smoothed my hands down the curve of her back and over her ass, giving her cheeks a light tap.

"Of course."

With a small laugh, she rested her head on my shoulder and gently traced the scar on my sternum.

"Do you know Valentina's parents?"

"I've heard of them but never met them. Why? Because Derek was part of Ares?" She nodded but didn't say anything. "Derek and his brother spared Maksim's life a few years ago. Killed off most of his family."

"Wow," was all she said, and I felt her tense.

"Yeah. And you, *preziosa*...did you know him? Is that why you're asking?"

For a moment, I thought she might say yes, her silence felt like a confession, but she shook her head.

Silas had confirmed what I'd already known and suspected.

Amara Carvalho was a woman without a past or paper trail beyond the last few years. But I'd kept my word and stayed quiet about her former ties to Ares.

Silas and I had been brothers for over a decade, and hiding something that vital from him felt wrong. But my love and loyalty for this woman ran deeper. My chest tightened at the realization of just how far I'd go to protect her. I only hoped that one day, she'd open up to me so that my love could extend to every part of who she was.

"Someone's calling you," she murmured, pressing kisses down my chest.

"You expect me to give a damn about a phone when I've got you here like this?"

Amara slid her tongue lazily across my skin, eyes lifted to mine from beneath her lashes. "It could be important."

"More important than my girl leaking all over me? No."

A flush of pink colored her cheeks as she lifted her hips and peeked between us, where my cum slid out of her and over my pelvis.

"Shit," she whispered, a small panic flickering as she tried to maneuver off me.

But I wrapped her in a bear hug.

I love you.

"That's beautiful. That's you and me."

She rested her forehead against mine, her curls fanning around us again, giving the illusion that we truly were in our own little world.

Maybe we'd stay a few more days. What harm would it do? Work could wait.

"It is," she whispered, kissing my chest.

My cell vibrated just as I rolled us over, and Blaise's name lit up the screen.

Paranoia gripped me when I noticed it was his fourth attempt to reach me. Only an emergency would warrant repeated calls while I was out of the office. Ice worked its way down my spine as I imagined the worst.

"Something wrong?" she asked, catching the shift in my expression.

"I think so."

I snatched the phone from the nightstand, and he answered on the second ring.

"They're dead," he exclaimed before I could get a word in.

"Who?"

"Two more dancers...and Ash."

THIRTY-SIX

Amara

"Amara, this is about your safety."

The elevator was taking its sweet fucking time to reach my floor. Not that it would matter, Santino hadn't let up since that call from Blaise. The entire four-hour flight had been a battle over whether I'd stay with him or go back to my apartment. One or two nights was one thing, but indefinitely?

No.

I wasn't ready to take that step, especially under the pretense that I'd be *safer*.

I'd been a helpless victim once.

I vowed never to be that woman again.

"How many ways do you need to hear me say I'm staying?"

"You're being stubborn, *preziosa*. Three of our dancers are dead. This isn't a coincidence."

Santino dropped my suitcase and boxed me in, his arms circling my waist, caging me into the corner.

"If something were to happen to you…I can't have that."

I gripped his collar. "I understand. I do. But—"

"Please don't give me that bullshit that you can take care of yourself."

My face tightened. "I *can*. I *have*."

"You're not bulletproof, Amara." He cradled my face in his palms, gentling his tone even as his words struck hard. "I know this is retaliation, but I can take anything. Fuck the business, nothing matters to me except *you*. And the only way they can hurt me, destroy me, is through you. I'd die before I let that happen."

Now wasn't the time for butterflies or the simmering heat his words always triggered but even pissed off, this man *still* got to me.

Which only strengthened my resolve.

"Hiding isn't the solution."

"You've been hiding for years."

Low blow.

He wasn't wrong, but it still stung like hell.

I take back the goddamn butterflies.

I broke out of his hold and snatched up my suitcase just as the elevator doors finally opened.

Santino slammed his fist against the railing. "Damn it, Amara."

"Is there a problem?"

Detective Braga, always showing up at the worst possible moment, extended his arm to block the doors from closing, his gaze shifting between us, sharp and intrusive.

"Everything's fine," Santino replied, voice like a blade. He stepped forward to grab my suitcase, but I yanked it back.

"I'll see you tomorrow night, Santino," I said, firm and with finality, meeting the betrayal in his eyes.

Call it pride or fear, but I needed space to think.

Even if it hurt him.

Even if it hurt me just as much.

"Amara, please—"

His frustration vibrated in his voice as he stepped in again, still holding tight to the handle.

"I believe she's calling it a night, Mr. Leone."

Santino steeled his shoulders, ready to charge the detective, but I stepped between them and cupped his face.

"Santi, give me tonight to think it over. That's all I'm asking. I promise."

His eyes hardened as they moved between me and Raymond. "Just tonight."

Santino exhaled, curling his fingers into my shirt and dragging me into his arms. "You call me if anything—do you hear me?"

Aware of the detective still watching, I pressed my lips to Santino's and gave a small smile.

"You too. It's not just about me."

With one last kiss to my forehead, he stepped into the center of the elevator and pinned Braga with a cold, lingering glare as the doors slid shut.

"Amara, is everything all right?"

Braga's voice cut into the silence.

"I spent all of last night and into the early morning at the scene a block from Illusion. Two more women from your club have been murdered."

"I heard," I said, turning toward my unit. "Look, it's awful what happened, but I just got into town and I'm exhausted. And—"

"Where did you and Mr. Leone fly off to, if I may ask?"

"Frankly, with respect, I don't think that's any of your business."

I set down my suitcase and fumbled through my bag for my keys.

"And I respectfully disagree."

I froze, waiting for the other shoe to drop.

"I informed Mr. Leone that I needed him to remain close for further questioning."

"We answered all your questions. There's nothing more to discuss."

"Three more of his employees are dead. So again, I disagree."

I twisted the knob and cracked the door open, officially done with this conversation.

"And curiously," he continued, "a colleague of mine in Philadelphia mentioned a case—strikingly similar to the one here a few weeks back. Strange, isn't it?"

His words caught me off guard. My heart skipped.

No. Don't show it.

Whatever he suspected, it couldn't touch me. Not without proof.

Serial killers were creatures of habit, leaving signatures. I'd always made sure to cover my tracks, my victims shared nothing in common except their cocks and their vile addictions to sexual violence.

Details that didn't always surface in investigations, especially in a city like Miami, with its murder rate and overworked PD.

But I'd slipped. I'd let emotion override logic, and carved the same phrase into each of them.

Death is mercy.

My pulse spiked as I turned back to face him. He was watching closely. Too closely. His graying brows twitched as he read every flicker of expression.

But suspicion alone wasn't enough. He had no evidence. I was just his neighbor, the woman who'd saved his son.

"Like I said, I'm exhausted. And as tragic as all of this is, it has nothing to do with me. Seems like confidential police business anyway."

The air changed. It was subtle, but sharp. Something shifted in his stance. He wasn't just a nosy neighbor anymore. Detective Braga was dangerous. And he knew far too much.

We stared each other down, neither one blinking.

"*Papai!*" Thiago's small voice echoed through the hallway as he bolted toward his father, an older woman scrambling to catch up. "*Papai! Papai!*"

Braga scooped the boy into his arms mid-air and turned him away from me.

The gesture burned red-hot in my chest.

Did he really think I'd hurt a *child?*

If I'd wanted to, I would've done it that night, when I found his son wandering alone in the hallway.

"I'm so sorry, Mr. Braga. Thiago said he heard your voice, and next thing I know, he's dragging a chair to the door."

Braga waved her off without looking. "It's fine. I was just heading inside." He met my eyes again, jaw clenched tight. "Have a good night, Amara."

This was a new threat, possibly worse than Luca.

But he wouldn't shake me.

"Maybe you should secure your door a little better."

I stepped inside and locked the door behind me, leaning against it with a thud. Santino had been right. Laying low was the smart play.

I couldn't afford to get caught with my ass out.

"*Shit.*"

I startled and jerked, slamming my back against the wall when I felt a brush of fur on my leg. Thank God it was only Phoenix...

Phoenix?

Adrenaline kicked in as I stared at my cat, trying to figure out why he was here instead of with Cambri.

"Phoenix, what the hell are you doing here?" I frantically scanned the room and flipped the light switch.

Darkness.

I kept flipping it, as if doing it enough times would magically trigger the electricity.

"It won't work."

Every ounce of breath left my body when I processed the intrusive male voice.

Fucking Luca.

"I suggest you keep still and think twice about what you reach for, or I'll put a hole through that pretty face."

He stepped out of the shadows, the barrel of a suppressor aimed at me.

I blinked rapidly, struggling to comprehend that he was in my home, threatening my life.

"What the fuck are you doing here?"

"Well, imagine my disappointment when I found out you flew out of town with my cousin...and didn't extend an invite. That's foul, Amara, considering *I* introduced you."

If Luca were smart, he'd keep his distance. But I knew him well. I was counting on his stupidity and ego to bring him closer and get him killed.

Phoenix circled my legs, and in an instant, a horrifying realization struck.

"Where is Cambri?"

Luca laughed outright and leaned back against the couch.

"There it is. Asking the important questions."

"If you hurt her—"

"Cambri and I go way back. I wouldn't hurt her...yet. But how else am I supposed to get you to cooperate if I don't have a bargaining chip?"

His words brought no comfort. Luca couldn't be trusted. If Cambri were fine, she would've called me. He was holding her somewhere. And I wasn't stupid enough to believe he'd just let her go.

With a hand hovering over my knife, I challenged him.

"You're pushing your luck," he warned as his aim steadied.

"Why are you doing this? You and I have never had issues."

"Correct. Until you co-signed my cousin kicking me out of *my* goddamn establishment. Santino humiliated me in front of some of my most affluent clients." He stepped closer. "And I didn't have to be a genius to figure out why. He's got his sights set on you."

Luca's face twisted with disgust. "A fucking stripper."

He was dead.

The pop of a bullet filled the air the same second I launched my knife at his face. I ducked, expecting another shot, but the room fell silent—except for Luca's gurgling and shallow, ragged breaths.

I crawled toward him, guided by the faint glow of a nearby outlet and the growing pool of blood below the blade jutting from his neck.

"Where is she?"

"Fuck...y-you."

Blood sprayed my face when he spit at me and grabbed for my throat, but only managed to fist a handful of hair.

I pried open his fingers. "Tell me what you did with Cambri, or I'll cut off your dick."

Laughter bubbled from his reddening mouth, forcing more blood from the wound. "He knows..."

Even dying, the bastard was playing games. I slammed my fist into his chest, and his body jerked violently inward.

"Who?"

Bloody gurgles muffled his response, but he kept trying to speak until one word came through, shockingly clear.

"A-Athena."

The last syllable was whispered on the breath of a death rattle.

I collapsed on my ass, eyes wide and unfocused as I processed the name I hadn't heard spoken out loud in years.

No.

She's dead. Athena is dead.

"How do you know that?" I crawled back toward Luca's lifeless body and pounded on his chest. "Who told you?" His face twisted under the sting of my backhand. "Tell me!" I cried, throttling his limp frame by the shoulders, his head crashing against the hardwood.

Over and over, until it was all red.

Everything was red.

Tears filled my eyes, distorting the mangled man in front of me. I slumped forward, resting my head against his still chest, sobbing as emotions ravaged my heart.

Luca couldn't have known who I was unless he'd been in contact with someone from my past.

I patted his front pockets, searching for a phone. Nothing. I flipped him over. Still nothing.

"We need to get out of here, Phoenix. We need Santino."

Staggering to my feet, I ran to the bathroom, tore off my shirt, and shoved it under the cold spray. I scrubbed down my arms with it, watching pink-stained water swirl in the sink. I kept scrubbing until the water ran clear.

The mirror called to me, taunted me, daring me to look, to catch a glimpse of *her*.

I shook my head and squeezed my eyes shut.

"No. Pull it together."

I bolted out the door, threw on a sweater, and scooped Phoenix into my arms. The hallway was silent. Vacant.

Good.

I sprinted past Detective Braga's apartment, praying he hadn't heard the chaos inside my unit. I half-expected his door to swing open, for him to step out and catch me with blood still caked in my hair. There'd be no talking my way out of it then.

And I'd be left with only one option.

It was one thing to dispose of predators, men who didn't deserve the air they breathed. But Braga was innocent. How could I condemn his little boy to a life without a father, when he'd already lost his mother?

I'd been left alone in this world. And if my story was anything to go by...I'd be no better than Ronan.

God, Ronan.

Could he be Luca's contact?

I flew down each flight of stairs, pulling my hoodie over my head as I neared the lobby, then slipped through the doors and into the parking garage.

Just a few more steps.

Relief surged through me when my car came into view. But before I could reach it, I was tugged backward into a hard chest. Phoenix dropped to the concrete with a startled yowl. I drew my knife and twisted, ready to drive it into someone's jugular.

THIRTY-SEVEN

Santino

I caught Amara's wrist when the blade was just inches from my face. Her other fist slammed into my chest as I wrestled the knife from her grip. She didn't recognize me, and fought me like a wildcat, punching, slapping, and landing a brutal knee to the groin that made me double over. Still, she aimed to stab me at all costs.

"Amara, stop! It's me."

She froze.

"It's just me, *preziosa*," I whispered, gently pushing the blood-stained hair from her eyes.

The knife clattered against the concrete with a sharp clang as she gasped, arms suddenly flinging around me. She buried her face into my chest.

"What happened?"

Her sobs grew louder, and the more I took in her disheveled appearance, the harder my heart pounded.

"Who did this?" My voice cracked as I fought to steady the tremble in my hands.

"Luca," she murmured against my shirt.

Blinding rage surged, eclipsing all rational thought.

I pulled away just long enough to unholster my gun, chambered a round, and started for the door.

"He's dead," she said, her voice flat, robotic.

"Are you sure?"

"I'm sure."

Amara's watery nod gutted me. I had to get her out of here. If there was one thing I knew about Luca, it was that he never moved alone. Someone would come looking for him.

Tucking her under my arm, I led her to the car. She was resilient, no visible wounds, thank God, but clearly in shock. Whatever had gone down had left her rattled.

I cursed under my breath. Had I been more insistent about her coming home with me, instead of giving in...she'd be in my bed right now, crying for a different set of reasons.

The only upside was that bastard was dead.

Phoenix leapt into her lap, and that's when it hit me.

"Cambri?"

Amara shook her head slowly, her gaze fixed on the windshield, squeezing the spotted cat tighter to her chest. I rounded the hood and got in, keeping quiet until we'd put several blocks between us and her building. She flinched slightly when I reached over and rested a hand on her thigh.

"Baby, whatever happened back there...it's over. You're safe now."

"You were still here," she whispered, squeezing my hand.

"Of course I was. You think I'd just go home and climb into bed? Blaise was posted outside your building. I was waiting in the garage, keeping watch. That's when I saw you running."

Her smile was faint, shaky. Tears gathered in her eyes as she looked at me, voice hoarse.

"Thank you."

———

Amara was mesmerized by the arsenal of weaponry I kept in the special storage room adjacent to my garage. Most had been brought over from my home in Naples; others I'd acquired through connections with Silas and Ares.

Even with Luca dead, it was clear he hadn't worked alone. There was no telling who he'd paid off to cause so much damage in such a short time. We shared blood, but our family knew the kind of man he was—a coward and a fool, one whose own father hadn't trusted him to take over the business.

An inventory check was in order.

I moved in slowly, and pulled her close, careful not to startle her, especially after everything she'd just been through. Amara's hands came up over mine, and I nuzzled into her slightly damp hair, grateful she was safe.

As much as I'd wanted to stay glued to her side, I'd given her space to come down from the adrenaline high without pressing her for details. But now, we needed to talk. We needed a plan.

"Talk to me."

She leaned into my chest.

"Physically, I'm okay. And I wasn't afraid of Luca...just caught off guard."

"Then what happened? Why were you so shaken up? Did he try to—"

"No. I never let him get that close." She twisted around to face me. "But he has Cambri. Or maybe she's already dead—I don't know. And I don't know what to do, Santi. We need to find her. I can't just leave her to whatever fate he's condemned her to. I owe her my life."

Where most would expect tears or a trembling voice, hers held nothing but fury and an unwavering determination to find her friend. Admirable, yes. But it broke me to see her clinging to that illusion of invincibility. She wasn't made of steel. She was flesh and bone. And she meant everything to me.

"I'm working on it. I've made some calls. But Luca's been off the radar since that night with Andretti. Was there anything he said, anything at all that could help?"

Maybe she didn't mean to, but the question struck a nerve. Amara stiffened and averted her gaze, her fingers bunching into the fabric of my shirt.

"No," she nearly whispered.

I lifted her chin with the tip of my finger, coaxing her gorgeous eyes to meet mine. "You can tell me anything. You know that."

She shook her head. "There's nothing to tell. This is about us —his way of getting back at you through me. Just like you said."

I wanted to believe her, to believe she wouldn't hold back information that could put her life at risk, but it was clear something had shaken her to her core. Whatever it was, it probably tied back to her past. But after everything she'd been through tonight, I'd let her sleep on it and press her in the morning.

"We're going to find her, *preziosa*. I promise. But in the meantime, are you hungry?"

The tension in her face softened, whether from the mention of food, the shift in subject, or both.

She nodded. "A little."

I chuckled and scooped her up, a plump ass cheek in each hand. "You up for some panna cotta? It's a dessert, and it's almost as sweet as you. Almost."

Her fingernails raked the back of my neck, sending a shiver and a jolt of heat straight to my cock, nearly tempting me into a detour to the bedroom instead of the kitchen. But I'd have my favorite dessert soon enough. For now, I wanted to introduce Amara to the one that had just been replaced.

After setting her on the countertop, I pulled open the refrigerator and scanned the shelves until I found what I was looking for.

"Giada keeps these stocked for me."

"Looks like cream."

"Precisely. Only tastier." I brought a spoon to her mouth, and she opened up for me.

"It's delicious."

I knew her emotions were still raw, so I wasn't disappointed by her lack of enthusiasm. Just sharing this part of me with her was enough.

I set the spoon down, not wanting to push her, but she reached for it and scooped up some more.

"Giada makes the best coffee and dessert?" she asked, taking another spoonful and bringing it to my mouth. I didn't hesitate.

"Tell her it's exquisite."

"You can tell her yourself in the morning. She'll be happy to meet you."

Amara leaned in and swiped her tongue over my bottom lip, savoring the bit of cream she'd just licked off.

"You had a little something."

A grin spread across my face as I framed hers and tugged her closer. "I think you do, too."

I'd never been a fan of kissing. The act was intimate—too intimate. A kiss felt hollow if there was no connection beyond a quick or decent fuck. But with Amara, it was different. Her lips were addictive, her tongue a temptation. I'd never tire of tasting her.

"*Mia preziosa...*" As I met her gaze, I was mesmerized. The fixture above us lit her eyes just right, making both striking colors sparkle beautifully.

"I love you."

The words slipped past my lips before I could stop them. But once they were out, I didn't regret them for a second.

"I love you, Amara," I repeated with a smile, savoring the way the words felt in my mouth.

"Santi..." she whispered, fresh tears sliding down her flushed cheeks.

"I do. *Ti amo, bella.* Stay with me."

Luca had come terrifyingly close to taking her from me. Life hung by a fragile thread. I knew that better than anyone. Living without Amara wasn't an option.

"I don't want you to say it back...not yet. Only when you're ready. But I need you to know how precious you are to me. That I'm yours in every way you'll have me." I kissed her, tasting the tears on her lips. "And you're mine, Amara. Only mine."

I stared at Cambri's text thread until my eyes crossed and the words blurred together, shattered by her last message.

> Cambrie: Love you, babes.

No response.

Guilt clawed at my insides when I realized I couldn't remember why I hadn't responded. Maybe I meant to and forgot, distracted by Santino, and by meeting Helena and Silas the night before our flight back to Miami. Two weeks had passed since I last heard her voice. Ten days since her body was found in the trunk of an abandoned car.

Luca. That goddamn bastard. She'd been dead from the beginning.

I didn't know what was worse, never finding her, or uncovering her horrific fate. I prayed to whatever god might listen that she hadn't suffered before he put a bullet through her head.

My throat ignited, and the tears I'd shed every day since threatened to fall again. I'd been drowning in grief and consumed by guilt.

Today was my first time stepping back into Illusion. I hadn't come to work, just to escape the suffocating walls of Santino's massive home. I needed to breathe.

Time had passed in a blur, painfully slow and yet somehow fast.

Luca's death left me shaken in more ways than one. He'd covered his tracks well, almost *too* well. Santino and his men had tracked down his closest allies and used creative methods to coerce answers. But none seemed to know anything. If they had, they would've sung long before losing vital body parts.

The what-ifs were maddening. Who had given him the information? And had he told them where to find me?

With the threat of unknown retaliation, we were on high alert. We'd hired extra security, not just for us, but for the club and the girls as well. Things had been quiet, but an uneasy energy still clung to the air, like the calm before a cataclysmic storm.

I dabbed the corner of my eye where a single tear had escaped and sighed at my reflection. There would be time to cry into my pillow later tonight.

My dressing room still felt like a sanctuary at Illusion, dancer or not. I came for the peace it offered, especially when Santino busy.

"Amara!"

Two urgent knocks hit the door, followed by a woman's frantic voice. I opened it quickly.

"Oh, thank God. I think I'm going to be sick, and Mr. Leone asked me to bring drinks out to his special guests... *Oh!*" She covered her mouth as a gag burst up her throat. "I can't do it. And everyone else is busy. And I—"

"It's okay. I got it. Where are they?"

"Thank you!" She blew out a breath of relief—then immediately regretted it, doubling over and fanning herself.

"The drinks are at the bar. And they're outside in Cabana A."

"Go home, Amy. I'll cover your shift today."

Her smile barely formed before her eyes widened, and she bolted for the nearest bathroom.

I expected to find Santino in the lounge, but he must've returned to his office. Amy's order was on the counter—a tray with two drinks and an appetizer.

As I crossed the spacious main floor, my gaze drifted to the empty stage and pole, a space I hadn't touched in two weeks. A strange sense of nostalgia washed over me, even though I didn't miss a single second of being objectified by the men who frequented this club.

Pushing the front door open with my hip, I stepped into the South Florida sun and immediately regretted not putting my hair up. The humidity was about to wreak havoc on my curls.

Cabana A.

My sandals tapped against the wooden walkway as I approached the green awning, where two people, presumably a couple, sat with their backs to me. The man was applying sunblock to his companion's beautifully tanned back and shoulders. He'd taken off his shirt, revealing a heavily tattooed torso. They looked like your typical Miami couple.

"Hey," I called as I rounded their table. "I'm sorry it took so long. I'm filling in for—"

The storm.

Glass shattered at my feet.

Like a gut punch, all the air rushed from my lungs as I locked eyes with someone I never thought I'd see again. Familiar blue eyes. No matter how much time had passed or how much he'd matured—like Derek—I'd never forget that face. That liquid steel gaze, framed by the darkest lashes.

Kai.

"Athena?"

I took off running before I could think. Emotions hit me from every direction. Maybe I imagined it. Maybe he wasn't really here.

But he'd said her name.

"Athena, stop!"

Again.

His voice was a blade straight to the heart. Part of me wanted to turn back and run to him. But it hurt too much.

Facing Kai meant facing my past. Facing *her*.

And she doesn't deserve to come back.

She was too weak.

That's why she's dead.

I crashed through the front doors, still sprinting, the world ahead of me a blur until I stumbled out of my sandal and nearly hit the floor.

Santino's arms caught me, hauling me upright in one swift, protective move.

His eyes darkened, his jaw tight at the sight of my tears. "*Preziosa*, who do I need to kill?"

I closed my eyes and slowly shook my head as more tears spilled over. But there was no time to explain. The double doors split open, and Kai stepped through with the woman beside him.

Instinctively, I clutched Santino's shirt, and that was all the reaction he needed. Shoving me behind him, he drew his gun and aimed it at my brother.

"You better talk fast."

The woman with Kai—his wife, the one from the portrait, stepped between them, gun already drawn, her expression fierce.

"You better be faster."

Kai tried to drag her out of the line of fire, but she refused to move.

"Amalia, no," he said, locking her into a bear hug, shielding her from Santino's aim.

Security surrounded us, the metallic *clicks* of chambering bullets cutting through the air. Tension thickened like smoke beneath the red haze of lights.

"Athena," Kai said, his voice softer now. Blue eyes pleading. He stepped forward with his hands raised. "Please. It's me."

I wrapped my arms around myself, holding it all in—holding *her* back.

Santino looked between us and gave a sharp signal to his men. "Amara, you know him?"

But I didn't answer.

I was drowning in a vortex of memories.

"You ever think of leaving this life behind?"

"Someday, Blue."

Breathe.

"Promise me something. If you ever decide to go… take us with you."

"Why? You'd miss me?"

Pain.

"When Kai and Derek find out what you've done, they'll kill you."

"Who's going to tell them?"

Dead.

"I'm going to break you."

"Get on your knees and call me sir."

Home.

"I promise, Kai Bear."

The dam burst. A sob tore from my throat as I ran straight into his arms and cried.

Kai hugged me so tightly I could barely breathe. But I didn't want him to let go.

"Athena, why did you leave us?"

It was the first time I'd ever seen my brother cry. I sobbed harder and buried my face in his shoulder.

"What happened?" he asked.

I dragged in a shuddering breath. "Ronan."

Kai's body tensed, and he gently set me down, brushing back my tear-soaked curls.

"Ronan," he repeated, a growl building in his throat. I nodded, and his jaw clenched. "Are you okay?"

A new wave of tears welled up and slid down my cheeks as I shook my head.

"No," I whispered, staring through him now. "He killed her."

"Who?" he asked, confused.

My throat burned. It nearly closed off as I fought to say it.

To say *her* name.

My name.

Kai gripped my shoulders, gently shaking me. "Who, blue? Who did he kill?"

Our eyes locked. "Athena...Me."

THIRTY-NINE

Lost Without You – Freya Ridings

Kai had been silent for what felt like hours, staring into the void, his jaw clenched so tightly I feared he'd crack his teeth. My tears had long dried as I laid out the tragic events of my life, holding nothing back. He confirmed what I'd suspected—Ronan was on the run after betraying Derek and getting involved in shady dealings against the organization. No one knew exactly where he'd gone, but from the few times he'd resurfaced, it was clear he still had ties to certain members and former partners who'd helped him with untraceable funds.

"Say something."

Kai squeezed his eyes shut and shook his head, gripping my hands. "Athena—"

"Amara...I'm Amara now."

He nodded and pressed a kiss to my skin. "Amara, why didn't you reach out? Derek and I would've come for you, no question. We would've taken his goddamn head if we'd known." His blue eyes brimmed with tears. "I'm so sorry. We should've suspected something. Should've confronted him. Looked for you harder."

"It's not your fault. He lied, just like he said he would. He made you believe I'd left with Ezra, left the organization, and didn't want to be found."

Kai's gaze dropped to the silk cuffs around my wrists before meeting my eyes again. He didn't have to ask. I saw the questions and anguish in his face.

"It's okay," I whispered as his fingers hovered over the edge of the fabric.

When he peeled them back, he slammed a fist on the table and jumped to his feet, pacing like a caged animal. Then he launched the chair across the room with such force that one of its legs snapped on impact.

"He's dead. All of them. When I tell Derek..." He turned to me, the rage softening as he knelt and took my hands. "You have to call him, blue. He'll be so happy to hear from you."

My heart galloped at the thought, excitement buzzing beneath my skin.

"I met Derek's little girl."

"You met Vali? How? Where?"

I smiled at the memory. "I was in Pennsylvania two weeks ago...where I also met Silas and Leni."

"You were so close."

I nodded and brushed his cheek as fresh tears welled. "Look at you, Kai. You were always handsome, but now...you're all grown up." We shared a soft, teary laugh. "And your wife—she's gorgeous. I can tell she loves you. The way she put herself in harm's way...I'm so happy you boys found love. You deserve it."

Kai glanced toward the bar, where his wife sat with Santino, and smiled. "That's my heart. But I don't deserve her. The things I've done...the things I'd do for her, for my family, for *you*. No, I'm just a lucky son of a bitch."

He squeezed my hands tighter.

"What about Santino? I know he's Silas's friend. Is he

someone special to you? I mean, I'd assume so. He nearly killed me when he thought I hurt you."

We both laughed again. I turned to look at Santino, our eyes meeting across the room. I owed him the truth now that he knew my real name, now that he knew I'd lied about Derek and Kai.

My gut clenched with guilt. He was in love with a woman who, technically, didn't exist. Maybe that's why I'd never said it back. The words were always there, resting on the tip of my tongue, but uncertainty, fear, and shame kept them caged.

Still, despite what Santino must have been feeling, he gave me this moment with my brother. That had to count for something.

"He is," I said softly. "Very special."

A calm settled over us as we sat in silence, watching our respective partners. Then Kai reached out and slid his phone across the table. Derek's name flashed on the screen. My heart thundered, but I drew a steady breath and pressed the green button.

"Hey, brother."

The gravel in Derek's voice sparked fresh tears—but the good kind. I once read that tears looked different under a microscope depending on whether they were born of joy or pain. After a lifetime of sorrow, I had no doubt these tears looked like a winter wonderland.

"No, it's not Kai."

I heard a sudden shift, like he'd stood up or changed positions—then silence, until finally...

"Who is this?" His voice had a frantic edge, like he *knew*.

I smiled through the tears.

"Me, Derek...Athena."

———

The woman in the mirror wasn't whole yet, but the fragments of her, of who she used to be, were peeking through.

Had she been here all this time?

For all the reasons life had given me to rage and cry, today, I had two more to smile…and feel a little less broken.

Derek booked a flight to come see me. By tomorrow night, I'd have both of my boys in my arms. My heart was so fucking full it could burst.

"Hey."

A soft knock at the door followed an unfamiliar voice.

Kai's wife, Amalia, stepped inside my dressing room. She was stunning, and a friendly but slightly cautious smile colored her face.

"We didn't really get a formal introduction out there, so I thought I'd drop by."

"Of course. Please, sit."

She respectfully declined and remained by the door.

"You know, Kai and I have shared everything since our wedding. But he never told me he had a sister."

I wasn't entirely sure how to respond to that, so I waited for her to continue.

Amalia's eyes narrowed slightly, as if focusing on something unknown, drawing strength to speak.

"But I understand. My little brother passed away about a year ago. We were very close…"

Her smile didn't falter, but it trembled just enough to reveal the depth of the scar his death had left. "I don't talk about him much either. But…maybe I should."

Her pain was palpable, and I dared to touch her arm, offering comfort. "I'm sorry."

She nodded and dabbed at the corners of her eyes.

"Amalia, do you want to grab lunch tomorrow? I'd love to get to know the woman who stole my brother's heart. Kai is a gem. Anyone he loves as much as he does you is someone I want in my life."

Her red lips curved into a bright smile. "Of course."

Illusion had remained closed for the day, and I was ready to head home, as Santino and I had a conversation pending. I hooked my bag over my shoulder and turned toward the mirror, combing through my curls with my fingers.

"It's your pick," I said, twisting my hair into a bun high on my head. "I'll take you wherever you want to go."

"I'm not familiar with anything around here, so surprise me."

"Hmm, I think I know a spot. Do you like Brazilian cuisine?"

Amalia didn't answer.

I found her reflection in the mirror. The need to ask what was wrong was unnecessary. Her gaze was fixed on my back.

On my scars.

Flashes of emotion crossed her features: rage, sadness, compassion.

Our eyes connected, but before I could say a word, Amalia approached and rested her forehead against my back, embracing me from behind.

"My god..." she whispered, swallowing thickly. "I'm sorry."

I placed a hand over hers. "Me too."

FORTY

Santino

The shower cut off, but it was another fifteen minutes before Amara emerged from the bathroom, steam still curling above the door. Her beautiful gaze was red-rimmed and slightly puffy. She'd been crying on and off for most of the day. Reuniting with her brother had brought tears of absolute joy, but those emotions were gone now.

Sadness lingered on her features.

"Come here, *preziosa*."

She meant to sit beside me, but I pulled her into my lap and wiped a lone tear from her cheek.

"Talk to me."

With a shaky breath, she touched my face. "I'm sorry I lied to you. I'm sorry if you felt I didn't trust you enough to reveal my name...my ties to Kai and Derek. It wasn't about you. I didn't trust myself," she said, kissing the tip of my nose. "I thought spilling blood and changing my name was the only way to reconcile my past and save what was left of me. But now I know I've just been running from who I was, from who I *am*. And I'm so sorry, Santi."

"Do you think I'm upset?"

She shrugged. "Maybe. You deserved the truth."

I ran my thumb along her bottom lip and rested my forehead on hers.

"Baby, I could never judge your choices, or how and when you chose to face everything you've been through. I knew you'd open up to me when you were ready. And maybe your hand was forced today...But I'm a patient man when it comes to you. I'd wait an eternity."

She exhaled a heavy breath and shook her head.

"I never thought I'd meet someone like you. That someone could love me when I didn't even love myself. Why are you so good to me?"

"*Ti amo.* It's that simple. I've never loved another woman besides my mother."

She chuckled and wiped at her tears.

"You came along and buried yourself deep in my black heart."

Her lips were soft, her mouth sweet. No matter where we touched, I felt connected to this woman, like she'd always been part of me, even when I didn't know it. Like we were always meant to be.

"Giada made some fresh panna cotta."

Amara laughed against my lips and nodded, shifting to stand, but I scooped her up and carried her to the kitchen.

"I could get used to this."

"Good."

I poured myself a drink and served her dessert.

"Amalia and I are meeting for lunch tomorrow. She seems nice."

"Debatable, considering she pointed a gun at my face."

Amara laughed and smeared cream on my lips.

"Well, to be fair, I'd do the same if someone threatened your life."

"Yeah? You must like me or something."

With her hands on my cheeks, she licked the white frosting from my lips, her eyes darkening.

"Something like that."

"Is that all?" I asked, pushing her robe off her shoulders. It slipped down, pooling at her waist on the counter. I flicked her exposed nipple with my thumb, then kissed the other until both peaked into taut perfection.

Amara reached for my glass of whiskey, took a sip, and pinched a small ice cube between her fingers.

"I don't know that I deserve you..." she whispered, tracing my lips.

"Bullshit. You deserve the world. And I'm going to give it to you."

I sucked the cube into my mouth, then brushed its cold tip over her nipple. She moaned at the chill, her fingers curling into my hair.

"All I need is you, Santi."

I cupped behind her knees and tugged her closer, alternating between her breasts. The ice melted against her warm skin, trickling in rivulets down her stomach.

"I'm not going anywhere, *preziosa*," I murmured, licking up the droplets as the shrinking cube slipped from my mouth, straight between her legs.

Her white thong was already damp before the melting ice, and I decided wetter was better. Spreading her thighs, I dragged my tongue over the soaked cloth, trapping it between my teeth.

"I need you to make it so I can't walk," she moaned, pushing my face closer to her pussy.

She didn't need to tell me twice. My favorite dessert was spread open, dripping, begging to be devoured.

I slid the fabric down her legs, tossed it aside, and pulled her to my mouth.

Every flick of my tongue made her jolt and cry out my name.

Amara never looked more beautiful than when she was drunk with lust, on the verge of coming undone on my cock or in my mouth. It filled me with pride. With purpose.

I wanted to break her, erase every scar, and rebuild her again and again—until it was only me she remembered.

"How about we make this interesting?"

When I pressed a kiss to her swollen clit, her thighs shuddered around my head. She was two tongue strokes away from coming.

"Interesting?" she panted, yanking my hair. "Like me killing you kind of interesting?"

I laughed and flicked her once more before reaching for another ice cube and sucking it into my mouth. With an ass cheek in each hand, I pressed the cold cube against her with the flat of my tongue.

"Oh...my god," she whimpered, leaning back on her elbows, head dipping. "Maybe you'll kill me first."

The droplets mixed with her arousal, and I'd never been thirstier. I lapped and sucked until my head was locked in a vise between her thighs, and she was cursing and praying in Portuguese.

"Santi, wait," she cried, scooting back as I continued drinking down every drop.

Gripping her knees, I pulled her back to my hungry mouth and spread her open.

"I haven't had my fill yet. Let me enjoy my own little creamsicle."

Amara couldn't help but chuckle between hard breaths and pleas for mercy.

It wasn't until she came apart again and reached blindly for a fork that I swept my tongue over her clit one last time and released her legs.

"You...were...this...close," she breathed, collapsing on the counter.

"I'll risk your wrath every time, *preziosa*, if it means getting my fill and making sure my girl is properly tongue-fucked."

She flashed me her brightest smile, and I couldn't help but do the same—only I felt the heat of that gesture in my chest, my heart swelling as my love for her surged and spread through me.

"I love you," I said, scooping her into my arms and carrying her through the house.

"Santi, I need you to know..."

Her voice was low, and I hung on her every breath, waiting to hear the words forming on her tongue.

"When I told you that I didn't deserve love...I also meant I didn't think I could love anyone either."

If my devotion to her proved I had a heart, then the crushing weight of her words solidified it—because I felt the jagged pieces unraveling.

"I told you once I'll take whatever you give and wait as long as you need."

Another soft smile touched her lips.

"Then it's a good thing I want to give you everything."

My dying heart thundered, and I placed her on the bed.

"What did you just say?" I asked, climbing over her.

Amara's warm touch on my face made my eyes close until she spoke again.

"I love you, Santi." She kissed me softly, nipping at my lip. "*Eu te amo.*"

"Fuck," I said, diving in, deepening the kiss and our connection.

I shed my clothes, and she locked her ankles behind my back as I slid inside her. "God, I love you."

My mouth closed over her nipple as I coaxed the sweetest fucking sounds from her lips. I couldn't get enough of her hands in my hair, her nails dragging across my scalp.

But tonight, I wanted more. I wanted to devour her, leave her in utter ruin.

With one hand, I trapped both of her wrists and raised them tight above her head.

I bucked into her, and she tensed.

Worried I'd been too rough, I slowed the next thrust, trailing kisses up her trembling abdomen.

Trembling.

When I looked up at her face, it was like a bucket of ice water had been dumped over my head.

"Amara?"

She didn't answer. Instead, she thrashed violently and screamed incoherent words.

"Amara!"

"No, no, please stop!"

Her flailing worsened the tighter I tried to restrain her.bAnd like a fucking lightning strike, it hit me. I let go of her wrists and shot off the bed. Amara curled into herself and cried.

"I'm sorry," she sobbed. "I didn't mean to...I thought...I don't know what I thought."

Kneeling on the floor beside her, I reached for a curl that clung to her tear-streaked face, and she jerked away.

"No, baby, I'm sorry. I shouldn't have held you down like that. I didn't know."

She froze.

Then lifted her teary gaze. And in the next breath, she launched off the bed and into my arms, holding on so tightly it was almost painful.

But I'd bear it—every ounce of it—for her. Whatever she needed. There was no pain she could inflict that would ever hurt more than the raw guilt of what I'd done. Just like that, I'd become one of her monsters.

"I didn't know either," she whispered, looking at her wrists and brushing a scar. "I spent so long tied down, and when you..."

"I'm sorry," I rasped, cradling her face.

Her tears rolled over my hands.

"They ruined me."

And I wrapped her in my arms.

"*Mia preziosa*, I can't erase what happened. But I'll spend forever loving every beautiful inch of you," I murmured, her soft cries shaking against my chest. "Showing you how deeply you've carved a home in my heart—until their poison can no longer reach you."

Her lips pressed to my neck, and I felt her body relax, molding against mine.

Amara wasn't the peace I thought I craved. Her touch was rage, passion, and pain. Like the collision of two storms, her love fed my soul and set the ashes of my heart on fire.

FORTY-ONE

> AMALIA: Running 15 minutes behind.

> ME: I'll grab us a table outside. Take your time.

Pulling out a chair, I sat facing the beach and closed my eyes, enjoying how the warm breeze lifted and tousled my hair. Life hadn't felt this complete, possibly ever. Cambri's death still hurt my heart, and I knew I'd feel her loss for a long time. But I'd been mourning for so long that I decided to let go of the pain, just for today, and relish all the good.

Santino and I were in a new place in our relationship. I never thought I was capable of love, let alone worthy of receiving it. Yet he changed everything.

I love him.

Nothing could sour my mood today. Lunch with Amalia. Then dinner with my brothers...

"Miss Carvalho."

Detective Braga's voice was the equivalent of screeching tires on hot pavement.

I hadn't seen or heard from him since that night outside my apartment—the night I killed Luca. Santino's cleanup crew, disguised as just that, had removed the body and any traces of death or struggle. They'd said a neighbor had hovered nearby and tried to question them, but they brushed him off.

I had no doubt the nosy neighbor in question was Raymond. Just like I had a hunch his being here now wasn't a coincidence.

"Mind if I sit?" He slid the iron chair out and sat, without waiting for a response.

"Actually, I do. I'm with a friend, so if you don't mind..." I said, motioning to the aisle.

"No worries. This will only take a second."

"How did you know I'd be here?"

"It's my job to know."

I leaned my elbows on the table. "Bullshit. You have no right to follow me. And I don't think that's very wise."

His thick eyebrow arched. "Is that some kind of threat?"

"Really?" I asked, letting out a cynical chuckle. "You show up and intrude on my space, but I'm the one making threats? But if you feel threatened, Detective, maybe that's a sign you should watch your boundaries."

Braga leaned over the table, meeting my steely glare. "Is that what you said to Luca Leone that night in your apartment?"

My heart stuttered for a millisecond at his admission, but I quickly reined in my shock.

"I don't know what you're talking about."

He tapped a small metal object against the table's surface. "Don't you?"

"No."

Relaxing in his seat, he opened his palm, and a familiar piece of jewelry rolled in front of me.

Luca's ring.

The Leone family crest was unmistakable.

"Is this supposed to mean something to me?"

"How about you drop the act, Amara...or whoever you are?

I've looked into your past and found a lot of holes—fabricated paper trails. But I'm not even here for that."

I said nothing and sat back, already contemplating escape routes and how to dispose of this man if it came to that.

"You haven't been back for two weeks—"

"So what? I'm a big girl, Detective. I'm allowed sleepovers for as long as I want."

"What of Luca Leone? The man who broke into your place and never came out?"

I wondered if he could hear how heavily my heart thudded.

"Again, you've lost me. But I think we're done here."

His fist rocked the small table. "Sit. Down. No one has seen that footage yet but me, and if you want things to slide in your favor, I suggest you cooperate."

"Fuck you."

The detective's mouth curved into a crooked smile. "I don't find joy in this, but it is my job, Amara. Your boyfriend's little cleaning crew left this ring behind."

"You were in my apartment?"

"That's irrelevant."

"You fucked up. Unless you have a warrant, you can shove that ring wherever you think it'll fit."

Braga's dark eyes narrowed as he exhaled a sharp breath. "Luca Leone was human garbage. But he's just the means to an end. What you did—what I *know* you're capable of—can't go unpunished."

Gripping the table's edge, I opened my mouth to speak, but another voice strangled the words in my throat.

"Is this man bothering you, *mo stoirín?*"

Pain.

Every muscle in my body locked up. I froze, paralyzed with fear, as Ronan's presence loomed over me like a storm cloud thick with death.

I was wrong.

Kai wasn't the storm.

It was him.

For years, I'd fantasized about this moment—how I'd react when I finally had Ronan Cain in front of me. All the ways I'd make him pay. How loud he'd scream.

But none of those revenge-fueled scenarios played out.

Instead, I was trembling. Helpless. Terrified. Prey.

"Look at you, my beautiful girl," he said, touching my cheek while I stood there, too stunned to stop him.

Detective Braga read the room and shot to his feet. "Who are you?"

"Oh, how rude of me not to introduce myself."

In the time it took me to blink away my tears, Ronan pulled out a gun and shot the detective three times. He collapsed instantly, the table toppling over with him as screams and stampeding footsteps erupted around us.

Mouth gaped open, I turned to face the monster who'd plagued my dreams, his claws buried deep in my soul for far too long.

"Ronan...what are you doing here?"

His large hands clamped around my arms, yanking me to my feet. "Finally retrieving what belongs to me."

"No," I growled, reaching for my knife, but he twisted my arm and slammed it to my back, jamming the barrel of his gun against my face.

"Don't get brave now, Athena," he hissed. "I may have come all the way here for you, but don't make me do what I should've done the night you rejected me."

I fought to break free, but he tightened his grip. Pain shot through my shoulder, so sharp I swore I heard something *pop*.

"Kill me. I'd rather die than go with you. *Do it!*"

His rumbling laughter chilled me to the bone.

"That's cute. You making a scene."

He waved over a man I hadn't noticed until now. "Check his pockets."

With his boot, he kicked Braga's body, flipping him over. The man crouched, pulling out the detective's badge and brown wallet.

Even with the gun pressed to my face, even knowing Braga was about to turn me in, I couldn't stop the flood of anguish at the sight of him on the ground, wheezing, blood pooling fast beneath him.

He'd been a good man. Just trying to do his job and do right by his son.

"He's a cop."

"Interesting choice of friends."

"He has a young son," the man added, holding up a picture of Thiago.

Ronan's maniacal grin widened. "You've got two seconds to decide if you want to come with me peacefully...or we pay the kid a visit."

As if stirred to life by the mention of his child, Detective Braga groaned loudly and reached out, pleading for his son's life. His tear-filled eyes locked onto mine, and he shook his head weakly before losing consciousness again.

I would never be able to live with myself if Ronan hurt that little boy...or robbed his innocence the way he had with so many.

"Okay...okay," I whispered.

Ronan's lips feathered along my jaw. "That's my good girl."

Then, like the spineless bastard I always knew he was, he struck me across the head with the butt of his gun. Pain exploded through my skull, brief and searing, then I collapsed into darkness.

FORTY-TWO

Drip, drip, drip.

My head throbbed, each drop reverberating through my skull like a drumbeat. I pushed against the cold ground, trying to sit up, but my muscles were weak, and my thoughts were in a haze.

"Where am I?"

Water rolled into my eye, and when I swiped at the moisture, it blinded me. Confused, I kept wiping at the relentless dribbling, but my vision only worsened. Slowly, I pulled my hand away from my face and gasped, horrified by the blood staining my skin.

It wasn't water.

And like a freight train from hell, the memory of Ronan crashed into me.

"Oh God."

The room was dim, with just a bed in the corner, bringing with it a twisted sense of déjà vu.

"This can't be happening."

Staggering to my feet, I shuffled toward a window, only to find it boarded with thick plywood. I wedged a nail through a small crack, hoping for leverage, hoping to rip the plank free, but the moment I applied pressure, it lifted my nail bed. I groaned in pain.

I slid down against the wall. How had I let this happen again? How had he found me?

More blood rolled off the tip of my nose, dripping onto my lap. That son of a bitch. He hit me even after I'd complied. But I knew that's what he wanted, what he'd always wanted. For me to submit.

I ripped off my shirt and pressed it to the wound.

"Broken...never weak."

Ronan would never have power over me again. I would never be a victim. Maybe I'd die fighting, but I'd take him with me.

"Santi," I murmured, resting my head against the wall. "I'm so sorry."

The door creaked open before I could drown in regret. I jumped to my feet, ready for death.

But it wasn't Ronan.

A man stood in the doorway, a black patch over his left eye, and a sinister grin crawling across his face.

Sasha.

The nightmare intensified.

My stomach dropped, and air caught in my throat, choked by flashbacks of his torture.

"Well, well. Look who it is," he said, stepping inside and snapping the lock shut. "Just like old times, eh?"

I was just a girl back then, weak and at his mercy. But not anymore.

"Fuck you."

"Oh, still got that mouth on you, don't you, witch?" He stepped closer. I stepped back. "But I know just how to break you in."

As much as I wanted to bathe in his blood for what he'd done, the scars he'd left imprinted on my body and mind, I had to stay calm.

"Please, just let me go."

Sasha threw his head back and barked a harsh laugh.

"Surely you know I can't do that. And I don't plan to. You owe me. Boss took my goddamn eye when you slipped away."

He lifted the flap of his patch, revealing jagged skin fused where an eyeball should have been.

I backed up another step. "You took everything from me, but I owe *you?*"

"As they say, an eye for an eye. I just can't decide which one I want. Blue or brown?"

A few more steps and he'd close the distance between us and decide my fate.

"What do you think? Which one's your favorite? Because that's the one I want."

"Surprise me."

His grin twisted. "Perfect. Now, get on your knees and—Call. Me. Sir."

I reined in my emotions with a deep, steadying breath. He wouldn't win this time.

Dropping to my knees, I leveled my gaze and held out my arms.

"Come and get me."

"That's cute, but I'll play."

I'd spent years reliving those horrific moments trapped with Sasha in that room, tied to the bedpost, naked, broken. I'd strategized every possible escape, every word or action that could have changed things. But blaming myself for their depravity wasn't the answer. Getting even wouldn't erase what he'd put me through...but damn, it would feel good.

He hurled himself at me, expecting submission, but my eye was on the blade at his hip. At the last second, I sidestepped, snatched the knife, and without hesitation, drove the serrated edge through his lower back, then again into his side.

Sasha growled, falling to his hands and knees.

"Look at you, crawling for me."

"Oh, you bitch," he snarled.

"Wrong."

I tightened my grip on the bloodied knife and buried it to the hilt into his ass.

The screams of dying men had always satisfied something dark in me. But Sasha's fed my soul.

"You're my bitch now," I said, twisting the blade deeper until his moans turned to strangled gurgles and he collapsed into a pathetic heap.

I straddled his torso and yanked his head back, pressing the knife to his throat.

As much as I would've loved to give him a more colorful send-off, maybe take his other eye and even out that ugly face, time wasn't on my side. Ronan could've heard his screams and might be kicking down the door any second.

The first layer of skin gave way under the sharp edge. But as I pushed deeper through tissue, Sasha found one last ounce of fight.

He twisted and plunged a hidden blade deep beneath my rib cage.

Pain knocked the air from my lungs. I collapsed, blood pouring from my side as I clawed backward and braced myself against the wall.

Sasha's throat gurgled with wet, rattling breaths as he bled out in a pool of his own filth.

"Shit," I breathed, clutching my side. My eyes squeezed shut as a wave of dizziness crashed over me.

Was I dying?

Was this how it ended?

Santi...

No.

Shaking my head, I forced my eyes open and dragged myself toward Sasha's body. My hands trembled with urgency as I patted him down.

When I felt his cell phone in his jacket pocket, I nearly cried out with joy—if I'd had the strength.

Two rings. Then his voice. And in an instant, I felt at peace.

FORTY-THREE

Santino

I launched my chair, shattering nearly every screen on the wall. My girl—*my preziosa*—was gone. In the hands of a depraved son of a bitch. The same man who'd destroyed her.

The thought was unfathomable. I'd never felt so fucking hopeless.

I didn't know how I was still breathing. I kept trying to shut it off, to block out the horrific thoughts of what could be happening to the only woman I've ever loved.

Four pairs of eyes watched me, each bearing different shades of sorrow.

Derek stood stoic against the back wall, his wife beside him. He hadn't said a word since we told him what happened. Kai's wife sat in his lap, arms wrapped around him, whispering in his ear every so often. She'd been the one to find that fucking detective on the brink of death.

At least the bastard had served a purpose, able to utter one name before he died. But once Kai and Derek explained who it was, knowing it had been Ronan felt more like a curse than an advantage.

If I was condemned never to see her again...not knowing her fate would've been a mercy.

"We can't just stand around here," Derek finally said. "There has to be somewhere to look. We can't let this happen to her again."

Evangelina rested a gentle hand on his chest. "I called in a few favors. Some colleagues are checking surveillance in the area, but it could take hours."

"She doesn't have goddamn hours."

"I know," she murmured.

As if realizing he'd raised his voice, Derek's scowl softened. He pulled her into a hug and kissed her forehead.

I looked away and slammed my fist on the desk. My phone shifted slightly under the impact. I wanted to hurl it across the room, to send it flying to join the mangled chair and shards of broken glass.

But I clenched my fists and reeled it in.

What if she escaped? What if she reached out?

Whatever news came next would come from that godforsaken device.

"I'm sorry." Amalia stepped toward me. "I should've been there. Maybe if I—"

"*Mi reina*, don't do that," Kai cut in, pulling her back into his lap. "What if you had been? Ronan would've killed you on the spot. You think I'd survive that?"

Kai's eyes flicked to mine, then back to his wife. His words weren't meant to hurt, but they did.

I folded my arms and began to pace. And as if some higher power heard my plea, my screen lit up with an unknown number.

My heart stopped.

Everyone lurched to their feet.

"Amara!"

Agonizing silence stretched for what felt like an eternity...

Then her voice.

"Santi..."

I clutched the phone like a lifeline, my chest tight, afraid that if I let go, or even blinked, I'd lose her again.

"*Preziosa*, where are you? Please—tell me you're okay."

"I just...I needed to hear your voice."

Her words shook, barely above a whisper.

I swallowed the fire in my throat. "Tell me where you are. I'm coming to get you."

She tried to hide it, covering her moans with a frail chuckle, but my worst fear was slowly unfolding.

"Baby, are you hurt?"

"Thank you for everything. For loving me...I love you," she murmured, ignoring my question, and confirming the truth I wasn't ready to face.

I grabbed at my heart, feeling like it was caving in.

"Amara, stop talking like you're leaving me."

"You're the best thing that ever happened to me, Santi," she choked out, her cries no longer masked.

I punched the desk. "*Fuck that!* Tell me where you are."

"I-I tried, baby. I tried to come back to you. I'm sorry."

No. No. No.

My vision tunneled. This wasn't happening. I couldn't lose her. I refused.

"Amara, let me help you." My voice cracked, softening, pleading, begging for a glimmer of fucking hope. Didn't she know? Didn't she understand that she was *everything*? That my life meant nothing without her?

"It doesn't hurt anymore."

I squeezed my eyes shut, swallowing what felt like razor blades.

"Drop me your location. *Preziosa,* please."

Silence.

"Amara!"

Soft whimpers filtered through. "I can't, Santi," she sobbed. "There's too much blood...I can't make it work."

"*Fuck!*"

"I'm s-sorry."

"No, *preziosa*, I'm sorry. I couldn't protect you like I promised."

My voice broke, vision swimming with tears as I sank to the floor. Her silence tore through me...until she whispered one last truth. A truth worse than death.

"He's coming."

Fire raged in my chest, snapping me back to my feet. I'd waited my whole life for Amara, and I'd be *damned* if I lost her without a fight.

"Listen to me, leave the line open and hide the phone. I *will* find you, even if I have to tear this entire city apart. Do you hear me? I'm coming. Hold on for me, *preziosa*."

I set the phone down, my hands shaking, and ripped open the metal closet, tossing two black weapon bags over my shoulder.

"Kai, Evangelina—trace that call. Find her." "Derek, Amalia, get the cars."

FORTY-FOUR

Derek Cain

Way Down We Go - KALEO

We split into two separate cars as soon as we got Athena's location. Santino, Eva, and I took the lead, speeding through rush-hour goddamn traffic. The cell phone she used pinged at some remote home about an hour outside the city.

I'd offered to drive. As upset as I was about losing her again, mere hours after learning she was alive, Santino was in worse shape. Years ago, I'd been in his shoes. I understood the desperation, the hopelessness, the devastation of knowing the person who meant everything to you was in danger.

Reaching across the console, I took my girl's hand, letting her touch anchor me, like it always did when the demons from that time in my life began to stir.

I was dealt a shitty hand as a kid, but none of those atrocities compared to the anguish of not knowing if I'd ever see her again. My worst nightmares weren't of my past or the monsters who stripped me of my dignity for sport. No, the nights I woke up screaming, drenched in sweat, eyes stinging with unshed tears... those were the ones where my little girl faded into ash.

One moment. One heartbeat. One goddamn slip to the left or right could've erased my entire world.

My whole heart lived in two people. Losing them was an unfathomable reality.

"Derek." Eva's voice broke through, soft and grounding, as her nails feathered across my skin. "We're going to find her."

I nodded, lifting my eyes to the rearview mirror. Santino sat in the back, posture rigid, jaw locked tight. He stared out the window, but I knew he wasn't seeing a damn thing. His mind was where mine had once been—on Athena.

"Five minutes out," I said, catching his attention. We met in the reflection.

"Do we have a game plan?" Eva asked. "We don't know what we're walking into. This is *Ronan*. Whoever's been helping him all these years probably has their hands in this, too."

I veered onto an embankment, killed the engine, and laced my fingers with hers. "There's no time to strategize. Athena's hurt, she's—" I caught myself, aware Santino was listening. "We work with what we've got." When I paused again, Eva's eyes narrowed. "You're staying."

"I'm not."

"Angel," I said, gently, "like you said, we don't know what we're walking into. It's too dangerous."

"Derek, that's bullshit. Stop trying to sideline me like I can't handle myself."

"Eva—"

"No. Would you say the same to Amalia? Would *Kai*?"

The car door slammed as Santino got out and started down the gravel driveway.

I cupped Eva's face. "There's no time to argue. I know you can handle yourself, but Vali needs one of her parents. I won't let her grow up the way I did."

That was all it took, the mention of our girl.

"Derek Cain, I swear to God, if you die in there..." She fisted my collar and slammed her lips to mine.

Time stood still with Eva.

I'd long committed her taste to memory, the way she felt, the way she melted into my arms, but every second with her still felt like the first. Electric. Warm. *Home.*

"One hour, tops," she murmured against my mouth. "Go find her. Come back to us."

"I love you," I said, exiting the vehicle before regret could root itself.

Kai and Amalia followed Santino as I caught up.

"I pulled the blueprints," Amalia said, holding out her phone. "It's an old manor—pretty straightforward. Three floors and a basement. Except..." She zoomed in. "This back corner is unaccounted for. The floor plan's missing about a thousand square feet. Not a guarantee she's down there because if Ronan thinks no one will find him, he wouldn't go through the trouble of hiding."

Santino studied the sketch, picking up his pace. "So we split up."

"Yeah," Amalia confirmed. "Kai and I take upstairs. You and Derek head down."

"One problem," Kai said, pulling a black jammer from his jacket. "Once we're inside, it's a dead zone. No signal in or out. If anything goes sideways, get to Eva at the end of the road."

"Start it up," I told him. "As far as we know, he's unaware Athena placed the call. We don't want to show up on their cameras."

He gave a sharp nod.

"Point of entry?" I asked Amalia.

"Eastern side door. Used to be an employee entrance. Feeds right into the kitchen and pantry. Less likely to be occupied... unless someone gets hungry."

"Noted."

Santino suddenly stopped, the home just visible beyond thick shrubbery.

We followed and waited, expecting him to speak or move. Instead, he let his head drop, the gun slipping from his grip and thudding into the dirt.

"I've seen and done a lot of shit," he said, voice rough. "None of it fazed me. But I can't—What if she's..."

Amalia placed a hand on his shoulder.

"I can't promise she's alive. Hell, I can't even pretend we'll all make it out. But I refuse to believe this was all for nothing. That everything we've been through, everything that brought us here, just dies now. Look around. We're all connected somehow. Like a perfectly spun web."

"*Mi reina,*" Kai said softly, "there's only one way I'm walking out, with you by my side or not at all."

Amalia pushed through the bushes and started toward the house.

"You still owe me a honeymoon, Cain. You're not getting rid of me that easily."

My brother chuckled and followed behind his wife.

"Ready?" I asked, picking up the firearm and handing it back. "No matter what happens in there, Ronan is mine."

Santino chambered a round. "Only if I get a piece of him first."

By the time we caught up, Amalia was wrenching her knife from a man's throat. His body lay sprawled across the threshold of the side door she'd mentioned. Kai stood nearby, wearing a grin that told me exactly where his mind had wandered in that moment.

"He the only one?" I asked.

"For now." She shrugged, wiping the blade clean on the dead man's pants. "He picked one hell of a time to step out for a smoke. But this confirms Ronan's not alone."

We all nodded in agreement.

"Watch your six, brother," Kai said, clapping my shoulder.

"You too."

I watched them ascend a shadowed stairwell, vanishing around the corner just before the second landing.

Santino and I followed Amalia's floor plan to the cellar door, but just as we were about to enter, we spotted three men passed out in an adjacent living room. They were stretched out across sofas and chairs, snoring, surrounded by empty bottles. Drunk. Easy kills.

"We might as well take them out now," I said, holstering my gun and drawing my favorite blade. "No sense in leaving a problem behind us."

Santino grit his teeth and pushed ahead, grabbing the first man by the hair and slicing his throat clean through, damn near to the spine. Without hesitation, he ended the second while I took care of the third.

We swept through a second room, cleared empty closets, and pressed on toward the basement. The spiraling staircase led us down, but it didn't take long to realize that Amalia's blueprint was outdated.

The entire basement had been converted into what looked like catacombs, narrow, endless, and winding. A quick escape wouldn't be an option.

"We're just going to have to go for it," I said.

"Agreed."

Before we could start kicking down doors, a shrill scream sent us sprinting forward.

"Amara!" Santino's voice echoed off the walls, blending with Athena's.

A fork in the corridor forced us to pause and listen. Her cries were both a beacon and a punch to the gut. She was alive. Hurt, but alive. That was all we could hope for.

Another scream pulled us left, toward the only closed door in that hallway. In a desperate, synchronized motion, we fired at the handle and kicked it open.

Athena and Ronan whipped around. She was straddling his abdomen, wearing only a black bra and underwear. Her skin was stained with dried blood, the side of her torso wrapped in a haphazard bandage.

But in that split-second of distraction, Ronan ripped the knife from his shoulder, presumably the one she'd stabbed him with, and raised it, aiming for her chest.

Santino's bullet tore through his forearm and slammed into the wall. Ronan yelped like a little bitch and dropped the weapon.

"Santi!" Athena staggered to her feet, nearly collapsing as he rushed forward and caught her in his arms.

"Fuck, *preziosa*, I found you."

She smiled through the tears and kissed him. "I knew you would."

My gun never left Ronan. The bastard who once dared call himself my savior. My father. His time was up. He was finally at my mercy.

But first...

"Athena."

She turned to me slowly, tears already spilling over.

"Hi, Derek."

After all these years, my sister was back in my arms, in my life.

My stomach twisted when I thought of how easily we'd let her go, how quickly we believed Ronan's lies. That she'd left. That she didn't want to be found. Maybe I'd felt abandoned. Hurt. Betrayed by yet another person I loved. But none of it had been true.

Kai hadn't gone into detail. Just said she'd crawled out of hell, a nightmare Ronan had set into motion.

"I missed you," she whispered, wiping a tear from my cheek.

I held her gently, afraid to cause more pain than she'd already endured. Her face was bruised and swollen, her lip split open, blood covering most of her skin.

"You need to get out of here. Get checked out."

She gave me a teary nod.

"You know," Ronan rasped, propping himself against the wall, "I'd hate to break up such a beautiful little family reunion, but I've got a hole in my goddamn arm."

"You need me to even you out?"

He tipped his head back and laughed. "Derek, my pride and joy. It's been a while, huh? How's that pretty little wife of yours? And my granddaughter?"

I vividly remembered the last time I'd blown out a man's kneecap.

James fucking Ford.

Fatherhood had always terrified me. Every man I'd ever known had failed me, beat me, destroyed any glimmer of hope or love I'd once craved, until I became nothing more than a vessel and messenger of death.

Maybe I could've forgiven Ronan for some of his betrayals. But what he did to Eva warranted a death of the slow, brutal, and creative kind.

"Go," I said to Athena, easing her frail frame into Santino's arms. "Get to a hospital. I'll see you later."

"Running again, *mo stoirin?*" Ronan chuckled through the pain, now with a hole in his leg. "You promised me a torturous death all that—*blah blah*. Isn't that what you said?"

Her eyes locked with mine, and a grin broke through her battered face.

"Promises kept."

I sent her a wink as Santino carried her out of the room. Ronan called her name in a sudden panic.

"Begging doesn't suit you," I said. "You knew this would be your end. And here I am, keeping my promise...and the one I made to my wife. The woman you sold to that Belov motherfucker."

He hissed, dragging his mangled leg as he struggled to sit upright. "Come on, son. You gonna let pussy ruin our relationship?"

I holstered my weapon and slowly unsheathed my blade. "You're talking too much, and I haven't even started. Maybe I should take your tongue first."

"You goddamn ungrateful son of a bitch. I should've let you rot in that home. Maybe that's what you wanted—to stay on your knees and become a whore too."

I swallowed hard as pure, unfiltered rage made my hands tremble at his words, at the memories they pulled from the dark. Gripping the leather hilt, I brought the knife to his throat and pressed until his blood dripped down my forearm.

"Derek."

Eva.

"I told you to stay in the car," I ground out, my eyes still pinned on Ronan.

"Eva, dear. So nice to see you again." He turned that same sinister glare back to me and whispered, "I'll be bonded out by morning."

I clenched my teeth. I wanted to tear this man apart. But I didn't know if I could do it if she asked me not to. Evangelina had that power over me. And he knew it.

"Derek, I had to make sure you were okay," she said softly, placing a hand on my shoulder. "And one more thing…" She leaned in close to my ear and set me free with three little words. "Get him, baby."

An ear-to-ear grin split my face. "That's my fucking girl."

"Evangelina! I'll have your badge, you little bi—"

Ronan made a particularly delicious sound when I shattered his other knee.

"Keep fucking singing."

"Shit…shit…" he panted, sweat beading on his face, rolling down and mixing with spattered blood.

A masterpiece in the making.

"Now, Derek, you didn't think I'd let you have all the fun, did you?"

Helena.

"Oh, fuck." Ronan began dragging himself across the floor, his ruined legs leaving streaks of red like the slimy fuck he was. "No, not that cra—"

"Careful. You know how I feel about being called crazy," she said, cool and brimming with barely restrained violence. "Makes me especially homicidal." She reached behind her back and pulled out a fucking katana. "On second thought, I'd love the extra motivation, since I brought my new favorite toy."

Ronan's breaths were heavy, his eyes wide and bloodshot as they flicked between me and Helena. I could almost taste his fear. And it was glorious.

"Eva! Evangelina, call for backup! You're a goddamn cop... don't leave me here with these—"

His eyes bulged from their sockets when I wrapped my hand around his throat and squeezed.

"Don't address my wife." I glanced at Silas. "Take her upstairs."

The door shut behind them, and I turned my full attention back to Ronan. His face was purpling, on the verge of passing out.

"Derek," Helena said evenly. "Let that man breathe—for now."

I released him, and he dropped to the concrete floor, twitching before gasping desperately for air.

"I'm glad you finally decided to join us."

"I would've sliced off your ball sack if you'd done this without me." Her grin twisted into a scowl as her gaze settled on Ronan. "He owes me. Isn't that right?" she taunted, circling him.

"P-please..."

It was almost tragic, watching how far he'd fallen. From the once-respected head of Ares to a pathetic man groveling for his life.

He reached for Helena's ankle. Without hesitation, she swung her sword, severing his hand at the wrist. The louder he screamed, the wider her smile.

"That was for Silas." She took his other hand. "And that one too."

I folded my arms, watching in utter amusement as she hacked away until both his feet joined the pile of severed limbs. Blood painted the walls, pooling in every crack of the concrete floor.

While Helena and I never missed a chance to sling insults at each other, we'd settled our differences years ago. At the end of the day, we were family, and she was like another mother to Valentina. Knowing my little girl had women like her and Amalia to look up to...well, it helped me sleep a little better at night.

"Don't fucking fall asleep on me. I could listen to you scream all day," Helena teased, pressing the bloodied edge of her blade to his throat. "What was it you said to me once?"

"F-fuck...you," he grunted, his eyes rolling back, then forward again.

She grinned wickedly. "No, that wasn't it."

Her sword sliced clean through his nose, and his shrieks filled the room like a goddamn symphony.

"That's the one—where you squeal like a *pig at slaughter.*"

"My turn."

Ronan only had a few breaths left in him. As much as I wanted to take my time and watch him suffer until I was satisfied, it was time to retrieve what I came for.

"You have something that belongs to me." I gripped his neck, watching as his bleary eyes met with mine. "Tell my bastard father I send my regards."

The sound of my blade driving through his rib cage was almost as sweet as the strained howls that tore from his mangled mouth. He spasmed violently as I reached in, my hand closing around his still-beating heart.

For a moment, his green eyes pulsed with terrified awareness…and then faded.

"For Athena," I said, releasing him, his lifeless organ still in
my fist.

"For my *father*."

Helena's katana caught the falling corpse with a clean slice.
Ronan's severed head rolled to a stop between my feet.

EPILOGUE

Athena

**Rio de Janeiro, Brazil
Six Years Later**

Forever Young – David Guetta Alphaville, Ava Max

Warm gusts of wind rolled over the surrounding mountains, blowing my curls in every direction. I closed my eyes and savored the scent of the ocean below.

It smelled like home.

It wasn't my first time back in Brazil after meeting Santino and all the events that followed—changing my life for the better—but it was the first time we were here as a family.

All of us.

I swung my gaze to the infinity pool where Valentina and her partner-in-crime splashed around, pretending to be mermaids. Well, Remi preferred to be a shark most days. The four-year-old was the spitting image of her mother, but with eyes as blue as the ocean, just like Kai. A smile crested my lips as I watched my niece dance to the music from a nearby speaker, followed by an amused laugh when she tossed Maksim's glasses over the pool's edge. From the day she was born, that little girl had given her parents pure hell. And I loved watching my brother be the best father, be everything he never had.

He and Derek deserved every bit of happiness because, despite the cards life had dealt, my boys had crawled out on the other side of darkness. We all had, in one way or another.

We'd severed our ties to a world that had once demanded blood in exchange for our souls. Maybe we didn't get to come back from the things we'd done, and one day, we'd have to atone for our past. But for now, we couldn't ask for anything more. The world kept spinning, brighter, happier, and we'd enjoy the ride until it was over.

Little hands tugged on my skirt. I glanced down, and another set of baby blues stared back.

"Giovanni, up from your nap already?"

The one-year-old had been asleep on a cot under the cabana. I lifted him into my arms and kissed his button nose. Baby Gio was the perfect blend of Kai and Amalia, and his broad, gummy smile resembled his late uncle's.

"Where's your mom?"

He giggled at the mention of his favorite person and instinctively searched for her, his gaze landing on his cousin and sister in the water.

"Don't worry," I assured him, placing a hand on my belly, "in about three months, you'll have your own best friend."

His giggles were contagious, and I tickled him some more.

"I don't know what's more beautiful, you pregnant with my child or the vision of you holding a baby."

The years gone by didn't matter. Santino's words always made my heart flutter. I grinned, wetting my lips in anticipation as he approached.

"Are you on baby duty, *preziosa?*"

I nuzzled Gio's soft black curls. "I am, but I don't mind one bit. This little guy is the sweetest kid in the world. He makes me so anxious to hold our little boy already."

Santino laughed. "And what if he's a hellion?"

"That's okay, too," I said, reaching for his chin to steal a kiss. My husband obliged, his hand caressing my belly.

Some days, I was still amazed I was someone's wife—*his* wife. We'd found love in the dark, at a time when the thought of being with a man was a literal nightmare. But Santino had taught me how to trust again, how to love again, and I'd spend forever repaying him for his unwavering devotion.

"I have two surprises for you, *amore*. But first, let me take Gio to his father."

"A surprise? What's the occasion?"

Santino shifted Gio into one arm and shot me a playful grimace. "Since when have I ever needed a reason to shower my wife with gifts?"

Laughing, I cupped his cheek and kissed him. "I love you," I whispered against his lips.

"You'll love me even more after your second gift."

"Can't wait."

Santino stole one last kiss before heading inside, but not without tossing Gio a good three feet into the air, catching him effortlessly, then doing it again.

My first-time-mom nerves spiked into overdrive.

"I'll kill him," I muttered with a chuckle, one hand over my belly.

Turning around, I let the stunning ocean view steady my racing heart.

"That makes two of us."

Amalia shoulder-checked me and leaned against the banister, Leni to my left, and Eva beside her.

None of us said a word as we watched the waves roll in below. I'd be lying if I said I hadn't felt apprehensive about joining their close-knit group, but they'd welcomed me with open arms. And over the years, our bond had only strengthened, like I'd been part of this sisterhood from the very beginning.

I rested my head on Leni's shoulder. "I heard Maksim's leaving for Moscow next week. How are you holding up?"

She sighed. "I'm okay. I think it'll be good for him."

A wistful smile touched her lips as she watched her son by the pool. Maksim wasn't that shy, withdrawn boy I'd met six years ago. He was handsome, driven, ambitious, with the world at his feet, thanks to an unexpected inheritance.

"The girls will miss him, though."

"They sure will. They love their Maxy," Eva laughed, waving to Valentina, who was squirting Maksim in the face with a water gun.

"Ready, *preziosa?*"

We all turned at the sound of Santino's voice. He stood with a duffel bag on his shoulder.

Apparently, his surprise required a change of clothes, but I couldn't imagine sleeping anywhere else when we had this beautiful home. Intrigued, I met him at the bottom of the small steps and took his offered hand.

"Where to?"

"You'll see."

Amalia followed, brushing her fingers over my belly as she side-eyed Santino with a teasing smirk.

"Wherever you go, make sure you're back by dinner tomorrow. It's our last night in paradise, and the last time we'll all be together with Maksim for a while."

"I can't make any promises," he murmured, pressing a kiss to my neck.

I giggled and shook my head. "Don't listen to him. We'll be here. Promise."

Amalia opened her mouth to respond, but her eyes suddenly widened as she looked past me. "Remi Isabel Cain!"

A squeal rang out behind me, followed by the rapid patter of little feet skittering across the pool deck.

———

We pulled into a quiet cul-de-sac in front of a small blue house. I didn't recognize the street or any of the homes.

"Where are we?"

"Wait here. I'll be right out."

I trusted this man with my life, so I didn't question him further. I watched as he disappeared through a white gate, only to return seconds later with a baby-faced boy who seemed tall for his age. His dark curls fell over his forehead, framing a beautifully bronzed complexion. My first instinct was to ask his name, but then I met his eyes.

"Thiago?" I turned to my husband, who wore a smug grin. "How did you find him?"

After Detective Braga's death, Thiago had been placed in protective custody. For a long time, the guilt sat heavy in my chest. I feared he'd become just another casualty of a broken system. It wasn't until a year or two later that we learned he'd been placed with an aunt out of state. They told us he was safe, happy, and well cared for. Still...I thought about him often.

"As they say, I heard through the grapevine he was vacationing with family. Pulled some strings, and here we are."

I approached the boy—the little escape artist I'd last seen as a toddler—and smiled.

"You knew my dad?"

"I did. We were neighbors. And he was a good man."

He nodded, a proud smile lifting the corners of his mouth. I was relieved to see that the mention of his father brightened his mood rather than dimmed it.

We spent the next hour with Thiago, taking him out for ice cream. I didn't know when, or if, I'd see him again, but he seemed to be thriving. That was all I could've hoped for. Finally learning his fate felt like closing the last open door of that chapter in my life.

"Thank you for that," I whispered, threading my fingers

through Santino's and kissing his hand. "I've always wondered about him, but I didn't know that seeing him in person was exactly what I needed. This must've taken a lot to coordinate... after all this time." I brushed my fingertips along his lips and sighed. "Have I ever told you you're the best?"

"Not today."

Taking advantage of the blacked-out windows and the raised partition blocking the driver's view, I straddled my husband's lap, an act that had become harder these days, but always worth the effort.

"Let me remedy that." I peppered kisses along his jaw, rocking against his hardening cock. "You're the absolute *fucking* best. I love you."

He squeezed my hips, holding me down over his erection.

"It's a good thing we're almost there, or I'd fuck you right here on the cabin floor."

Grinning against his lips, I ground harder over him, teasing until his deep growl vibrated down my throat.

"Why wait?"

"No time for me to fuck you the way you deserve, *preziosa*," he said, gripping my neck and tightening his hold on my thigh. "And I'll never half-ass making love to my wife."

His teeth tugged gently at my lip.

"Not a single day will pass where you question my love. You hear me? Whether I'm fucking you bent over our bed or taking my time devouring you on the kitchen table—and everywhere in between."

"The. Absolute. Fucking. Best," I echoed, punctuating each word with a nip up his neck.

I'd been so focused on humping my husband, I hadn't noticed we'd turned onto a narrow dirt road flanked by thick trees until the car jolted to a stop on the uneven ground, jostling me in his lap.

Santino held me close and kissed my forehead. "Surprise."

"Where are we?"

"Come on."

We stepped out, and the car pulled away without a word, just as he'd likely instructed. Suddenly, it was just the two of us, standing in the middle of what looked like a jungle.

"I haven't knifed a man in a few years, baby," I said dryly, eyeing the trees. "But this is a little suspicious. Lucky for you, I never leave home without my blade."

He let out a booming laugh and tugged me through the brush until we reached a small clearing. There, high atop a rocky incline, was a large property nestled into the mountain.

It was our rental home.

"How the hell did we get back here?"

"You trust me?" he asked, threading his fingers through mine as he guided us deeper into the trees.

"Of course."

In one swift motion, Santino lifted me bridal-style and carried me across the road onto another dirt path. We walked several minutes in silence until the forest broke open again, and the sound of rushing water caught my attention.

He set me down gently, and I turned to face one of the most breathtaking views I'd ever seen: a crystal-blue lake crowned by a cascading waterfall.

"It's yours."

"Mine?" I breathed.

He dropped the duffel to the ground and took my hand.

"Yours. I purchased the land, house included, and renamed this little slice of paradise after you, Athena."

The name no longer made me flinch or recoil. I had come to embrace my resilience, forged in hell.

I'd learned to love her again.

To love myself.

Amara had kept the light on for me all those years. She was exactly who I needed to be at the time, strong, whole…fighting my demons while dancing with them through the flames. But her time was over.

Athena was here now. For good.

"Santi, this is incredible. Thank you."

Again, my feet left the ground as he lifted me and carried me into the cool water.

"Wait, our clothes—"

"Not important," he said, wading deeper until the ripples reached his waist. "*Mía preziosa*, all of this is yours. I told you I'd give you the world, didn't I? I thought this little corner of what was once your home would be the perfect addition."

Santino and I spent most of the year enjoying the Amalfi Coast, alternating between our homes in Philadelphia, Miami, and now, Brazil.

"It's gorgeous," I said, combing my fingers through his hair. "But you know I don't need the world...not when I have everything I want right here in my arms." I placed a hand between us, feeling our son's lively kicks. "And right here."

A riveting smile spread across his face.

"I know," he said softly. "Just as I know there are things, painful memories, you'll never forget. But I'm going to overflow your cup, *amore*. Until all you see and feel...is us." His hand pressed over mine, resting over our baby. "Our love."

"I love you," I whispered again as he submerged us beneath the water and kissed me, palming my ass until the need for oxygen forced us to the surface.

"Perfect. Just the way I like you, dripping wet." He licked the droplets from the crook of my neck. "Fuck, I love you."

I threw my head back as his mouth latched onto my sensitive nipple. He nipped at the drenched fabric, swiping it with his tongue, and teasing it to a peak with his teeth. Pregnancy hormones made me insatiable some days. I wanted to jump my husband's goddamn bones at every turn. The bigger I got, the more creative we became to accommodate my growing belly.

And I fucking loved it.

We stripped, letting our clothes drift downstream. The duffel bag made total sense now.

"If you don't fuck me in my own lake soon, I'll kill you," I warned between shallow pants.

Santino laughed as he guided us toward the tumbling water.

"Ready?" he asked, ducking beneath the rushing spray and reappearing on the other side.

A small cavern was carved into the rock, with the falls acting as a curtain between us and the forest beyond. He laid me down on the slick stone and wasted no time diving between my thighs.

"Oh, fuck," I whimpered as he feasted, throwing one of my legs over his shoulder.

"Sit up," he snapped, licking a hard line up to my clit. "Eyes on me. I want you to watch while I eat this sweet little cunt of yours."

My belly made it difficult, paired with my trembling thighs, but I still managed, clutching his hair and watching him devour me like his favorite dessert.

"I've been dying to taste you all day, *preziosa*," he groaned. "Downside to vacationing with family..." He spread me open and sucked hard. "Can't have my *fucking* pussy whenever I want."

A moan tore from my throat. "Fuck...fuck. So good, baby."

"Eyes, Athena."

"I can't," I whined, thighs quaking as they closed around his head with every sinful stroke of his tongue.

His wicked laugh pulsed against my clit and sent me hurdling over the edge. I imagined the euphoria of diving off a cliff into the ocean felt a lot like this. Rising so fucking high, only to free fall back to earth.

With Santino's name on my lips, I collapsed onto the rock, heaving for breath as he lapped up every drop. The more I tried to squirm away, the harder he yanked my legs open, feasting until I teetered on the verge of another explosion.

"Open up for me."

He pried my thighs apart, stroking himself as he slid the head along my dripping slit.

"I need you, Santi."

He slapped his cock against my pussy, making me jolt.

"Say it."

"Fuck..."

Another slap. The metal of his piercing clipped my clit, forcing a ragged cry from deep in my chest.

"Wait," I whimpered, a shaky laugh catching in my throat.

"Beg me."

The sound alone, the slap of his cock against me, made me feral.

"Fuck me, Santi."

Slap.

"Say please," he growled, his own need burning through every word.

I bit my lip and spread wider. "*Please.*"

He filled me in one stroke, shifting my hips and sinking deeper. My back scraped the rock, the sting blending with pleasure as he lifted my legs to his shoulders. Each thrust rocked me to my core, sending pressure through my belly and dragging another orgasm from my body.

"That's my girl," he praised through clenched teeth.

"*Eu te amo muito.*"

Santino lowered my legs, flipping me over and hauling my ass back, driving into me again.

There were still nights when I woke up drenched in sweat, screams caught in my throat, haunted by old nightmares. But they came less and less. And Santino was always there. Strong arms. Soft whispers.

His love had saved me.

With a loud grunt, he spilled inside me, fucking me until every drop was spent.

The rhythmic sound of the water soothed us as he rested his palm on my belly. Our son had a habit of falling asleep after sex. We joked it was the way we rocked his little sanctuary.

Maybe there was truth to that. I laughed at the thought.

Santino smiled, tugging me closer.

"You're so fucking beautiful. Pregnant with my child, properly fucked, and my cum dripping out of your body. Life is good, *preziosa. Ti amo.*"

I turned to him and cradled his face. "It is. Thank you," I whispered, resting my forehead against his, tears in my eyes. "For this beautiful life. Because of you...I found my way back to my family. And I found my way back to myself."

When one door closes, another blows wide open...

EXTENDED EPILOGUE

Maksim Belov

**Next Generation
14 Years Later**

THE SEVERED HEIRLOOM SERIES

OHMAMI – Chase Atlantic

"I can't believe you didn't tell me you were coming! We would've picked you up."

Even though my mother had visited Moscow just three months ago, her voice betrayed her emotions. I caught the shudder when I told her I'd be in the States for the rest of the summer. After fourteen years away from the place that broke me and the people who helped piece me back together, I was finally home.

Aside from my parents, I hadn't kept in touch the way I

should've. Work kept me busy, and the girls were too young to form any lasting connection beyond the occasional Christmas card or congratulatory message for life's new milestones.

I was happy. Things were good.

Until Mom got sick.

I wanted to be there for her, the same way she'd always been there for me. The love and patience she showed me when I was a cynical little asshole with a chip on my shoulder was a debt I'd never be able to repay. But I'd be by her side until the very end.

"I wanted to surprise you."

She was quiet for a moment.

"It's the best surprise," she sniffled. "I'm glad you're home."

"Me too. I'm just a few blocks away. I'll see you soon. *Ya tebya lyublyu.*"

"I love you, too."

I ended the call and slid the phone into my pocket, lifting my gaze just in time to catch the driver hitting the gas, trying to beat the yellow light. There was no way in hell he'd make it.

"Slow the fuck down."

Too late. He was going too fast to brake in time. Tires screamed across the pavement, and a sudden rumble of motorcycles echoed nearby.

"Shit!" he shouted, just before a body smashed into the windshield and was launched several feet into the air. The impact cracked like thunder, whipping me forward against my seatbelt.

The driver jumped out of the car. I followed, rubbing the back of my neck where it had taken the worst of the jolt.

A mangled motorcycle lay crushed against a street sign, debris scattered across the intersection, and in the middle of it all was the unconscious rider.

A woman.

Her helmet was still on. She wore white riding gear, and I could only hope it had protected her from the worst of the crash.

"Oh God, you think she's dead?" the man stammered, dropping to his knees and reaching for her helmet.

I snatched his arm back.

"Don't fucking touch her. You'll do more damage than you already have."

"Shit, man. I'm sorry, I—"

"What the fuck!"

We snapped our heads up as another woman stalked toward us. She tore off her black helmet, and long, dark waves tumbled free, streaked with blonde that framed the dangerous scowl on her pretty face.

"I'm sorry," my driver muttered. "I didn't mean to—"

"*¡Hijo de puta!*"

Blood spattered across my face as she swung her helmet and smashed it into the man's head. He dropped like a stone, knocked unconscious by the blow.

"No, no, no, no, no," she cried, falling to her knees beside her injured friend.

"Don't touch her—" I started, but a switchblade was suddenly in my face.

"Back the fuck up!"

Tears welled in her furious blue eyes.

"I'm calling for help..." My voice faltered as I looked at her more closely.

It couldn't be...

Her eyebrows lifted, her expression shifting as if she came to the same realization, and shot to her feet.

"Maksim?"

"Remi."

"Oh, my God. Maksim!"

She kept talking, but her voice faded beneath the roar in my ears, because my gaze was locked on the broken woman on the ground.

A cold shiver ripped through my chest.

No.

My little *kolibri*.

My hummingbird.

Valentina.

The past had this way of making its rounds and coming to collect. I always knew Derek Cain would kill me someday.

To Be Continued...

The Severed Heirloom
Scarred Angel
2025
Book One
https://mybook.to/4pos

Severed by Vengeance
Book One
Available in KU, Paperback, and Audio
https://mybook.to/sBwGhxh

**Tempted by Blood – An Enemies to Lovers Dark
Romance**
Book Two
Available in KU, Paperback, and Audio
https://mybook.to/Muh2n

**Bound by Betrayal – A Marriage of Convenience Dark
Romance**
Book Two
Available in KU, Paperback, and Audio
https://mybook.to/ovi3OR2

ACKNOWLEDGMENTS

It's surreal to close the final page of this series. Words will never be enough to express my gratitude to all those who immersed themselves in this universe and loved these characters. Thank you from the bottom of my heart. But this world has more stories to tell, more pages to burn, and more love to make you kick your feet. The Severed Heirloom is coming soon!